ALL THE WAY HOME

Also by Ellen Cooney
Small-Town Girl

ALL THE WAY HOME

Ellen Cooney

G. P. PUTNAM'S SONS
New York

To Connie

Library of Congress Cataloging in Publication Data

Cooney, Ellen, date.
  All the way home.

  I. Title.
PS3553.0579A8   1984   813'.54   83-24768
ISBN 0-399-12915-4

Printed in the United States of America

CHAPTER ONE

At eleven A.M. on Saturday, May tenth, the day of the game, sailing barely higher than the prickly dark peak of the town hall roof and the three church steeples competing with each other for sparks from the mild morning sun, a public relations blimp appeared in the air above Currys Crossing, Massachusetts. It was the size of a small factory, the shape of a submarine. It was an utterly soundless gray balloonish thing that dangled from its underbelly a white banner, sixty feet long, that said in monstrous red letters, NOBODY BEATS THE BELLES. In the bottom right corner of the banner, just below the outline of a small handbell in a circle, there was a signature in brilliant blue. New England Telephone. A thrill went straight through town. Out came people from houses, stores, the post office, the bank, the bars, the beauty parlors, the gym, the electricity plant down by the river where everyone expected it to tangle in the wires and explode. Cars stopped at green lights, brakes screeching. Children climbed up on fences to get a better look. Those too young to read decided it had come from outer space and stretched their arms upward, begging to be taken aboard.

Inside the hospital, nurses wheeled patients to the windows, where the oldest men teamed up to operate the controls of an invisible army tank, pretending it was Germans.

Looking out from his office at the *Clarion,* sportswriter Rollie the Fist Pelletier, fresh from eating breakfast birthday cake in honor of turning fifty-eight, ground his teeth together as the big gray blob passed by. His pulse was racing. His stomach burned. They never should have let it come to this. Even if they fired him he shouldn't have let it come to this; and he had to look away, reaching into the desk for his stomach pills.

Next door, in the high school parking lot, the Currys Crossing Marching Band, hard at last-minute rehearsal, dropped their instruments to the ground in awe. "It's Goodyear!" cried a girl with a clarinet, her jaw wide open. Fifteen-year-old Brian Griffin, who played bugle, sniggered defensively. "It ain't Goodyear. It ain't anything but a balloon. I could pop that thing with a dart, easy." Brian Griffin's mother, Patsy, who drove the school bus, played center field for the Spurs. All winter he'd been timing her bench-presses. Holding down her ankles for sit-ups. Hiding the Twinkies she kept trying to smuggle in. He was going to die of shame if she made a fool of herself out there. If any of them did, God. He had twenty dollars riding on the Spurs. Screw the telephone company. The Spurs had it. Gussie Cabrini was a genius, a queen of the game, and what was more, she knew what she was doing. Tingles of excitement shot down his back as he raised his bugle. "Screw you!" he shouted. "If we knew you was comin' we'd a got a B-52! Ten of 'em! A whole screwin' *fleet!*" He shoved the bugle to his lips and puffing out his cheeks in agitation, bleated wildly toward the blimp's rear end. The drummers rolled their drums and the band took up again with vigor.

They could hear it plainly a mile away on Anthony Street, where six houses stood three to a side on a short dead-end road. The road stopped at a clump of woods at the edge of a sand hill leading to other people's backyards. Twenty-five-year-old Evelyn Brody had lived all her life in the last house on the right.

She was sitting cross-legged on her kitchen floor, hands on her knees, palms up. Her eyes were closed. She was sweating heavily. Her shoulder-long light brown hair was pulled back into two braids that had loosened during her exercise routine. Wet strands clotted around the sides of her face as if she'd just been swimming. She was doing everything in her power to slow down her heartbeat, trying to remember the way Gussie had said to do it. Concentrate. Breathe like you're in the bathtub and there's nobody home but you. Breathe like it feels good. In and out, in and out, there's nothing in your head but blankness; fog; it's all steamy, it's like the end of summer when it's been raining all week. That's you. Cloudy. Heavy and light, there you go floating and you're rolling, you're airy and free, rolling high, higher than earth, you're . . .

"Mama, what's a blimp?"

Evelyn's eyes popped open. Up went her heartbeat again. Four-year-old Kate plopped down in a chair at the table as her mother forced herself to her feet.

"A what?"

"A blimp."

"You been over at the Arbises'?"

Kate nodded her small, perfectly round face. Her blue eyes, Danny's eyes, were glittering. "We been helpin' Mr. Arbis clean his car. Uncle William too, and everyone. It's a black car, Mama. Mr. Arbis said it used to belong to the cops. He just fixed it. He said Daddy could buy it cheap but Daddy said it's bad luck to have a police car. It's real big. But it's not so big's a blimp."

Evelyn went to the sink and poured a glass of water. There were four hours left until the start of the game. She had no idea how in the world she would ever get through them. She was still breathing hard, too hard to swallow, and spit out a mouthful through her teeth. Kate squealed with delight.

"Can I do that too, Mama?"

Turning to face Kate she let her sudden anger flare. "Did somebody call somebody a blimp? Who? Was it Mr. Campbell? Did he say it about somebody on the team?"

"Nope. Mr. Campbell said the blimp's the best psych-out he ever saw in his life. What's a psych-out, Mama?"

"Who did Mr. Campbell call a blimp, Katie?"

"Nobody." She spun around in her chair as the back door opened and seven-year-old Mundy charged in.

"She see it?" Kate shook her head.

"See what? What the hell are you two . . ."

"Hi, Ma," said Mundy. "We were just helping Mr. Arbis polish the car he fixed. Uncle William did the whole fender by himself." Thin earnest Mundy, his dark hair spilling into his eyes, planted himself directly in front of his mother and wrapped his arms around the tops of her legs.

"You're the best second baseman that ever lived, Ma," he

said. As Evelyn stooped down to hug him he gestured behind
his back and his sister climbed up on the kitchen table, quietly
pulling the curtains closed.

"Mundy, did somebody out there call somebody on the
Spurs a blimp?" asked Evelyn.

Mundy looked up in innocent shock.

"Then how come your sister comes in here wanting to know
what one is?"

"I was just makin' some nice conversation, Mama," said
Kate.

"Then how come you're closing the curtains? Okay you guys,
out with it. What's going on?" Evelyn cupped her son's chin
and tipped his head slightly backward. "You two go near Mr.
Monopoli's rose bushes?"

Mundy opened his eyes wide with insult. Kate slipped off the
table. Bounding across the room she shinnied herself up her
mother's leg.

"We *love* you, Mama!" she cried.

Mundy heaved himself against her, trying to steer Evelyn
around so she would be facing the blank wall above the sink.

"Show us how you're gonna scoop up a grounder, Ma," said
Mundy, struggling to get her down to the floor.

"I read the words myself!" Uncle William, who was eighty,
appeared in the doorway. He held his scrawny arms over his
head like a prizefighter. "I saw the sign up there and I read it.
Ain't nothin' wrong with my eyes, Ev." He drew himself together, proudly opening his mouth. "Nobody be . . ."

He didn't finish. Coming up behind him Evelyn's husband
Danny McGrath, with Allison, the baby, under his arm like a
football, reached forward and clamped a hand over Uncle William's lips. Uncle William's honorary purple baseball cap with
the big white S toppled off his head. He let out a muffled grunt
of surprise. The baby howled.

"Enough!" Evelyn peeled off her children. Before they could
stop her she rushed to the window and yanked open the curtain
and looked. Danny McGrath let go of Uncle William. The
baby hushed. The huge wingless wonder, dripping its awful
message, slowly and quietly floated over Anthony Street. A
shadow came over the house.

"Nobody beats the Belles," said Uncle William on a fast rush
of breath. "That's what it says all right."

"I thought you might not want to see it, Ev," whispered Danny. "Ev? You okay?" When she turned from the window there was no trace of color in her face. Her husband put a hand on her shoulder, his expression softening as though he meant to make a joke. "Ev, listen."

"*Ah! Ahhhhh! Aaaaaaaaaahhhhhhhhhhh!*"

The three neighbors in Tim Arbis's yard next door lifted their heads and listened to the shriek.

"Sounds like Evvie's taking a look at our visitor," said Tim.

"Yep."

"You ask me, the whole thing's getting a little out of hand. First they're going at this thing like it's the goddamn World Series. Then Rollie the Fist starts carrying on like a banshee in the paper, acting like he's going to have a coronary if a bunch of girls play a game. Then they got to have a parade. A parade for Christ sake. And now this." Tim Arbis, who nevertheless looked delighted at the course things were taking, leaned against the Plymouth in his driveway as the banner in the sky set off a gentle, rippling reflection across the spit-polished black hood. "What do you say, Nate? You going to the game?"

Sucking on an unlit cigar, Nate rolled his eyes and shrugged. He was a lean, deeply tanned, trimly muscular man of fifty with a stomach as flat as the day he'd married Juney Zarella twenty-four years back. He was wearing, as he wore every weekend, a white golfing cap, a thin pastel cotton shirt with a small animal woven on the breast pocket, impeccably creased khaki trousers and a pair of expensive leather loafers his wife had bought for him on her last trip to Rome. Nate Campbell, Superintendent of Roads for as long as anyone could remember, folded up like a lawn chair and eased himself into the back seat of the car. He stretched his long legs out the open door.

"I do believe I may take a stroll on down there, Mr. Arbis," he answered in a slow drawl. Tim Arbis came from Tennessee and Nate Campbell never let him forget it. "Just to see if the ladies truly do know what they are doing."

Sitting on a big rock at the end of the driveway, old Joe Monopoli laughed from deep in his expansive belly. He was baggy all over. His pink bald head, ringed by a half-moon of white hair, was beaded, as usual, with tiny drops of sweat. On Anthony Street they called him Joe the Rosarian. One spring a photographer from the *Clarion* had come to take pictures of his roses. The pictures had not been printed, but Joe still had the glossies framed in his living room. He grew red ones, hordes of them.

"Whatsamatta you Arbis? Course he's goin'. He's related to the pitcher. You think he's gonna play golf while his brother's kid's the pitcher?"

Nate shrugged. "Nancy Beth got an arm, Joe. But she's got no endurance. Three and a half, four innings and she's a jellyfish."

"So they take her out," said Tim. "I seen that kid pitch. Now I ain't saying there's anything respectable about the game of slow-pitch."

"It's a *hitter's* game, Arbis," said Nate with scorn.

"Nothing so respectable about that," continued Tim. "Can't bunt, can't steal, takes out all the fun. On the other hand I have seen that kid pitch. It's like she's having a dialogue with the ball. You can almost hear her out there: 'Now you get along 'cross the plate and give Mama a nice little pop to short field' or something like that. And I'll be damned if she ain't pretty good. So they put her in a couple innings, they take her out, they put her in again."

"Can't very well do a thing like that, Mr. Arbis, when you only got one pitcher."

"They got *one* pitcher?"

"That's what I'm telling you, Arbis."

Tim studied his greasy fingernails. "I still think they got a team that can play some halfway decent ball, even if it's only slow-pitch. Okay, they ain't ever played before but I've seen them practicing now and then when I'm taking a car out. They got guts, I'll give them that. Matter of fact if my girls were old enough I'd send every one of them straight to Gussie Cabrini and let her teach them a thing or two. Gussie got no manners but she knows something about playing ball."

Nate bolted out of the car and faced Tim with extravagant swagger. "You want to lay something on that, Arbis?"

"Oho! So he's turnin' on his own relation!" cracked Joe.

Arbis folded his arms across his chest. "Can't say I'd mind if I do, Mr. Campbell."

"Heya, Juney!" called Joe, waving. June Campbell was

coming out of her house next door at number two. She was wearing an elegantly tailored pantsuit in pale green, her favorite color. It fit her small body with absolute precision. She carried a small brown purse which matched the smooth dark leather of her low-heeled shoes. She'd been to the beauty parlor and her hair, the color of dry beach sand, looked as though it had been embroidered.

"Isn't that something?" she called, pointing up to the sky. "I never saw anything like it since the time we went to the Super Bowl!"

Nate Campbell squinted across the yard at his wife. "Where you going, Juney?"

"Bye, dear. I left some sandwiches for your lunch." She slid into the car and poked her head out the window. "See you at the game!"

"Juney, wait a second. Where are you going?" But she started the car against his voice and backed out of the driveway, rolling down the street without a look back. The car disappeared around the corner. Nate kicked idly at the edges of a small pool of oil seeping from under the Plymouth, and gestured toward the house across the street. "The girls home?"

"You mean the nurses?" answered Joe. "I saw the two 'a them leave for work four, five hours ago."

Nate grinned. "So what're they planning, to play ball in their uniforms? Can you see it, a ballgame with a couple of nurses in the outfield?" His cigar wagged in the corner of his mouth. "What're they going to use for catching a ball? A bedpan?"

Joe shook himself red with laughter.

"Wait a minute. Wait just a minute here." Tim came between them like a referee. "Thought we were laying a bet. Do we have one or not?"

Nate pressed his thin lips together. "What do you have in mind, Mr. Arbis?"

"I'm going with the Spurs. I'll go you, uh, I'll go you ten bucks."

Nate slapped the side of the car and let out a howl. "All these years, Mr. Arbis, and you are still talking like you just came out of the hills. What's ten dollars between friends? I am truly appalled."

Tim flushed. "Twenty."

"Fifty."

Tim threw a quick glance toward his house as if it were listening and added in a low mumble, "Fifty it is, Mr. Campbell."

Nate grinned. "What about you, Rosarian? You in?"

Joe shifted uncomfortably. "Naw. Tell you the truth, I already got one."

"Hoo-ee!"

"Who you been talking to, Rosarian?" demanded Nate.

Joe patted his stomach, working his mouth as though he were chewing on the answer. "Willie Brody. Willie, he come over my house last night and I let him know I was makin' a little deal with some friends 'a mine. Willie wanted in. I let him."

"Some friends of his, you hear that, Mr. Arbis? Just what I love, discretion. C'mon, Rosarian, we know who your friends are. Cabrini. Poli. Your thirteen cousins still in the old country. I know all about you Italians. It's just like in the movies. You stick together like you got the same nose. So what did Willie-Boy put up? His teeth?"

"Couple a hundred."

"Who you doing business with?"

"Nolan."

"Chocko Nolan?" Tim whistled softly. "Chocko's wife Birdey is playing for the Spurs. So's his sister-in-law."

Joe spread his arms out wide to indicate he had no part in anything less than honorable. "I stay outa other people's marriages. It's Chocko's money. He makes up his own mind. He's the one 'a come to me. I tell him, 'Chocko, these girls of ours, they 'a goin' to stew the tomatoes off the telephone company.' But Chocko, he don't wanna listen." Joe leaned back in the sunlight. He took another look at the warning in the sky, and gleefully muttered something terrible in Italian.

One thing Avis Poli knew but never said about her married daughter Angela was that whenever Angela was around, Avis felt herself to be at her very best. Angela understood her. Not that Leo after twenty-six years ever gave her a reason to think he didn't understand her, or even slipped up now and then like some of the others by bringing home chocolate malted ice cream when the smell of malt made her sick or leaving the car windows open when she never did get over the time the stray cat got in late one night and came creeping up her shoulders as she was starting the engine. But a man, even Leo Poli, could only go so far. A man just could not go beyond a certain point in the comprehension of a woman's mind. Perhaps it was in their genes. But it seemed an easier thing by far to get along with a man than without one, God knew. It was why women married them. There was romance, there was the adventure of learning him: the pull of his words; the trick of his mind unfolding itself to hers; the many amazing and new motions of a body she would come to memorize as well as her own and after twenty-six years if Leo pulled a hamstring or got a crick in his neck it might as well be happening to her too.

Not that there wasn't the unpredictable. Just when she thought she had him down, off he would go in a new direction. One year it was martinis after supper. The olive had to be placed just so, the ice cubes just such a size, for Leo had thought it was time they came up in the world. Coming home from the priests to a martini after supper had meant something distinguished to Leo, for hadn't he said every time he tipped back the expensive martini glass, "Imagine, Avis, what the priests would be thinking if they could see me right now!" Avis didn't have to imagine. Avis knew that the priests were in the rectory doing exactly the same thing without wondering what anyone thought of it. It was stature Leo wanted. He was the church's man, the one who got the heat going at Saint Michael's and kept the pews repaired and the grounds pretty and after a few years the priests had made him custodian of all the church property for life. All the respect he could take they gave him, the whole parish. Somebody who needed a little advice, or a few dollars for the electric bill when a husband was unemployed, could as easily go to Leo as to one of the priests. Lord knew everyone knew him. If the priests minded that Leo's hand got shaken Sunday mornings more often than theirs, they never said. But was it stature?

Another year it was tennis lessons for the kids. Ten dollars an hour and all the way to Brookline. Then they had to have rackets and fancy colored balls and the girls had to have whooshy little dresses and the boys those cotton shirts that cost as much as five steaks apiece. Frankie, the third-born, ended up on the pro's list of the thirty best players in the state but Frankie was good at anything that needed fast feet and short rounds of intense concentration. The rest of them couldn't care less about tennis. Leo used to sit on the sideline while Paulie struggled with a racket twice the size of his head and Mary-Susan made the pro lose his temper with her serve, saying to the other fathers, his eyes wet with pride, "Those kids are *mine.*" The only reason Leo gave up on the tennis was that Angela told him that if she had to waste one more Saturday in Brookline she was going to enter a convent, one that didn't allow men, even fathers, to visit.

No, Avis Poli could not say that her husband had ever bored her. All she could say was that it was different with a woman. With men you could cover up, you could put emotional clothes over the things you had inside you, down so deep that half the time you didn't even know for yourself that they were there. But women knew. Women never let you get away with anything. Like the stray cat. The night the cat sneaked in the open window of the car (she had been on her way to her sister's because one of Birdey's kids had swallowed a nickel and nobody could figure out what to do except to call Avis) it had been a shock, a horror, it was straight out of an Alfred Hitchcock movie. Into the house she'd gone, half-hysterical, and Leo looking up from his newspaper in the kitchen had at first thought she'd set her clothes on fire. Getting up he sniffed around for the smoke, and learning what it had been, all Leo could do was tell her at least it was a cat, not a murderer, and march outside to take the thing away. Angela was still in high school. She came downstairs to her mother, listened with patience, and without a word she laid a hand on Avis's shoulder where the claws had been. Then she wiped them away. In that moment Avis felt something stirring inside her, so large that she had to look away. It was the first time anyone had cut clear through Avis Poli and looked into the core of her self. It was done with a simple motion: Angela could have been brushing dandruff off her mother's sleeves, or brushing away a mosquito. Avis thought no more of the cat. It was nothing, it was silly, it was something to laugh about at the dinner table. Afterward Leo would say every now and then what a fine thing it was to see the two of them together; and later, when Angela had gone to Dallas with her husband and Avis would say how she'd left an empty place that never quite filled up, Leo might almost see what she meant.

But oh, ho, what a thing it was to have Angela home right now, seeing her mother like this! The boys, George and Frankie and Paulie, all home since the night before, let it show that they were tickled pink with their mother. The three of them had got together to buy her yellow roses, her favorite, the biggest bunch she'd ever got in her life. The boys made her feel like a prom queen. Mary-Susan, home from college, brought her a good-luck card signed by all the girls in her dormitory. Leo had the priests say a special Mass earlier that morning and to Avis's shock she woke up to a pot of tea on a tray beside their bed. Alongside the tray there was a gift, wrapped in expensive gold-colored paper. It was bulky around the corners, for Leo had wrapped it himself. Inside was a floor-length silk cloud of a nightgown in the exact shade of pink Avis loved. "It's size twelve," Leo said before she could look. He was carrying on worse than the boys. "None o' your old clothes're gonna fit you anymore, Avis. Wish I could give you a hundred dollars for every pound you lost. You'd be rich!" She had to try it on even before the tea, and she had to smile to herself as she remembered that the best part of living with Leo was that she never could exactly predict the times when he'd fall in love with her all over again. "What would the priests say, Leo?" she'd teased.

But then there was Angela, coming off the plane with her babies. Avis's throat had filled as she came forward, and no one could say that Angela was not a beautiful woman, a bit fuller around the face; a touch of gentle, maternal excess in her breasts; a clear steady beam of the unmistakable light that was Angela, and as she flung herself in her mother's arms she looked as pleased as if she was looking at the face of God Himself.

"Thirty-four pounds, down the drain," said Leo, taking the babies in his arms.

"You'd think it was your father losing the weight," Avis said. It was hard to stop thinking herself too fat. It was hard, no, impossible, there at the airport, with thousands of things going on inside her, to say anything that meant anything at all. She wanted to simply and purely open her mouth and say that all the months of it, all the straining and struggling and black bitter moments when her body rose up against her with a force it took everything in her soul to contain, all of it, everything was worth that moment: Angela coming off the plane with her babies. The feel of her arms and the old familiar press of her body. The smell of her hair, the amazing rush of affection that came over Avis like the feel of coming into a warm lighted room after too long a walk in fog. Angela was going to stay a month. There was nothing to say. Angela's arm around her mother's waist said it all. Avis sighed a long deep sigh and swished her feet around in the water. It was starting to get cold. She'd been in there at least an hour. But as she reached forward to pull the plug she heard a scurry in the hallway and the crash of an open hand against the door. Only one hand in the world sounded like that. It belonged to her sister Albertina. Birdey. The only woman on the team to sew perspiration shields into the T-shirt armpits of her uniform. Avis suspected her of putting them into the crotch as well but Birdey denied it. As usual she sounded breathless.

"Avis, Avis let me in!"

"I'm taking a bath. I'm all the way across the room from the door."

"Mother of God, Avis, I ran all the way over here. Open the door! Avis? Have you got the shade pulled down?"

"No, Birdey. I got the shade wide open. I'm showing the whole neighborhood my tits." She smiled. Birdey hated that word, it drove her crazy.

"She's got the shade down," said Birdey to someone else. Her voice nose-dived into a peculiar whimper, muffled but distraught even for Birdey. "She's in the tub."

"Mother?" Angela now. "Mother, turn up a corner of the shade and take a look out the window."

The two women outside the bathroom door heard a slight splash of water, the sound of a rising body, and a long moment of silence during which Birdey Nolan clasped her hands to her heart, pressed her head against the door, and shook all over as if she were freezing.

"What's that? Angela, what's she doing?" The big gulping sounds echoed through the hallway with shattering force, undoing every nerve in Birdey's body. "Avis?"

"She's laughing, Aunt Birdey," said Angela. "Laughing her head off." Her look told Birdey that she might as well do the same. Birdey promptly burst into tears.

In Tim Arbis's front yard Nate Campbell was giving a golf lesson to the four Arbis daughters, Ivy, Holly, Camellia and Patience, and Mundy and Kate McGrath. They were lined up in a row with branches Nate had whittled down for clubs. Beside them on a pair of lawn chairs, Joe Monopoli and Uncle William Brody were making golfballs out of balled-up strips of aluminum foil. The winner would be the first child to hit the blimp.

"Swing!" cried Nate, swinging a real club to show them how. They all but ignored the police cruiser pulling up in the driveway. Officer Raymond Kuzick climbed out and walked toward Nate with a look of stupefaction.

"That Plymouth," he said, pointing to the car he'd parked behind. "That's the one stupid Bolton wracked up. I'd know that car anywhere. Hole-eee. Last time I saw this car it was wrapped around a telephone pole with its guts out. Where's Arbis? I got to talk to Arbis about this car. Best piece of work he ever done."

"He's taking a shower with his wife," said Nate.

"I'll wait."

"Come off it, Kuzick. You didn't come over here to look at a car."

The cop reluctantly moved his eyes. "Morning Joe, morning Willie. Hey, kids! What's going on, Nate, you switching careers? This your kindergarten? Seriously though. I heard you were looking for me."

"You know what I love about you guys? You guys are so prompt. Last night I was looking for you. Eight o'clock this morning I was looking for you. And here it is, damn near noon, and here you are, Kuzick, showing the face we all love and admire."

"Get to it, Nate. I got things enough on my hands without you smart-assin'. Bunch of kids were carousing last night up hospital hill and broke six windows in the maternity ward. Don't get your lip up, they're outa-towners. We got them. And now this. This—this shitbox in the sky. It's like we're getting invaded or something. The whole town's going nuts. And now we got to bring in the extras for the parade. Then the game. Christ."

"The life of a cop is truly one to be envied, Kuzick. I envy you with my whole heart."

"What did you want?"

Nate took him by the elbow and steered him back to the cruiser. He lowered his voice. "Think you ought to take a ride by River Road. Just a ride."

Ray Kuzick tipped back his hat and ran his hand wearily along his forehead. "Kenny Dorn been around again?"

Nate shrugged. "Can't say for sure. McGrath thought he saw his Mustang when we were working a hole on Water Street. Danny called to him but he never slowed down."

"Shit, Nate, would you? With a warrant on you?"

Nate shrugged again. A quick look of contempt came over his face, replaced by thinly hidden impatience. "Just take a ride, that's all I'm saying."

"I probably will. But the place is covered anyway."

"Covered? What covered?"

"It's Gussie Cabrini and that team of hers. They take turns sleeping over. Somebody's watching the house all the time. They stay out of sight so the kid doesn't catch on. Matter of fact, it's your neighbors who usually guard the place. Those nurses. Last time I went by, they made me show my goddamned badge. You ask me, that house is covered better than a bank."

"My wife's gone over there," said Nate. "She's gotten real attached to the kid."

"I'm telling you, it's safe. We got an assault'n battery out against Dorn. But you know how it is, Nate. You been around. Happens all the time. You get a marriage going bad, and one wants out and the other don't, and—hell, anything can happen."

Nate took a sharp breath and shook his head. "We're talking about a kid. A kid, Kuzick, who landed in the hospital with a bashed head. I don't give a good goddamn about marriages going bad, all I know is what I hear, and I heard, way back, that Kenny Dorn wasn't going to take it easy when he didn't get custody. Sandy's half out of her mind worrying he'll come back. Juney's gotten real attached to her."

"C'mon, Nate, be real. What do you think, Dorn's coming in with a shotgun? Think he'll do something nuts?"

Nate scowled. "We got some scared women up at that house, Kuzick. My wife's one of them. How'd you like it if it was yours?"

Kuzick, who was unmarried, turned back toward his car. "Maybe I'll mention it to the chief."

Nate swung up his club and waved it warningly in the air. "Don't talk to me like that. Mention it to the chief, you might as well mention it to one of those kids over there. I've done you boys plenty of favors. You don't need me reminding you of a single one."

"C'mon, Nate, this ain't no time to get political."

"A *ride,* Kuzick. Take a ride by River Road. Covered or not, check it out up there. Got it?"

Kuzick, with an exaggerated huff, yanked open his car door and slid in. "Tell Arbis I want to talk to him."

Nate toyed with his golf club and nodded. As the cruiser backed out of the driveway he called after it, "You want to lay a little something on the game?"

Kuzick waved an arm out the window. "Got it all taken care of," he said.

Nate lit his cigar and turned back to the golf game to see Camellia Arbis trying to strangle Kate McGrath with her tree branch. Kate kicked her neatly in the knees and laid her flat in seconds.

Little Patience Arbis was throwing tin foil balls at Uncle Willie, who threw them right back. Nate was glad all over again that he and Juney didn't have children of their own. He swung his club in the air as if he meant to remove all their skin and they rushed back into a line, and stood there poised at attention.

"First one to hit the blimp gets a quarter," he said, and disappeared into the house to find Arbis.

"So they brought in a blimp, big deal," said Danny McGrath, stripping off his jeans for a clean pair. In honor of the Spurs he was wearing purple underpants. The silky feel of them had embarrassed him earlier that morning, but now he couldn't take his eyes off himself. "All it is, Ev, is a hunk of hot air. You don't have to take it so—so personally."

"I knew Drago would do something. I just knew it."

"So they got Drago. Same thing all over, a hunk of hot air. You go in there being scared of Linda Drago and you might as well not even bother playing. Hey, what're you drinking? Is that coffee? Gimme that, Ev. You don't drink coffee before a game. You're thirsty, suck on something sweet. Here." Danny stuck out his lips in a damp pink O. Wrapping his arms around her hips, he pulled her close.

"No fucking before a game."

"Who said anything about fucking? All I want's a kiss. C'mon, Ev. Remember the first time I had to go golf a real game with Campbell? And I dreamed about walking in there carrying my clubs in Mundy's diaper bag?"

Evelyn giggled in his arms. "In the dream you were running all over the green trying to find the goalposts. But then you couldn't figure out why you had to have goalposts because you were wearing your baseball cleats." She kissed him. She kissed him again.

"Okay, Ev. There's a pop fly a mile up and it's coming down like it's on fire. Looks like it's going to short or center but you're already backing up. Here it comes. What do you do?"

"Call it."

"Who you calling it to?"

"The air. I'm not looking at anything but the ball."

"Where's your hands?"

"In the air. Over my head. Like this."

"Lower. Hold them like that it'll bean you."

"Like this." Evelyn held an imaginary glove slightly above her upturned face, and positioned the other hand close to it.

"It's a scorcher, Ev." Danny made the sound he made for the children when playing fire-engine. "Where's your feet?"

Evelyn ground her feet firmly into the floor, one just in front of the other, and as Danny made a popping noise she trapped the imaginary ball neatly.

"The runner, Ev! Quick! The runner on third is going home. What're you thinking?"

Ev brought back her arm and lunged forward. "I'm thinking this one's for Avis." Avis Poli was the catcher.

"She faking you out?"

"Who?"

"The runner on third. You overthrow. Avis scoots after it and the sweetheart's home free. You throw to third but it's behind her and off she goes. Where's your pitcher?"

"She's gone to the bathroom. Too much coffee before the game. I'm going to throw it home, Danny. Avis'll get it."

"What's the worst you could do?"

"I know, I know. I'll be careful."

"So say it."

"Look before I throw."

"Say the whole thing, Ev. Look me right in the eye and say for once and for all the wrong thing you have sometimes done out there at second base. Go on, Ev."

Evelyn flushed with anger and gritted her teeth. "I get a little ruffled."

"And what are you feeling in your gut about this runner, say it's the winning run. Top of the seventh. The heat is *on*. You just made the second out. You're sweating so hard it feels like grease. The whole town's watching you. Your own children. Uncle William's shitting in his pants he's so nervous. The runner on third is one very fast lady. She could slide home quicker than you could blink. What's going on?"

Evelyn took a very deep breath and stared hard at her husband. "I am going to throw the ball to Avis. Avis will tag the runner at the plate or the runner will return to third. I am going to throw the ball directly into Avis's mitt. I know it by heart. I'm not going to fumble the ball because soon as I get the thing I hold it tight as I'd hold the baby."

"Okay. You got a grounder coming your way and it's so hard the pitcher feels like it took off her eyelashes going by her. Runner on first. You're playing close to the bag. What're you doing?"

Evelyn quickly spread her feet and scooped up the imaginary grounder, and with a fast, gracefully accurate, semicircular movement of her whole body she planted the edge of her foot on the imaginary base.

"Out!" cried Danny. "Okay, long whopper to right. No runners. Where are you?"

"Spreading back for the relay."

"Where's the pitcher?"

"Covering second."

"How do you know? You look?"

"I'm looking at the ball. I just know."

"Okay. You got a crazy chop looking like it's a snap for the pitcher but it bounces and gets right by her. Runners on first and second. You're on the bag but . . ."

"It's mine. Right here. My glove's on the ground and I got the base and I whip it to first."

"Why not third?"

"Can't take the time to look. I whip it over to first."

"Double play!" Danny shouted, his fist in the air. "Okay, no runners. A whacker out to left. You back up and catch it pretty from left field with the runner rounding to third. What're you doing?"

"Letting her have it."

"How come?"

"Too risky to run her down. We've practiced a hundred times but running her down means four of us on it together and we end up looking like clowns."

"Okay. High one to center. Runner's closing in on you fast. She's big, she looks like a freight train. You both got the same shot at the bag. What do you do?"

"Scream."

"After that."

"Block. Go for the tag."

"Ump is calling her safe and you know damn well you got her."

"I'm *not* going to lose my temper."

"While you're going for the tag she steps on your hand. You feel like your fingers are gone. Ump is still calling her safe."

"So let him."

"Okay. You're terrific, Ev. You're great. Let's fuck."

"*Danny!*"

CHAPTER TWO

From the summer she was pregnant with her first baby, her son Edmund, until the moment Uncle William discovered Gussie Cabrini in the motorcycle wreck, Evelyn Brody's favorite way of living was asleep. She was good at it. She had a routine. Midmorning nap in a corner of the sofa while the baby chewed plastic clothespins at her feet. Afternoon pickup at three, upright in a kitchen chair in case anyone passing by took her for lazy. After-supper rest in twilight—the best—when Danny, pushing himself away from yet another meal, pulled the children to him like a man who loves to swim slipping at last into clean familiar water, and they left her alone beneath a belly of pillows; out of it; safe; and even, it was possible, happy. She never dreamed. She would not have been able to bear it if she had dreamed.

Uncle William, her father's uncle, had been part of her inheritance. He had just turned seventy-nine. The weight of his age sat on his shoulders with unrelenting heaviness, a sort of growth in reverse that kept on pushing him downward. With his bent back he could no longer walk without stooping. He had a worn, elasticized appearance. His face looked like old wallpaper and his skin hung in sags but there was still the very pale blue of his eyes; there were still the thin hairs curling at delicate angles up and down his arms, over his crinkly hands and yes, there was still the dreamy smile playing at the corners of his mouth, now bashfully, now clear as the moon. It was here

that once, twice, a hundred times a day she came face to face
with the ghost of her father: cool, serene, untouchable. Although the look of him was as familiar to her as her pillow it
never stopped taking her by surprise. She spent most of her
waking moments trying to avoid it. The house where she lived
had been hers as a girl. She had been an only child.
  Every morning after breakfast, Uncle William reached for a
big plastic bag, kissed the children, and left for work. His job
was finding things. He covered the same route daily, a quarter-
mile loop that took him through all the backyards of Anthony
Street, into the woods at the end of the road, down the sand
hill, up again, back home. Into the bag went rags, rocks, coins,
pigeon feathers, baseball cards, pieces of colored glass, small
objects like gauze pads from the hospital supply cabinets that
the nurses, Hannah and Peggy at number three, stole and scattered over their lawn. Evelyn had once tried to remember how
all this had started, but gave up. She threw away most of the
things Uncle William brought home. She never tried to stop
him from trying.
  It was the end of May. Uncle William wasn't due back for an
hour. She wrapped the baby, Allison, in an old sheet and went
out to the back porch. It was warmer outside than in. Behind
the other houses on Anthony Street, patches of newly turned
earth, poked here and there with tomato stakes, brownly
churned in the sun. Evelyn thought that if she stood very still
for a while she might see green things popping up from the
ground like the children's jack-in-the-box. It was all very fertile
and muck-happy and ripe. Lawns were clipped and hedges
were trim. In her own backyard where weeds were thick, her
son Mundy's tricycle lay on its side, rusting. Her daughter
Kate's wading pool was spilling cracked, plastic fishes into the
mud. It had not been an easy winter. She had tired often and
without much effort. In the stretch of ground where she had
once tried to grow petunias there were weeds the size of lettuce
heads. The uncleared trees and bushes beyond the yard seemed
to be moving in closer. The yard was smaller. Right before her
eyes the yard was shrinking away like Uncle William. She
would have to put up a fence. She'd been saying so for years.
  Mundy and Kate, jackets unzipped, ran to her from the
front of the house. Evelyn stirred with resolve. It was not too

late to go downtown. They could go downtown that very moment. They would plant some flowers. Tomatoes. Pumpkins. Spinach. Crisp, elegant pea pods. She would pack up herself and the children and go downtown for seeds. She would buy a rake and a spade and a pair of cloth gloves to protect her skin, which rashed easily, and a plastic wheelbarrow for Kate, and a floppy sun hat for Allison, who was still bald, and a watering can for Uncle William, and a little shovel for Mundy, and a big shovel for herself, and a pail for Danny, who could pick fresh salad greens for dinner. She would stake her tomatoes just like everyone else on the street. She had no idea how she'd get the weeds out. Dig from the bottom? Pull from the top? She thought she might borrow Danny's bulldozer and get it done all at once. At the same time she could clean out the dead trees, creeping with their long-clawed arms closer and closer toward the house. She could put in a sandbox with the wood left over from building the fence. She might even paint the porch.

Grunting, Allison filled her diaper. Her wrappings dampened and stank. Mundy flung himself onto the ground. Kate flung herself on top of Mundy. It was probably too dangerous to put in tomato stakes. The children might be impaled. All the same, she would talk to Danny about the bulldozer. At twenty-five, Danny McGrath was the youngest man ever to be Assistant Superintendent of Roads in Currys Crossing. She was sure he'd take care of the weeds and the old trees. He could do it for the town, he could do it for his own backyard. Kate and Mundy rolled across the yard in a heap, gathering mud in their clothes and hair. Evelyn was right. Tomato stakes were out of the question. She shifted the baby to her hip.

"Edmund! Katie! Zip up those jackets, we're going downtown."

Mundy and Kate looked up with the look small children have for adults they love but do not believe. Evelyn sat down on the step. In a minute she would clean the baby. She would wash the children's faces. She would bring the baby carriage out of the basement and get the children into their hats and fix a bottle of juice for Allison. They would all go downtown. Uncle William came slouching toward her, dragging his plastic trash bag. Mundy and Kate rushed for it. It was empty.

"You got to come with me quick, Ev," he said. It was nearly

time for her nap. It was no time for her to hike through the woods to help him drag home some big thing he'd found, an old tire or the body of a raccoon. They always held funerals for Uncle William's dead animals but today she was not in the mood. Once, just after Mundy was born, he had found a bank safe with a door blown clean off its hinges. It had hardly rusted. They dragged it home on Evelyn's old sled, and half the neighborhood helped Uncle William get it up to his room. They had planned to call the police about it, but didn't. Uncle William kept it cleaner than his teeth.

"Come on, Ev." He scowled, tugging at her sleeve. She was wearing an old wool jacket of Danny's over a flannel nightgown which was tucked into a pair of jeans. She rarely dressed during the week. She liked clothes that were easy to get out of, for her naps. But she gave in. She always gave in to Uncle William. She rewrapped the baby. With the children trailing, she followed him into the woods. The last image of her ordinary life was the sight of Uncle William in a small clearing, pointing inside. Instinctively she pulled the children behind her before she took a step closer.

The motorcycle, a medium-sized street bike, was an obscenely tattered heap of black and silver wedged between a large rock and a tree. Huge ruts gutted the dirt where the wheels had tried, and failed, to turn. One bare leg, bent sharply backwards at the knee, was poking out of the wreck, and it was the smooth and evenly tanned leg of a woman. Evelyn touched it like a girl in a story trying to get a genie out of a lamp. The leg was still warm. She gave the baby to Uncle William and sent them away to get help. It took many tries but she rolled the bike away. She was sure that she knew at once who it was. She had not known she was back in town. She had not known she drove a motorcycle. She had not seen her for over three years but there had been a time, a long, long time, when there was nothing about her Evelyn had not known as well as she knew herself. Augusta Cabrini. Her friend with the glorious name, back again on Anthony Street. She was wearing a dark pair of gym shorts and a filthy white jersey and a pair of sneakers. There was no way of knowing how long she had been lying there.

Evelyn took off her jacket and laid it across her friend's

shoulders. She sank to her knees. She knew what to do. She had been in a place like this before, down on her knees, talking to something that did not answer. She did not try to move her. She called her Gussie, and she kept on talking. Gussie, I've got three kids now. Gussie, the new family that moved in next door is named Arbis. They come from Tennessee. They've got four girls, all named for flowers, dear God, open your eyes!

Her eyes stayed closed but she was breathing. It was slow, it was faint, but it was breath.

An ambulance came. Familiar and unfamiliar faces, lured by the wail of the siren, watched from the edge of the woods as Gussie was loaded inside on a stretcher. Uncle William and the children stayed up in the road with their hands across their mouths. Before going back to them, Evelyn looked around in the bushes for Gussie's helmet. There wasn't one. A tow truck came to haul away the bike, and rumbled down Anthony Street with its orange lights flashing. Across the street, old Teresa Monopoli came out to her porch, crossing herself as it passed. When she met Evelyn's eyes she crossed herself again, and lowered her head in prayer.

She had been named Evelyn for a small fishing boat her mother remembered from a harbor she had known as a child. It had never been clear to Evelyn whether the boat was real or imagined. It could have been a picture on a postcard, an illustration in a favorite book. It could have belonged to a sea-splattered lobsterman with kind and gentle hands who lit up in smiles when he saw her, and reached into his pockets for candies or gifts from the shore. Evelyn could only guess. Her mother told her little. The boat was called the *Evenly.*

Evenly, explained Shirley Brody, was the way she had planned their lives to run. Evelyn grew up believing it would someday come true.

Shirley Brody had been a Thompson of the New Bedford trucking Thompsons. Evelyn remembered her mother's father and brothers as a blur of badly made dress suits, sitting uncomfortably around the table for Sunday dinner. All she could remember of them were the tattoos over their wrists. Kinship began and ended with the blue eagles and flame-colored tiger heads that startled her whenever one of her uncles reached for the salt shaker or her grandfather stretched across the table to touch her cheek. She could never tell, overhearing their conversations, if they meant their wives or their trucks when they said things like, *Babette's got a stick up her arse today,* or *Millie's purring like a pussycat.* Evelyn did not dislike them, the way she did not dislike slush in the road in February. They were one more thing to put up with. Her mother hid the good lace tablecloth when a Thompson came to visit, and shuddered when they drank their beer out of cans at the table. She once told her daughter she had married Franklin Brody because he was the first entirely non-Thompson man she'd met.

Franklin Brody was born in Currys Crossing, and as far as Evelyn knew he had never been away from home. He had worked in the paper mill across the river. When Evelyn was twelve he was promoted to shipping supervisor. Shirley Brody donated all his old denim work shirts to the Salvation Army and bought him two dozen white ones with button-down collars. Everyone else's husband wore permanent press by then but Shirley wouldn't hear of it. When he took one off she folded it into a cloth bag and when the bag filled she sent it to the cleaner's. Back they would come in cardboard boxes, stiff and shining, hand-delivered for the whole street to see.

When Evelyn was twelve years old they bought a car, a brand new white Oldsmobile with silver trim and red leatherette interior. The hubcaps were bright as mirrors and Uncle William kept them clean. Nate Campbell came over to help dig up turf for a driveway. In a burst of good humor Shirley unpacked her daughter's first pair of booties and attached them by their laces to the rearview mirror.

Franklin passed his driving test flawlessly. Gasoline was cheap. The whole world lay open before them, as smooth and easy to understand as the Esso maps Evelyn traced, and studied, and memorized. There was nowhere they would not go. Their first trip made Uncle William carsick. Their second trip made Shirley come down with palpitations of the heart, and she made a rule that her husband was not to drive over forty miles an hour. Evelyn's father tried to keep it, and failed, ripping over the highway with the ease and the comfort of a trucker. That was all Shirley needed. Another trucker. They stopped going out on trips. Shirley said it didn't matter. Why should they have to go anywhere when they had already arrived? Shrugging his shoulders Franklin said she had a point. Evelyn secretly, longingly, kept on reading the road maps. Uncle William kept on shining the hubcaps.

On Saturday nights they all got into the car, looking over the dashboard at the darkness creeping in from the woods. Evelyn's father turned on the radio. It was as good as going to a concert. Evelyn saw her father and Uncle William in tuxedos, turning over their tickets to ushers who knew their names. Her mother's jewels would glitter at the nape of her neck, dropping starlike into the soft thin fabric of her ballgown. "Turn it up louder, Frank," Shirley would say as she pulled off her gloves. Uncle William played drums in the back seat. Shirley was the horn section. Evelyn was all the strings. Franklin Brody as befitted a man of his authority and character was the conductor, tapping the tips of his eyeglasses against the steering wheel to keep time.

Like her father, Evelyn's mother had worked in the paper mill. She went in right out of high school but she had ambitions. She hadn't meant to stay long. Five years after she started she was taken off the third-shift dyes and put on the second-shift dyes. Then she moved into Quality Control. Franklin said she was the best inspector they ever had, but she did not have many friends. Unlike the others she was a woman of manners. She was not going to spend her whole life on the line. Like a queen she was going to walk out of there, like she owned the place.

Evelyn liked her best when Shirley sat at the side of her bed after a concert, imitating Gladys the packer on line five who thumbed her nose every time Shirley walked by, or Sally the shredder, the foreman's adulterous girl, rushing to hide the sugar cubes whenever Shirley took her coffee break. She was a fine and gifted comedienne, Franklin said. She could imitate anyone. She was a regular act in a nightclub, and at times such as these he could almost forgive her for not allowing him to drive his own car. Standing in the doorway of Evelyn's room, watching his wife make him laugh, Franklin would soften his look, and crumble with affection, and believe whatever she told him, even when it came to her hands.

When Evelyn was fifteen, her mother was laid off with a pension. She did not walk out of the mill with her head held up like a queen. She only came home one day and never went back. It was a silent, secret rule of the household that none of them ever mention why.

If there had existed a way to surgically remove a pair of hands and replace them with a new pair, Evelyn was sure that her mother would have given her eyes to pay for it. Shirley Brody hid her hands the way she learned to hide her ambitions, but it didn't stop her from talking to them. She talked to her hands all the time, roaming through the house with a vocabulary she had learned from her brothers. On a good day she only whispered. On a bad day Evelyn stayed out of the way. She kept it to herself that she loved her mother's hands. She pitied them, she adored them, she wrapped the tough hard muscles of girlish longing around them as if they were exotic animals caged in a zoo. She believed that the paper dyes had not ruined them. The paper dyes had rendered them magic. No other girl in the world had a mother with hands like the hands of Shirley Brody. When they sat in the car for concerts, warm and safe and comfortable, Evelyn put down the strings to watch them move. It was the only time Shirley took off her gloves. In the shadows they looked like two tiny saddles, two saddles that straddled the backs of invisible horses and sometimes the horses had wings. Through the air inside the car they paced, they ran, they soared, they took her crashing through the wall of everything that was ordinary and flew her off like dreaming. Evelyn tried to be careful about watching her mother's hands. It was important not to let on. Her father kept his eye on her, calling softly, "Hey! Where're those violins? Violins taking another rest back there?"

Outside the car Shirley kept her gloves on. She had drawers full of gloves, countless gloves, white ones, beige, blue, black. When she became an inspector in the quality-control department she bought new, expensive gloves: green suede the color of the sea, lavender, peacock blue, doeskin brown. When she left the mill and decided to learn to drive the car she bought a pair of thin, tan leather ones with straps across the back that really buckled.

"Just because we don't live in Paris is no reason we can't be stylish," Shirley Brody said.

Her voice comes to Evelyn out of the walls. Evelyn believes that her house is full of ghosts. All day they flit in the corners.

They crowd the furniture. They hover over the necks of her children. Here is Franklin, shaking his head from side to side. Here is Shirley, looking for the keys to the car. They talk and talk. A smile creeps across Franklin's lips. He has an idea: listen. He wants to sue the mill.

Union representatives gather in the kitchen, drinking coffee. Evelyn watches their wrists for tattoos, but finds none. She chooses, for the moment, to trust them. She is the girl in the fairy tale whose father wears a suit of armor. She imagines him urging his fast horse onward, charging the factory while trumpets play in the background and the world cheers. He raises his sword and lawyers come running. He telephones the doctor for copies of Shirley's X-rays. The union representatives talk money across her mother's best lace tablecloth. Her father is there in the middle, conducting things. At the height of it he climbs up on a chair and clears his throat.

"They're not going to get away with this!"

He plans and plans. A lawyer really does come. Shirley is away on a driving lesson. Franklin talks with Mr. F., the lawyer, about rights of the plaintiff. Uncle William talks with Mr. F. about the Red Sox. Franklin mentions the chemicals in the dyes. He explains that Shirley Brody has given up her hands so that the daughters of wealthy men could write their letters on pretty-colored stationery. Eloquence comes into his voice. He is flushed with belief and passion.

"You must be Irish," the lawyer says. "Only an Irishman can talk the way you do. What county you from?"

Blushing, Franklin changes the subject. The lawyer says maybe they've got a case. Shirley comes into the house. The lawyer wants to take a look at her hands.

She is wearing her tan suede gloves with the dark leather patches on the palms. Mr. F. reaches into a breast pocket for a thin pair of glasses. He puts them on. Shirley pauses, watching him the way a small animal watches its killer. She tells her daughter with her eyes that it feels the same way it feels in department stores, where the clerks with their pale, beautiful hands guard the cases where they keep the gloves. All the cases are locked. Only the clerks have keys. They poke each other in the ribs when they see Shirley Brody coming. What kind of a woman tries on a pair of gloves with gloves on?

Franklin bites his lip with impatience.

Shirley tugs at one thumb. For a wild moment Evelyn believes that she is really going to go through with this.

"If it's paralysis, we'll really go for the bucks!" cries the lawyer.

Shirley loosens the gloves at the tips of her fingers. She moves slowly, deliberately. When Franklin can't stand it any longer, he jumps out of his chair and flies at her.

"We'll be rich, Shirl, rich!" He grabs her and pulls her hands apart. He fumbles with her wrists. The lawyer's glasses are cloudy with steam as he steps in to help. They nearly have her, but they don't have blind panic on their side. Shirley slips out of their grip and flees. Franklin sinks into his chair. The lawyer reddens with embarrassment. He gathers his papers into his briefcase and hurries away.

Franklin goes upstairs. He knocks at the door of their bedroom three hundred times. Evelyn counts. Shirley does not give any sign that she hears him. Hours later, Shirley comes out. She brushes past her husband and runs down the stairs. Looking for the car keys she pulls on her gloves. Franklin is shouting at the top of his lungs. She can't drive the car, she's only had a couple of lessons. What is she trying to do? Get herself arrested?

"I'm a Thompson," Shirley reminds him. "Where I come from, Thompsons get arrested all the time."

Uncle William finds the car keys and hands them over. Evelyn wonders: Had Father hidden them?

Alone, her mother walks down the gravel path to the driveway. She gets into the car. She turns on the radio and a band plays. Smoke spurts from the shiny tailpipe in frisky clouds that quickly disappear. She drives away, smoothly and efficiently, as if she's been driving all her life. The car glides down Anthony Street and for a moment, watching in the doorway, Evelyn feels proud. She imagines her mother in the cab of a rig, in a flatbed truck with an engine as big as a jet. Behind the wheel of such power her mother shimmers with confidence. Perhaps she might drive all night.

All night, Evelyn waits. Franklin waits. Uncle William waits. They keep their heads low. They hold tightly to pieces of furniture. They say nothing. They take care not to look each other in the eye. When they finally hear the sound of wheels in the driveway they leap to their feet, stunned.

The windows turn orange with light. The blazing, blinding light freezes them, transfigures them. The policemen in their heavy boots leave the lights going as they try to walk softly up the steps of the porch. The doorbell begins to scream. Its screams grow louder and louder, and Evelyn must take her hands away from her ears to let them inside. She knows what they are going to say. Her heart knows, her whole body knows. The policemen, whose eyes have been humbled by the sight of sudden death, hope it will be a comfort to know that she died right away. They found the car against a tree, not two miles from Anthony Street, with its smooth engine still running. They are big men, clumsy with feeling.

Instantaneously, they say.

Later, Franklin sits in his overcoat in the low armchair they never used except for company. He is still wearing his hat. It's the same hat he got married in. He has pulled it down low over his eyes the way they do in detective movies. The paper-stiff collar of his shirt shines whitely in the shadows. Evelyn kneels at the side of his chair. He has something to say to her. She is seventeen years old. In half a year she is going to marry Danny McGrath, but she doesn't know this yet. She thinks she knows what her father is going to say. He will say that it wasn't time for her to be out in the car. All she'd had was a couple of lessons. He will shake his head from side to side. He will say, "Should've gone after her, Ev."

Her father speaks, and this is before she has been to see the doctor, who will tell her that it wasn't only in her mother's hands. It was everywhere. "You can imagine what happened to your mother if you imagine the roots of a very old tree with no room at all left to grow," said the doctor by way of explanation.

Her father wants to speak.

She will marry Danny McGrath because Gussie Cabrini tells her to. They are all seventeen years old. Gussie's family has already moved away from Anthony Street, but she has not left Evelyn entirely. It is a small and quiet wedding. Nate and June Campbell give them a breakfast on their patio. For a wedding present, Nate will hire Danny to work with him on the roads. June will send over wallpaper samples and charts of paints. "You'll probably want to do over some of the rooms," June tells them. They do. They buy new furniture. They put down new rugs. They rip out the old kitchen cabinets and put in new ones that Danny builds himself from a kit. Uncle William stays in his room a lot. He has kept Franklin's clothes even though none of them fit right. He prefers to roll up the bottoms of Franklin's trousers and the sleeves of Franklin's shirts than give Franklin up altogether. He begs Evelyn to send the shirts to the cleaner's the way Shirley used to, but Evelyn thinks she knows where to draw the line. She launders the shirts herself. June comes by and takes away everything belonging to Shirley except her gloves. Uncle William gets the gloves. Then there is nothing left to do. Life runs smoothly, evenly. She naps three times a day.

She is eighteen when her son Edmund is born. She calls him Mundy. Three years later, Kate is born, and three and a half years after Kate, Allison. Evelyn has never neglected her children. She has never missed the fixing of a single meal. After a while, when he no longer remembers his life before his marriage, Danny runs out of ways to try to get her to sleep less often. He stops trying to make her laugh for no reason. But sometimes in the morning as he leaves for work he catches her watching him. Pausing in the doorway, he watches her back as if he were talking to her with his heart. He tells her that he is going to come back. He promises. If she lets him, he wraps his arms around her, and tells her that just as sure as his eyes are blue he will always, always come back.

Franklin Brody, who will leave the house in his overcoat and the hat he got married in, has something he wants to say. In three days his body will turn up at the edge of the river, bloated and bloodless and cold. In a minute, Evelyn plans, he is going to say her mother's name. He will take off his hat and coat. He will undo the stiff white collar of the shirt and he will remember that earlier that day they saw Shirley Brody's body put into the ground. He will remember that it is not everyone in the world who is dead. Shaking his head from side to side he will say that they should have gone after her. They never should have let her drive the car. He looks up. There is nothing going on behind his eyeglasses. Finally, helplessly, Evelyn realizes that she has no way of knowing what he is thinking.

Her father speaks. "My name didn't used to be Brody. It was your grand-dad that changed it. I don't recall what he changed it from. All these years, Ev, and you never knew."

All this night he sits in the chair, trying to remember who he is. Uncle William is up in his room, lying across his bed in his old black suit, his funeral clothes. In his hands are Shirley's leather driving gloves. He is fastening and unfastening the buckles across the back. Evelyn tries to rouse him, and fails. She hurries back downstairs to her father. She helps. If the memory of a name is all he wants, she will give him one. She looks through all the drawers for documents but there is nothing to find. Her parents had grown up with immigrants. They picked their lives as clean as chicken bones. Then she coaches, jiggling the invisible strings of her father's memory. She is the girl in the fairy tale trying to guess the name of Rumpelstiltskin. O'Brodie? Broderson? Broderleigh? Broderino? She goes through the telephone book, down on her knees, talking to things that don't answer: Broderick, Brodeur, Brodoff, Brodsky; and her father goes on sitting there, shaking his head from side to side with his hat on.

Because Peggy Glazer, the emergency-room nurse, was Evelyn's neighbor, she broke the rules and allowed Evelyn to go to the waiting room with Gussie's family. They were all there. Her sister Christine. Her brothers, Carl and Rio. Her parents, Victor and Marina. Carl was thinner, harder. Christine was dressed in a light wool gray suit with a skirt that opened down the side of one thigh. Christine worked for a bank in Boston. Evelyn had heard she'd been divorced, but she didn't show it. Rio still looked like Gussie. Victor's hair had whitened at the edges. Marina was Marina, distant, beautiful, silent. Victor held out his arms. Christine eyed her warily because they had always disliked each other but her look softened quickly, as if she had just remembered that Evelyn Brody had buried both parents in the same week.

"We're grateful to you, Evelyn," said Christine.

Carl nodded in his artificially charming way. At thirty-four, fit and well-oiled, he was the front man in the family's real estate business. His pale-green shirt was real cashmere and his dark flannel slacks looked as if they'd just come off an ironing board. He wore a signet ring on his baby finger and a gold chain around the neck of his sweater. Evelyn could not imagine anyone wanting to buy a house from this man.

"They've got Gussie in the intensive care," said Victor. His voice cracked with the strain of his fear. He brought his hands to his eyes. His shoulders wavered but he did not cry.

"Did she say anything to you, Evelyn?" Marina Cabrini was standing in a corner of the room with her back to the window. Her hair was pulled harshly off her face into a tight knot at the nape of her neck. Her skin was the color of an almond, smooth and unmarked. It was a face that Evelyn had always imagined a painter spending a lifetime trying to paint. Evelyn shook her head.

"She never woke up." Marina turned away, but then there was Rio. They closed their arms around each other and held on for a long, long moment.

"Gussie came home yesterday afternoon, Evvie," said Victor wearily. "She was planning to call you."

Carl started pacing up and down the small room. Christine opened a magazine. Rio sat down, folding his arms and legs as if he were disappearing into himself. "Things didn't go so well for her in Arizona," said Victor.

Carl made a sound like air coming out of a balloon. He fisted his hands. "Things didn't go so well, Papa? Is that it? How long you going to let her pull the wool over your eyes? All that money we spent on that girl and she shames us. Does she come home like we want her? Pah! She comes home with her tail between her legs. She's gotta go play ball, she says. Play ball, Papa. She's your goddamn daughter and you let her—"

Marina Cabrini held up a hand. "Carlo. Carlo, stop this."

Carl set his teeth together and stormed out of the room. A nurse came in with a tray of coffee but no one touched it.

"He doesn't mean anything, Papa," said Christine at last. "He's upset."

"Evelyn, Gussie got dropped off the team," said Rio quietly.

Victor spun around. "It was that coach! That coach out there hated Gussie. Made her life hell. Gussie was the best one they had and the coach got jealous."

"Papa," began Christine, but he stopped her.

"All her life all she wanted to do was sports. Sports this, sports that. Okay, that's what she wants to be, that's what she gets. An athlete. A pro. First, when I hear she wants to play pro ball, I'm a little against it. Gussie, you're a girl, I tell her. Not a man, a girl. She tells me girls play pro ball. Girls even win, she tells me. I see how she wants it. I'm her Papa. You want to go play with those Saints, then play with those Saints, I tell her. So they're all the way in Phoenix, Arizona, so what? Get me a box seat. You know how it was, Evvie. You remember. The basketball. The field hockey. The races she beat all the boys in. Every time she was the best. You know the look in her face when she picked up a baseball bat, it's what she loved. She used to tell me, Papa, think if I was a musician. If I was a musician I'd play music all the time, except I'm no musician. I play ball.

"So play ball, I tell her. She's out there, playing hard as any man. Her knee goes out on her. She's in pain half the time she's playing but she keeps on playing. She's swinging like a pro. She's got this batting average I can't believe. She's the best. Then she comes up against this coach. He gets her thinking she's no good. Makes her life rotten."

"No, Papa. That's not how it happened," interrupted Christine. "There was a coach like that when Gussie was in high school. But there's no coach like that now."

"No coach?" echoed Victor, dazed and sad.

"There's no jealous coach," Christine repeated slowly, as if she were talking to a child. "Gussie messed up all by herself. I don't know what really happened out there, she never tells me anything I can believe. For all I know, she never even played on a team. She was probably robbing banks. God knows she's the type."

"What an asshole you are," said Rio. He sighed wearily, as if he had said the same thing a thousand times before. "I suppose you're going to say that we should have dragged her home by the hair and chained her to a desk in the office. Is that it?"

Christine flashed him a look of contempt. "If she had a job, she wouldn't be out wrecking motorcycles."

"A job? Is that all you think she needs? A *job?*"

"We made her a good offer, Rio. It's not my fault if she wants to throw her life away. For a whole year she hasn't even bothered to answer Mother's letters."

"Mother's letters," said Rio with a laugh. "We know about Mother's letters. We—"

Stiffening in her chair in the corner, Marina cut him off with a sudden, lashing word in Italian. Christine began to redden as the air filled with the crackle of her mother's voice. Rio disappeared into himself like a little boy. Victor rolled back his head with grief and closed his eyes. Evelyn quickly, reflexively covered her ears with her hands. She tried to make herself small. She began to bring her mind into blankness. She knew how. She was good at it.

CHAPTER THREE

The telephone company's blimp stayed in the air for fifty-five minutes before turning around like a whale and heading back to wherever it came from.

Avis Poli was sorry to see it go. She had been hoping that the thing would remain, dramatically and meaningfully, right over the playing field until the end of the game: the better the challenge, the sweeter the taste of victory, she thought, and she was not sure if she had just made up the phrase or had heard it before and filed it away for a time such as this. Victory. It was not a word she had ever used before in any direct connection to herself. Her sons, yes: it was the stuff that ran through the fabric of their everyday lives. From the time they were old enough to go out of the house without her, it had been one round of victory after another. First it was the small things—the thrills of fear in their faces as they plunged into the road for themselves, defying the traffic with their little fists raised and holding up their hands in triumph when they made it to the other side. With the girls it had been different. Angela and Mary-Susan would no more expect the traffic to harm them than they would expect one of their brothers to come at them with a shotgun. And when the boys were older it was the larger things: games in the schoolyard; football in the streets; leaps into the river from the quivering branches of trees with their very lives hanging in the balance. It never mattered what the particulars were. What mattered was the principle.

It seemed to Avis that they carried in their genes some mysterious but indelible inheritance that made them believe that life was as divided down the middle as the back of a skunk. On one side were the winners. On the other side were the losers. Sometimes they took turns winning and losing but the principle remained the same. They never questioned this. They accepted it as simply as the law of gravity. Certainly all her sons had their own special personalities. George was broody and liked his privacy. Frankie was never still a minute. Paulie was picky, especially about his clothes. Paulie changed his clothes three or four times a day. But Avis could say in all honesty that her boys were a far cry better than some of the others.

Birdey and Chocko's sons, five of them, were as capable as bulldozers when it came to something like carrying on a normal conversation. When they talked at all they talked into their new, broad, strong chests and although it gave her pleasure to look at them it was difficult to run into one of them on the street. "How are you, dear?" *"Rrrf."* "Tell your mother I want her to call me." *"Kayk."* Any old lady who needed help cleaning out her attic would be sure to get it by asking Birdey to send over one of her boys but all the same, and Avis couldn't help but feel a little guilty at admitting it, for after all they were part of her own flesh and blood, she really did believe that Birdey's boys were, when you got right down to it, boring. Not that she would ever say so. Birdey adored them. If any woman on earth was made to be the mother of five sons, it was Birdey. They in turn had put their mother up on a pedestal, tiptoeing around her as if she belonged in a glass case in a museum. Avis could honestly say that there had been many times when she would have liked nothing better than to see Birdey stuffed and put into one. ·

How Birdey had ever stuck it out with the team was beyond Avis. Maybe it was the attention. Birdey had been the girl with the prettiest dresses, the prettiest bows in her hair, the prettiest way of dropping her knees if a curtsy would bring her attention. But there had been nothing pretty about what they'd been doing for the last four months. The first time Birdey looked in a mirror after a workout she nearly fainted at the sight of her bloated, red face and the queer way her chest was heaving. Avis expected her to quit there and then. Later, when the practices had gotten more serious, Avis just stood back and waited for Gussie to kick Birdey out. Wasn't she the one holding up batting practice because her bra strap came loose? Wasn't Birdey the one who couldn't bear to wear a glove over her half-inch fingernails? And didn't Birdey herself, begging Avis to run some more hot water for a bath because her bones were all undone, say that the whole business was crazy and all she cared about was losing a few pounds and buying a few new dresses? Somehow Gussie had put up with her. Somehow Birdey had stuck it out. They had all stuck it out.

It seemed now, as Avis picked her way in a half-trot along the river to Sandy Dorn's house, that it was like some grand, incomprehensible scheme requiring the most careful attention, like a wedding or a church bazaar; no, better than that—like a trip around the world or running for representative or liberating a country. It was grand. It had taken everything. It had clicked steadily onward until at last here it was, right up to the brink, up to the day of the game with not even three hours to go. No matter what the worst of them said, no matter what Rollie the Fist Pelletier had done to try to stop them, they were going to see this thing through to the finish. Avis began running faster.

The sun was hot on her neck and the river was glinting beside her. The great willow trees along the bank passed by in a rush of soft green. Under her feet the damp sandy path yielded with the feel of a trampoline, now accepting her, now flinging her upward, and as she tossed her head back in the breeze she looked up at the hole in the sky where the telephone company's blimp had been, and she told herself that for the first time in her life, the thing she wanted more than she had ever wanted anything was the thing she was now calling victory. Even as she said the word she felt a thrill. She felt giddy all over. Slowing down, she walked the last hundred yards to Sandy's cabin. She was breathless as she climbed the steps. Her loose, lightweight sweatsuit felt warm and a little damp. She hoped she had not overdone it. Gussie had warned them to take it easy before the game. But Gussie did not have a sister like Birdey.

Up on the porch, Avis rang the bell to the back door. Her friend June Campbell, wearing her favorite pantsuit, let her inside. A kettle was boiling on the stove. Sandy's five-year-old son Jeremy, looking, Avis immediately thought, ever so much better, was bent over the kitchen table, coloring a large pencil drawing of a blimp. The boy was dressed in his honorary Spurs junior-sized uniform, with his name stenciled across the back of the shirt. It was a gift from June. Jeremy's face was almost rosy as he put out his arms to Avis.

As always, she took him to her with a hard pang of emotion, nuzzling his face with hers. Her fingers went at once to the side of his skull where the injury had been. She saw with pleasure that the bones had finally hardened. There did not seem to be a scar. After all, she thought, fractures heal. Even in a child pain comes and goes. The world was full of it. You grow up believing you can spot evil a mile away, you think you can sniff it from a distance the way you smell a dead animal and you come to find out it's not that easy. The givers of pain passed you by on the street as ordinarily as the givers of strength. Kenny Dorn was as good-looking as any one of Birdey's boys. He smelled good too.

Avis bristled at the thought of him. Leo and the priests, pitying Sandy Dorn and sponsoring Masses for the safe recovery of Jeremy Dorn, had all the same been ready to rush in with forgiveness for Kenny Dorn. There was a time for everything, they said; a purpose for everything under the heavens, as though their heavens, busily keeping the stars in place and the oceans flowing, saw no reason at all why a grown man should not be forgiven for bashing the head of his small son against the walls of his house, once, twice, repeatedly—and Avis knew all over again that no matter how often Leo and the priests came at her with their scriptures she would never stop damning the life of Kenny Dorn for what he had done to that boy.

Not that he had gotten away with it altogether. There was a warrant out for his arrest. No one knew for sure where he was. No one was certain he would not come back. And if he did, and if he came back with his hand out for forgiveness, what was the use? What good were the priests with their mercy, the police with their warrants, when right in front of her, coloring a picture with his crayons, was a boy who would spend the rest of his life with the knowledge of terror and pain? What about his dreams?

Avis clasped her hands together, and kissed the boy once more. Bringing her a cup of tea, June said that she couldn't get over the sight of the blimp. The blimp had taken up Jeremy's whole window. The blimp had made him smile. Avis wrapped her hands around the warm mug. Low-sounding grunts were coming from the front room of the cabin, where Sandy, the shortstop, was doing push-ups. Avis warned her not to overdo it. The last thing they needed was their fastest player throwing out her back. Sandy laughed breathlessly. She was a small woman with back muscles as tough as electrical wires. She was only five-feet-two, but she did not believe herself to be short. Avis sipped her tea.

"I've been thinking a lot," she told June. "I've been going over in my mind all morning how boys are different from girls. I think we raise them differently."

June beamed with fondness, sending Avis a look that meant, Of course you have, dear. Avis understood that the look would have been exactly the same no matter what she might happen to say.

"How's Birdey?"

Avis shrugged. "The same. Last night she shaved her legs twice. She keeps wishing we had decided to wear shorts instead of breeches. Thirty-eight years old and she still acts like she's a pom-pom girl."

June cupped her small, exquisitely chiseled chin with her hands and smiled. "Now, Avis, she's only nervous. You know what I think? I think Birdey secretly wishes she could be more like you."

Avis looked up quickly, scoffing.

"She's ten years younger than you and that means a lot. You should hear her these days when she talks about you."

Avis made a clucking sound with her tongue.

"For heaven's sake, Avis, she makes you sound like you're a movie star! She practically calls you Sophia Loren. Avis Poli, you can't sit here and tell me you don't know how proud everyone is of you, Birdey especially."

Avis blushed.

"Stand up," commanded June, wagging her finger. "Since when are you so shy?" She clapped her hands together and called for Sandy. Jeremy put down his crayon and squirmed with anticipation. Huffing heavily, Sandy bounced into her kitchen. Avis rose.

"Tell us how much weight you lost," said June.

Avis protested. "You asked me already. Yesterday."

"I forget. I never was any good at numbers."

Sandy Dorn scooped up her son. "Guess how many pounds Avis lost!"

The boy screeched with delight and remembered. "Avis used to be *fat!* And she ain't anymore!"

Sandy rolled him around and tickled him the way he loved it all over his belly. "Guess how much."

Jeremy took a deep breath and blurted, "Eighty-ten hundred!" It was the highest number he could think of.

"That's right," said June.

"Right!" cried Sandy.

Avis couldn't help it; she went into a glow all over. Sandy tumbled into a chair with her son holding on as if she were a merry-go-round, and in a burst of enthusiasm the two of them turned into a whirl of arms and legs, hugging, tickling, playing. Avis met June's utterly satisfied look and the two women grinned at each other.

"I bet Angela is thrilled to be home," June said. "And those boys of hers! Pretty as their mother. I was just saying to Nate the other day how I'll have to get Grace Pandy to make an especially nice quilt for Angela before she goes back to Texas. I think I'll ask her for one like she made Jeremy. I would have done it this morning when I stopped by Grace's, just before I came over here, but you know Grace. She was all dathered up over the game. I had a little something for her, one of those medals I brought home from Rome. It's just a tiny thing, a Blessed Mother, the kind you can pin on your bra. Grace said it was just what she needed. All she could do was stand in front of the mirror and say how if anyone told her when she was twenty that when she was fifty-two she'd be playing on a softball team, she would've had them committed to a mental hospital. Her husband Marko, God rest his soul, would turn over in the grave if he could see her. But like I was saying to Nate . . ."

There came a very small catch in Juney's voice, a sudden quivering, and without turning to look behind her, Avis sensed with horror that something dangerous was moving in fast. The back door slammed shut. Avis heard the clumping sound of a heavy pair of shoes or boots; they all heard it, and in that moment Avis saw something she had hoped she might never see again: the change in Jeremy Dorn. It was not that the boy merely went pale. It was not that he merely looked frightened. He clutched at his mother with a single, utterly desperate cry of terror, and as he closed his mouth again he appeared to have been drained of everything that was childhood. Avis's stomach turned over at the sight. The footsteps approached. Sandy went rigid. Avis motioned to the bedroom door with her eyes and Sandy rose with the boy. June rose also, and without a word reached to open the silverware drawer. Avis reached for the telephone. A hard knock sounded against the hollow kitchen door. Sandy began to bolt for the bedroom but the front door suddenly flew open and she was halted in mid-flight with her son a small round ball clinging tightly. Avis looked up in confusion. Someone rushed across the front room and even as the back door was slowly creaking open there appeared from the front a woman in a leaf-green jogging suit and the purple and white cap of the Spurs.

"Patsy!" cried Avis. Patsy Griffin, solid as a barn, pushed back her cap and stood in the middle of the kitchen with her hands on her hips.

"I heard a car down the road," she said, and even as she spoke there was the back door coming all the way open, and there was June with her hand in the silverware drawer, and there was Patsy looking like she was ready to bring down the roof if it meant keeping Jeremy Dorn from hurt or fear, and there to their amazement stood Officer Raymond Kuzick.

"Christ, can't anybody around here answer a door?"

They all seemed to burst at once. They looked from each other to Kuzick and back again and there wasn't anything to do but put their hands to their faces and let out sighs of relief. Sandy freed her son and he went like a dart for the policeman. Kuzick welcomed him up on his hip. He took off his hat and put it on the boy's head. Jeremy turned and beamed down upon the women. Kuzick just stood there trying to look like he knew what to do with himself. Patsy broke the tension with a half-laugh and plopped down at the table as though she'd been invited over for lunch.

"Nate sent you," said June flatly.

"Hey, pal," Kuzick coaxed Jeremy. "How about you get to wear that thing outside?"

The boy slipped down and scooted out to the yard.

"Don't you go dropping it in the river, it's the only one I got!" Kuzick turned back to June. "I just wanted to drop by and say good luck to the ladies," he said.

"Sure." Patsy rolled her eyes with disbelief.

"Let's have it, Ray," said Sandy sharply.

"Look," he shot back, not unkindly. "You've got every right in the world to your feelings, but I saw it too. I know what Kenny Dorn did to that kid." At the sound of her former husband's name, Sandy brought back her shoulders stiffly, as if, Avis thought, she was about to make a throw to the plate. But Avis had to give a little credit to Ray Kuzick: he wasn't any lunk.

"So how come the bastard's not in jail?" said Patsy, clenching a fist as she spoke. Avis noted the way Patsy kept her eyes set firmly on the open window to watch Jeremy. So did June.

Kuzick spoke softly and without visible emotion. "Danny McGrath thinks he saw Kenny's car. He's not sure. Could be he's back in town. Maybe not."

Sandy, with a great effort, collected herself. She looked at him squarely. "Jeremy is going to be sitting with Nate and Juney at the game. I'd be grateful if you or, or someone, might be not too far off. He'd never come anywhere close to Jeremy with Nate around. But . . ." Sandy faltered.

"Not that it's any consolation, Sandy, but if he does, he's not going to do the kid harm. I've seen this kind of thing plenty enough. My guess is if he's in town, he's sniffing for something else." Avis could not tell by his look whether he really meant what he said. June pushed back her chair and went to Sandy, taking her gently by the hands and steering her away from the kitchen. Kuzick allowed himself a short smile in her direction.

"Hey, Sandy? Listen, uh, I just want to say, good luck. You just get out there and play some good ball. If you ladies whip the pants off the telephone company, I'll feel better every time I got to pay my phone bill." He reached up to tip his hat, but remembering it wasn't there, he flashed another smile and left quietly.

It was time to dress for the game.

CHAPTER FOUR

While they waited, Gussie lived. The torn side of her face healed slowly, and it was hard to tell what was skin from what was scar. She had broken three fingers, an elbow, many ribs. The hearing in her left ear was completely gone. Her left leg had been smashed almost flat. The nurses kept it wrapped in thick layers of gauze and plastic, safe as a relic. Hovering nearby they stood guard against infection. Victor Cabrini turned grizzly with beard. Marina stayed in the waiting room at the end of the hallway, speaking to no one. Rio paced the halls and stairways and would not sit still. Evelyn watched carefully. In a week, Gussie was moved from intensive care to a private room with a view of the maple trees that ringed the parking lot. Hannah and Peggy took a very comfortable armchair away from a doctor and brought it to Gussie's room for their neighbor Evelyn. They brought Evelyn meals on trays and made sure she ate them. When there was nothing left in Gussie except pain, Evelyn turned her eyes away, but she kept on sitting beside her.

By the middle of June Gussie was eating real food. By the Fourth of July she was sitting up in bed. Her parents and her brother went back to their offices. For the first time in more than six years, Evelyn was having trouble falling asleep. She could hardly sleep at all. She was too busy to sleep. She was making plans.

In one version of Evelyn's plans, Gussie returned to Anthony

Street, the only place where she had ever been happy, in a wheelchair. Evelyn and Danny brought her home like their new baby, wheeling her inside with nervous pride. They spared nothing for her comfort. Evelyn cleaned the whole house. She even put up new curtains. The children were crazy about Gussie. Mundy and Kate stopped fighting. Allison learned to stand up by balancing herself against the armrests of the wheelchair. Evelyn herself learned to change Gussie's bandages. Mornings, before the summer heat drove them inside to sit by the fan and drink cold tea, they all worked in the garden. Gussie, although she never had one of her own, loved gardens. Gussie was sick to death of the desert, and supervised the planting from her wheelchair. Evelyn pulled weeds. The children helped put in the tomato seeds, the summer squash, the lettuce. There would have to be flowers. Gussie would want flowers that were big and bright and lasting. They would go to the library to read seed catalogues, and if Evelyn happened to ask, Gussie would tell her that she would be nowhere else on earth except Anthony Street when those seeds came up in blooms.

In another version, Evelyn sat in her usual place by Gussie's bed in the doctor's armchair. Gussie's family had gone home. Late, late into the night, the two of them talked. Evelyn stopped remembering that in their childhood, Gussie talked hardly at all. Evelyn forgot about the silences, the days with Gussie when Gussie put the whole of herself into the race she was running, or the game she was playing, or the new round of exercises she was putting her body through. Gussie had not believed in talk. Talk was only a necessity, like money. Evelyn planned that the sound of Gussie's voice closed all the spaces between them, and somehow, somewhere in the desert, Gussie had learned to use words. Evelyn sat at the side of Gussie's bed. Gussie would reach for her to come closer. The skin of her face was blistering, her teeth were gritted against pain, and the effort to speak was enormous, but Gussie was strong. She came through. She talked.

In Evelyn's mind there has been no motorcycle, no accident. They are two girls together and Evelyn's father has not yet bought a new car. Uncle William is not seventy-nine years old, but much, much younger, young enough to give Gussie lessons in throwing a football, swinging a bat, twisting her body in a slide to home plate. Evelyn is the one on the sidelines, cheering. Evelyn is the one keeping watch, the lookout ready to make them stop the moment she sees any member of Gussie's family except Rio anywhere near. In the corner of the Brody yard nearest the woods, Uncle William shows Gussie the best way to field a grounder, steal a base, make a tag. Evelyn is giddy with fear. All of this has been forbidden. Gussie has never told her what they've done to her the times they've found her out, but each time she has disappeared into her room for a day, or two days, or a week, and they won't even let her come to the phone. Marina Cabrini pays a visit to Shirley Brody. Marina has hired a lawyer. She will prosecute the next time Uncle William breaches her trust, she says. No more coaching. No more workouts. Does Shirley Brody get the point?

Shirley Brody promises that Uncle William will stop. He does not. He brings Gussie to the river with a stopwatch and lets her run until she drops. Shirley smacks her lips over a word like *prosecute*. She pulls down the window shades to thumb her nose at her next-door neighbor with the beautiful clothes and the husband setting up a new business. Shirley tells Evelyn, "You know what I'll do if she comes over here one more time with her uppity ways? I'll prosecute, that's what."

Shirley lets Gussie do chin-ups on the bars of her clothesline. When Uncle William teaches Gussie the way to tape her wrists and ankles before a baseball game in the schoolyard, Shirley lends them the tape. Franklin looks the other way. Evelyn goes on standing guard, following Gussie from one neighborhood to the next. Boys let her into their hockey games when the river freezes. If they don't, they will find their hockey sticks broken in half. Some of them bleed from the nose. Gussie has a fist and a temper they all fear. Evelyn makes a list of the people Gussie has sworn not to hurt. They are: Evelyn, Uncle William, Shirley, Franklin, Rio, Victor. Evelyn sees with satisfaction that her name is at the top of the list.

One Christmas, Uncle William gives her a set of dumbbells, which she keeps hidden under her bed. Evelyn goes there often, curling up in a chair to watch. She keeps count of the lifts as Gussie's muscles strain, and her body ripples, and her breath comes and goes in short, deep huffs with the regularity of music. Evelyn listens for footsteps outside the door, for they have told Gussie's family they're doing homework. Evelyn does two of every assignment. She has learned to imitate Gussie's handwriting perfectly. Gussie leaves her education to Evelyn, who teaches her French verbs between lifts of the barbells, history dates as she hangs upside down from Shirley's clothesline, geometry on the way home from basketball practice.

In the two kitchens side by side, supper is on the table. Marina Cabrini, rushing home late from the office, has heated a pot of soup. Shirley Brody cooked a pot roast with potatoes and carrots. The smells combine, rich and compelling, and standing on the sidewalk in front of their houses Gussie and Evelyn cannot make up their minds where to eat. Shirley goes to her window. Marina goes to hers. They wave their arms, calling for the girls to come in. Marina is dressed in her business clothes. Smoothly, trimly, beautifully, she waves her arm in the window, and her hands are strong and white. Evelyn knows that in the round, clean glasses at the Cabrini table the red wine catches the last rays of the sun and shimmers with light and life and clarity. Evelyn tells Gussie that she feels like soup. Pleased, Gussie runs to Shirley for pot roast. When supper is over Evelyn helps Marina wash dishes. When they are finished, Evelyn takes a long time saying goodbye.

In her hospital bed, Gussie lay on her side facing the wall. The sheets were pulled up to her chin. All that could be seen of her from the doorway was the jumbled mound of her black hair, spilling over the pillow as if it had just been poured from a bucket. She was motionless and silent. The room was dark except for thin streaks of sunlight coming in from the cracks where the drawn shades didn't quite meet the window frames. The narrow table at the foot of the bed was crammed with drooping flowers in vases with yellowing water. In between the vases were untidy stacks of greeting cards and letters, many of them still in their envelopes, unopened. At the side of the bed, the armchair held an untouched breakfast tray. Even the cold scrambled eggs smelled of hospital. Under the tray, their corners sticking out haphazardly, there were more unopened envelopes with strange, exotic stamps. In the far corner of the room a huge, horseshoe-shaped wreath gave off a weak scent of roses. The roses were yellow and the banner around the top was bright scarlet. The white lettering across the banner said, *Saints.* Evelyn went into the room on tiptoe.

"Gussie? Are you asleep?"

She did not turn her head. Her voice was low, hoarse. "Yes. Fast asleep, Ev. I'm dreaming."

"Why were you on Anthony Street on that motorcycle?"

"There's no motorcycle in this dream. Want to know what there is? Ice cream. Blueberry ice cream. Thickest blueberries I ever saw in my life."

"You weren't wearing a helmet. I looked all around for one."

"Did you bring me ice cream, Evvie?"

"I brought my kids. My kids and Uncle William are down in the parking lot. They want you to look out the window and wave to them."

"I'm tired, Ev."

"But they put on clean shirts just to see you. Uncle William even brushed his teeth without being told."

"I'm tired. If you brought ice cream, why don't you give it to the nurses."

"Nice wreath, Gussie."

"What wreath? There's no wreath in this dream." Without another word, Gussie lifted her head and plunged under the pillow. There was nothing left to say.

Evelyn went to see Rio Cabrini.

Like his brother Carl, Rio worked for the family. He lived alone, four blocks from Anthony Street, in an abnormally tall, hundred-and-twelve-year-old house that looked as though it had been plopped down in Currys Crossing by the producers of a horror movie. Rio was doing it over. Evelyn had never been there before, but he had been doing it over for as long as she could remember. He had painted the outside white with white shutters. The front porch was missing. A short wooden ladder reached to the wide oak door, and Evelyn walked through an empty, shadowy series of rooms that smelled of sawdust and rotten wood. She found Rio in what was going to be the kitchen. He was flat on his back on the floor, staring upward, smoking a cigarette and absently flicking ashes onto the cracked old linoleum. He looked up at Evelyn without surprise.

"Tell me what you think of the color green," he said, propping himself up on an elbow. The smoke of his cigarette curled into the air like thin blue fingers. "It's an excellent color for a tree, but what about my kitchen? I can't make up my mind what'll happen to my stomach if I paint it green." He stubbed out his cigarette and jumped lightly to his feet. His black hair fell in a jumble to his ears and curled, the way Gussie's hair curled, thickly and warmly around the open collar of his shirt. His eyes were Gussie's eyes, black and bright. He smiled at her.

"You didn't show up to talk about my walls, did you, Ev? Christ, it's dark in here. Come on out to the back porch where it's better."

Evelyn followed him out to a wide old porch opening onto a stone path leading into his garden. Evelyn blinked in the sudden light, gasping with surprise when she saw what was out there. The garden was running riot with flowers. Color burst off the ends of stalks and wildly sprang toward the sun. Some of the blossoms were enormous and bulging, some were quiet and small, some reached up from the green blades of grass like the clear eyes of a very small baby, and ivy grew over the round stone wall that enclosed it all. Over the top of the wall she could see apple trees dotted with fruit, and an unusual blue in the sky through their branches. Rio pulled out an old straw chair and she took it.

"It's beautiful, Rio. I had no idea."

Rio lit another cigarette. Shrugging, he lowered himself to the porch step. "Doesn't take much. The ground here is good."

"I wish I knew names of flowers. I'm thinking about planting some myself."

"You didn't come by to ask me the names of flowers, Ev."

With great effort, Evelyn took her eyes off the garden and faced Rio. "It's Gussie. She won't talk to me."

"And you think I will?"

"I'd appreciate it."

"Have you talked with my mother?"

Evelyn shook her head.

"Poor Ev," said Rio softly. A hard, tight look came into his face. "That's real slate I got up there." Squinting, he craned his neck back, trying to look at his roof. "Big slabs of slate. Been there since 1863. Mother's worried about them falling off. Every time she comes over here, she puts a book or something over her head so she won't get hit. You have no idea what she must look like to my neighbors. If it's windy, Mother uses a soup pot. She goes straight to the attic to rap on the roof to see if they've loosened."

"Oh, Rio, she does not," sighed Evelyn. "That doesn't sound like your mother at all."

"You're right. We won't be hard on Mother. She can't stand it that I bought this house. It's too kinky for her to have a son carrying on with a house instead of some nice girl with a fortune. But this thing with Gussie is getting to her. Mother's patience is wearing thin, even for Mother. She wants Gussie home and straight to work."

Evelyn sat forward. "Work?"

"Out of touch, Evvie. You are definitely out of touch. Wait a minute, I want to show you something." Rio went into the house and came back with an unsealed envelope. He pulled out a letter and held it out to Evelyn. "Read this. From Mother to Gussie. I found it with Gussie's things after the accident."

Evelyn handed it back. "It's in Italian, for God's sake."

"Oh, sorry." He folded it together and slipped it into his back pocket.

"Aren't you going to tell me what it says?"

"Mother has set up an office for Gussie at home. She's got her eye on some land by the river and she wants Gussie in on it. Mother's been trying for years to get Gussie involved in the business. Poor Mother. She hadn't counted on the motorcycle."

"Is that why Gussie came back? To work for your mother?"

Rio shook his head with a laugh and stubbed his cigarette out on the step.

"Then why?"

He lit another one. For what seemed a long time he stared out into the garden, exhaling noisily. At last he turned around.

"Do you know where the Saints are?"

Evelyn eyed him blankly, then thought of the letters under the breakfast tray, the armchair, quietly collecting dust. She had a quick, colorful image of an entire softball team hiding in Gussie's hospital room, invisibly and magically urging her safe recovery. She shook her head slowly.

"On tour," said Rio. "Australia. Japan. You name it."

"They went without Gussie?"

"They left a day or so after Gussie left Arizona. It's simple, really. They cut her from the team."

Evelyn's face twisted with confusion. She stammered dumbly.

"She was benched a couple of months ago. You can call it a slump if you like. Other than that, you know about as much as I do. You know how Gussie holds on to her words. She won't give anything away unless she has to."

Evelyn went back to the hospital. She had no idea of what she might say, but she took the stairs to the second floor two at a time and hurried down the hall to Gussie's room. The door was half-closed. Evelyn reached to push it open and a white-sleeved arm shot out from behind her. Hannah Wally took hold of her wrist.

"Gussie's got company," said Hannah. She pulled Evelyn away from the door. "What've you got in the bag?"

"Ice cream for Gussie."

"I'll put it in the freezer, Ev. You can come back later, or you can wait. I'll let you wait in the nurses' lounge if you like."

"Come on, Hannah. Let me in."

Hannah folded her arms across her chest and looked firm. Taking the ice cream, she steered Evelyn to the tiny lounge behind the nursing station in the middle of the corridor, sat her down in a chair, and told her to stay there until she was sent for. The instant Hannah was out of sight, Evelyn crept down the hallway to Gussie's room. She made herself small in the doorway and looked in.

A woman was leaning against the chrome radiator by the windows. She appeared to be in her mid-thirties. She was not especially tall or short, but there was in her manner the quiet ease of a woman who is utterly at home in her body. She was dressed for the hot August night in a loose, sleeveless cotton shirt and a knee-length skirt that was decorated with row after row of bright, healthy, spectacularly embroidered flowers against a background of pale green. It was Rio's garden, wrapped around her hips and delivered to Gussie's bedside to cheer her. All Evelyn had brought was blueberry ice cream.

Evelyn recognized her at once. Miss Linda Drago, former director of girls' athletics at Currys Crossing High. Linda Drago was laughing. She had broad, pleasant features and the kind of face that belonged to people who get their maple syrup straight from the trees. Linda Drago did not look as if she would have any trouble felling a tree all by herself.

It was a harsh, mocking laugh. "You quit, Cabrini? You *quit?*"

Gussie answered in a low mumble. Linda Drago took a step closer to the bed.

"Christ, look at you."

Evelyn heard a slight, muffled sob that seemed to come from under Gussie's pillow.

"You're pitiful, Cabrini. Pitiful. A shot at the top with the Saints and you throw it away. You think I don't know the score? It gets a little rough out there and you can't take it. Hell, I used to think you were a winner. I got girls working for me who'd whip you easy when it comes to guts. I got eighteen-, nineteen-year-olds who'd give anything for a shot at the Saints. Just make sure you never let any of my girls look at your face. Christ, look at you."

The sounds from the bed were like growls. Drago put her hands to her face and laughed again.

"I'm surprised, I'm really surprised. Pisses me off when I think about the time I wasted on you. What for? So you can lie here like a loser?"

Evelyn put her hand on the doorknob.

"Don't, Evvie. Please," said Hannah softly behind her. Evelyn let go, hating nurses and their silent feet.

"Gussie's crying, Hannah."

Hannah pressed her lips together thinly.

"You know that woman in there? Drago?"

Hannah nodded. "She used to be at the high school. That was before I came here. I don't know Linda well. Mainly by reputation. She's a coach now. Softball. I used to play a little before I came to work here. Have you ever heard of the Belles?"

Evelyn sighed. Softball was what Gussie had done miles away in the desert. The last thing Evelyn wanted to hear about was softball.

"Come back tomorrow, Ev," said Hannah.

Evelyn dreamed:
Gussie's leg has healed. The motorcycle is as good as new.

One morning Evelyn shows up for a visit, but Gussie's room is empty. The bed has been freshly made. The floor has been mopped and polished. The nurses treat Evelyn with slick, professional kindness. They bring her to a window. She can see Gussie outside, walking away from the hospital. Her motorcycle is parked under a tree. A small crowd has gathered around it. Gussie approaches them. They are women wearing bright silk jackets and matching caps. They are waving banners that say Japan, Australia. Their mouths open wide with laughter.

Gussie leaps on the motorcycle and turns on the radio. She waves her arms in the air, swaying her body to the music. Then she pulls on her gloves. The motorcycle engine roars. Dust rises up from the ground. The nurses call Evelyn's name. Hannah and Peggy take hold of her with strong, soft hands. Evelyn does not want to leave the window, but she is certain that they will split her apart if they pull any harder. She yields. She will do whatever they tell her.

At the end of the summer Gussie was released from the hospital. The plaster casts came off her arm and hand. Her ribs had healed. The scars on her face had faded to a dull pink. She walked with a thick, wooden cane, dragging her useless left leg behind as if it belonged to somebody else.

She saw a physical therapist daily. When she was not in therapy she was at work in her family's business. Her father told her that she was doing so well he would make her a full partner by the time she turned thirty. She looked almost pleased to hear it.

CHAPTER FIVE

"Looks like you gals got yourself a beautiful day for a ball-game," said Rollie Pelletier, the sportswriter, unpacking a large battery-operated tape recorder in Avis's living room. By the look of him, Avis thought, he had probably been up all night praying for a thunderstorm. Avis settled into a corner of the couch, next to her sister, and invited Rollie to take the matching chair nearby. Birdey sat up very straight with her feet crossed politely at the ankles. She had flung on an old raincoat belonging to Leo, a yellow plastic thing that crinkled every time she moved. She was doing her best not to move at all. The raincoat covered her uniform. Birdey had thought it might be bad luck to let anyone see her dressed before the start of the game. "Just like when we were brides," she said. Avis, still in her sweatsuit, was on her way upstairs to get dressed when the doorbell rang, and to everyone's surprise Rollie the Fist Pelletier came in looking for a pre-game interview just, he said, the same as if they were pros.

"Don't you mean to say 'men'?" Avis couldn't help saying.

But really it was a rich and splendid day. The sun was beaming. Under the vast blue cloudless sky the green had come into the trees practically overnight like a long cool drink of something vital. What was it Leo had said, making fun of the Irish priests? Mellifluous. "Sure and it's a mellifluous mornan, Avis! Couldn't a done it better myself!" Avis had a pretty good idea what Rollie Pelletier would do if she told him a word like mellifluous: have it all over town by nightfall that Avis Poli committed adultery, or something worse.

She eyed him with suspicion. Whatever it was that had made Rollie Pelletier change his attitude, Avis was not about to trust him for one minute. Not even a month ago the very man was screaming in his newspaper articles that not only Currys Crossing but the entire civilized world would come grinding to a halt if they let those fool women go ahead and have a softball team. As if anyone could stop them! And it had been Rollie Pelletier who tried getting the Selectmen to deny the Spurs a permit to use the ball field. It was Rollie Pelletier who went through the ordinances with a fine-tooth comb, yelling high hell when he discovered that it said, *to be used freely by those men and boys committed to public recreation, this field shall be maintained by the town in all seasons.*

"Not a thing about women!" proclaimed the *Clarion*, and the whole team practically had to hold Gussie down to keep her away from Rollie Pelletier's office. She wanted to put dynamite under his chair. In the end she went to Boston to see a lawyer who personally went to visit the Board of Selectmen, the president of the newspaper, and Rollie Pelletier with the news that the term *men and boys* had been declared by the United States Congress to be a generic one, applying to all manner of human beings, and if Rollie Pelletier or anyone else dared to try depriving the Spurs of their constitutional rights, the Supreme Court itself would hear about it. The *Clarion* had complied.

Catching Avis's look, Birdey poked her sister in the ribs. Birdey was dying to get her name into the paper. While Rollie breathed testily into his microphone Birdey leaned over and whispered in Avis's ear, "Remember what Gussie said. Just look at him like he's a grape."

It wasn't difficult. With his balding, oval-shaped head, and his bland eyes, and the deep, almost crimson flush in his cheeks, Rollie Pelletier *looked* like a grape. Thinking the same thought, the two sisters quickly looked away from each other, biting their lips to keep from laughing out loud.

"Either of you ever have any experience with one of these things?" said Rollie in the tone of voice that Avis used on her grandchildren. Birdey smiled sweetly.

"Why, of course. That's just what we bought our kids for

Christmas toys. Avis and I have five apiece. But I have five
boys. Do you want their names?"

"Mr. Pelletier doesn't want us talking about our children,
dear," said Avis, emphasizing the *Mister* to let Rollie know he
was not going to find anything but the coolest formality in her
manner. "We haven't got much time. In fact we have hardly
any time at all. Why don't you just ask us some questions, Mr.
Pelletier?"

"Thank you, Mrs. Poli," he answered icily. "All you have to
do is speak clearly. You can make believe it's not even here.
Now, why don't we start with the beginning. What was it Augusta Cabrini did to tempt you into, uh, athletics? I take it neither one of you was ever inclined that way before."

His lips curled at the corners. He looked like a bad-tempered
little boy who was about to tell a dirty joke.

Grape, said Avis to herself.

"Bingo," said Birdey, sitting forward. Fixing her eyes on the
tape recorder, face flushed, Birdey was all ready to run with it.
Avis sat back. When Birdey was excited like this she was better
than the movies.

"Bingo?" asked Rollie Pelletier.

"We played every Tuesday down at the church. We had a
ball. Then one night just before Christmas, along comes these
two nurses, straight from the hospital, and before anybody
knew what was going on, they climbed up to the caller's booth.
Father O'Malley, that's who was calling, almost had heart failure. Nobody in eight years had ever interrupted a game. But
there they went. Said they had an announcement.

"It was Gussie. Course, we all knew Gussie Cabrini was just
out of the hospital after her accident. Nina Mason, the girl with
the harelip who's the bookkeeper for the Cabrini business, you
know, they're in real estate, they own half the town plus five or
six miles down on Cape Cod. Poor Nina had a sister who was
friends with my second boy, Charles, so I heard regular what
was happening. Not that Nina would ever so much as say a
single word against a Cabrini! You had to read between the
lines.

"Hannah and Peggy, they were the nurses, got up there like
the Red Cross asking for blood. They said if anyone wanted to
help Gussie Cabrini they should come to their house on An-

thony Street the next night. By their faces you'd of thought Gussie was at the door of death. Now it just so happened that Mrs. Flynn, that's the woman who's housekeeper at the Cabrini house, though what Marina Cabrini thinks she's proving with a housekeeper is not for me to say, but Mrs. Flynn ran into me at the supermarket that very next morning and when I happened to mention the nurses at bingo, out she bursts in tears. Didn't want to talk about it, she said. God love the poor girl, she said. She's very religious. Then she told me it would take a miracle and a half to get Gussie back to where she was.

"So I talked about it with Avis and we went. Not that I had any special feeling for the Cabrinis, but if I had half their money I'd get me a housekeeper too. Avis and I decided that if we could do anything at all to help Gussie we might as well."

Pausing for breath, Birdey flashed Rollie Pelletier her most dazzling smile. Rollie was ready to change the subject, but Birdey ignored him.

"Well! We got there to the nurses' house and to my surprise there were about twenty-five or so of us. They passed around these trays of little sandwiches and hot cider with cinnamon. Absolutely delicious.

"Gussie wasn't even there. After everyone settled down, along comes Evelyn Brody. Now I had not seen much of Evelyn Brody since, well, since the funerals. Her parents, I mean. Both in the same week. That poor girl. She was doing all right though. Very calm. She gave a little talk and I tell you the tears were flowing by the time she finished. I don't know about Avis but I was *moved*. Evvie told us how Gussie was in a very deep state of acute depression, and if somebody didn't do something soon the girl would be recommended by the psychiatrists for some kind of institution. That did it as far as I was concerned. Never in all my life did I have to consult a psychiatrist with what's personal. But let me tell you, I have heard stories. The last thing I wanted was to see that poor girl in a straitjacket. That's what they do. She was practically a stranger to me but after I listened to Evvie, she wasn't a stranger anymore. I would've taken her into my own house if it would've helped! But let me tell you, the last thing I expected was what Evvie told us."

"Oh?" Rollie raised his eyebrows and sat forward. "The cure, I'll bet."

"Softball," said Birdey, smacking her lips with wonder. "She wanted us to get together and form a softball team. I'd heard of weird cures for depression but this was a first. I don't know about Avis but I just couldn't get over it. Then the nurses got up and gave us this very clinical talk about modern techniques and I could see for myself they were serious. They said the best way to undo the sort of depression Gussie was in was with something that was familiar. What could be more familiar to Gussie than softball? It made sense. Of course, she wouldn't be able to play for herself. It's a wonder she can even walk. Her leg's smashed pretty bad, you know. It's like a story I read once, or maybe it was a movie, about this famous piano player who wakes up one morning and his hands are paralyzed. Come to think of it, it was depression. He was in love with this frowzy French singer with red hair who disappeared during the war. He hadn't heard from her in months. As it turned out, his hands came back right after she did. They went all over the world together, giving concerts. So I said to Avis that we'd better sign up. A whole bunch of us signed up, and Evelyn went to see Gussie the next day. This part is really clever. This part's where the ulterior motive comes in. Gussie believed that the whole thing was Evelyn and the nurses' idea, and they wanted her to coach. At first she said no. That's depression for you. Once you're in a depression, the word yes goes right out of your vocabulary. Can't eat, can't sleep, can't clean the house, can't do even the things you like. I'm telling you, I'd rather have leprosy. You know what I mean?"

"I write about sports," said Rollie simply. Birdey nodded sympathetically.

"After a while, Gussie gave in and the next thing we knew we were having practices. You ever try playing softball in the snow?"

Rollie shook his head with profound indifference.

"My kids, I have five sons, all thought I was nuts. Chocko, that's my husband, was dead against it at first but my boys talked to him about it and he came around. My boys taught me a few things to get me started, like, well, everything. And that's that." She fell back in the couch, looked at her watch, and patted Avis on the knee. Avis appeared to have been dozing. "It's almost time to go," said Birdey sweetly. "Any more questions?"

Rollie opened his mouth but Avis, getting up, waved a hand to stop him. She had to get dressed. Albertina needed some time to herself before the game. She was sure Mr. Pelletier had gotten all the information he needed for a really fine article. Scowling, Rollie snapped off his machine. Avis breathed a long low sigh of relief. She had been worried that Birdey, carried away with her tale, might tell more of the truth than she had. Avis glanced sideways at her sister. Birdey pulled the raincoat more tightly around her waist, almost shyly. There was a girlish glint of happy expectation in her eyes.

Oh, I'm hard on her, thought Avis, as they saw Rollie Pelletier to the door. As soon as it closed behind him Birdey tore off Leo's raincoat and tossed it to the floor with a grand swagger.

"Thank God that's over," gasped Birdey, pretending to feel put-upon. Avis had a pretty good idea what kind of story Rollie the Fist would make out of what Birdey had told him. It made her shudder to think of it.

Wrapped in an oversized raincoat indoors on a lovely spring afternoon, Mrs. Albertina Nolan shared with us some of her thoughts on her softball team, her teammates, and life in general . . .

"Oh, Birdey," sighed Avis.

"What?"

"I thought for a minute you were going to tell him the truth. About Sandy and everything."

Birdey ran her tongue around her lips. She looked delighted with herself. "Sounded pretty good, didn't I?"

"Pretty good." Avis gave her a squeeze. Birdey caught hold of her sister's arm and held it.

"Tell me something, Avis. Is it true that Kenny Dorn's been around here?"

"Who told you that?"

"Never mind. Is it true?"

Avis wagged her head with impatience. "I've got to go get dressed. This is no time—"

Birdey clutched her arm more tightly. She had a firm, surprisingly solid grip. Avis couldn't remember ever noticing her sister's strength before.

"I won't let go until you answer me, Avis."

Reluctantly, Avis nodded. "Danny McGrath thinks he saw Kenny's car."

Birdey let go, leaving red marks on Avis's flesh in the shape of fingers. "I'm going to tell my boys to watch out for Jeremy."

"Fine."

"So get dressed, will you? I spend half my life waiting for you, Avis Poli. Hurry!"

Muttering under her breath, Avis went up to her room. Her uniform had been laid out on her bed. She closed the door and locked it. Her shoes lay side by side in front of her bedside table, cleated ends up so they wouldn't dig into the carpet. It was a thick, rich carpet the color of wet moss. Avis had bought it for Birdey's fortieth birthday. It hadn't been Avis's fault that the carpet fit her own room better than it fit Birdey's, and it hadn't been Avis's fault that Birdey's least favorite color was moss green. Birdey had given the carpet back to Avis with singular silence. Avis thought it was the kind of rug that made feet glad to be feet, and was happy to have it. She untied her sweatpants and let them fall. She looked down at her belly.

It still felt like looking at a stranger's. Even without sucking in her breath she could stare and stare at its simplicity, its gentle little roundness, its utterly amazing lack of too much fat, and it came to her that no matter what happened this afternoon, no matter what Linda Drago's Belles might do to run the Spurs ragged, humiliate them in front of the whole town, steamroller them all over the field or even, the possibility existed, God knew, win the game, she, Avis Poli, who four months before could hardly manage a flight of stairs in her own house without stopping to catch her breath, had this: the sight of herself with her pants down in front of the mirror. And look who was looking back! Look who met her stare without curling her lip in a sneer, without sending her into a frenzy of unhappiness that always ended in the bathroom, her own fingers stuck down her throat as though she had just swallowed a piece of rotting meat and must force it out even if it meant reaching all the way down into her guts and retching and reeling and shivering on the bathroom floor, alone with her tears and the huge heavy useless blobby thing that used to be her belly.

Avis untied her shoes and kicked them off and stepped out of her sweatpants. She put her hands on her hips and shook herself. No fat rippled. No jeering children's voices rose up out of her past with their stinging singsongs that had echoed and ached in her head all through her childhood. No more watching Birdey pick slim-waisted dresses off department store racks while she had hers made special. Shapeless. No more coming into a room at a party as the chatter ceases. No more did her own children introduce her to their new friends as their eyes said, "This is my mother. Don't let her gross you out." Avis hooked her thumbs in the elastic band of her underpants and gently pulled. There was a loud rap on the door.

"Mom? It's me, Paulie. Aunt Birdey says to hurry or she'll leave without you."

"Tell Aunt Birdey she can . . ."

"What?"

"Tell Aunt Birdey I'll be right down." Avis peeled off her underpants, letting her hands run slowly down the length of her new and still-strange body. She took off her sweatshirt and unhooked her bra, letting it fall to the floor, and turning this way and that, she studied herself in the mirror. True, the stretch marks were there, probably forever: pale and haphazard, the scars ran like random indentations across her belly, beneath her breasts, down her thighs, even, if she looked closely, in her upper arms where the fat had given way to firm muscular strength but left its traces in tiny seams. Leo, who had lately been asking her to come to bed without her nightgown, said she looked like a road map. Leo liked to make small automobiles out of his hands and throw off the blankets and go for a drive over her body. Sometimes he started at the knobby hills of her knees, sometimes at the twin oceans of her eyes, revving up his engine as he careened around her smooth almost-flat belly and slowing down because she liked him to come into her slowly; she liked for it to last.

Avis gave a little sigh and sank down to her knees beside the bed, resting her forehead at the edge of the pillow. Her fingers very gently glided over her stiffened nipples, making circles, making small ripples of delight that made her moan. One hand lay flat against her belly, rubbing. Her knees parted. She let her other hand float to the center of her body, to her soft damp curly hair, and her hips started swaying as if she were listening to music. Her fingers pressed, and as the tender wet feel of herself spread from between her thighs to her knees and upward in a smooth, sweet wave to her breasts, her shoulders, all of her, her fingers took hold of the throbbing tip of her clitoris and stroked and stroked and stroked and there came over her a wonderful trembling as she brought herself to where she was aching with pleasure and soaring with every nerve in her being and faster and faster her fingers touched, played, danced, flew and just when she knew she could bear it no longer she plunged one, two, three fingers deep into herself and burying her head into the pillow she cried against it as her body climbed and peaked and exploded in a dazzling burst that left her melting and melting and melting. Her hands lingered where they were. As her heartbeat slowed and her breath returned to normal she brought her fingers slowly out of herself, and the bedroom door began to vibrate under the weight of Birdey's pounding. Avis dove for her clothes. Hurriedly she pulled on underwear, white socks, the purple T-shirt that said *The Spurs* in two-inch-high white script across the front and her number, 18, on the back. Scrambling into her white breeches with the thick purple stripes up each side, she scooped up her purple stirrups and pulled open the door. Birdey, caught in the middle of a knock, came tumbling in fist first. Avis grabbed her neatly and plopped her onto the bed.

"If you kept me waiting one more second, Avis, I wasn't going to give you what I was going to give you."

Avis sat down beside her, eyebrows raised, and slipped her feet into the stirrups, tucking the tops into the elasticized bottoms of her breeches. Birdey held out a closed hand and slowly opened it to reveal a thin silver chain with a small heart-shaped locket. Birdey dropped it into Avis's outstretched hand.

Instantly Avis's eyes filled. "Mama's necklace! Oh but Birdey she gave it to you. This is your favorite." Avis touched it with deep affection and put it up to her neck. "Thank you."

Reaching up to fasten it Birdey quickly added, "Don't think you can keep it, either. I just want you to wear it today. For luck." She clicked the snap closed.

"Then I have to give you something, too," said Avis, running to her bureau for her jewelry box with her sister right behind her. She fished around in the heap of old earrings, costume bracelets and stickpins that had seen more use as her daughters' playthings than decoration for herself. She drew out a gold-colored ring with a simple green stone and offered it to Birdey.

"Papa bought me this when I turned thirteen. I think it'll fit you."

Birdey squinted. "Where'd he buy it, the five and ten? Let's see what else you've got."

They rummaged around as though they were playing dress-up until Birdey landed on just the right thing, Avis's fifty-dollar pearl earrings Leo had bought her for Angela's wedding. Birdey had had her eye on them ever since. Avis protested. Birdey held firm. Avis said only a nut would show up for a softball game in fifty-dollar earrings. Birdey said wasn't that Avis all over, selfishness and deprivation. Avis said it took one to know one. Birdey said if Avis didn't let her wear them she, Birdey, would take it back that Avis was godmother to every one of her sons. Avis allowed that she would do likewise. Birdey put on the earrings. Avis pointed out how the whole team, probably the whole town, would die laughing when they saw her. Birdey, raising her hand to strike her sister but thinking better of it, gave Avis a pat on the back and said in her most jarring voice that that was just the sort of thing Avis ought to know about, having people laugh at you. Whereas she, Birdey, having always been *thin*, had no reason to worry about . . .

Birdey's hands flew to her face. "Oh, Avis! I didn't mean it, oh!"

Avis stepped back, blinking and swallowing hard.

Birdey removed the earrings and dropped them back into the jewelry box. She reached for her sister's hand but Avis pulled away. "Avis, please, I say these things that hurt you and I'm sorry. Avis?"

A small smile flickered over Avis's lips. The stinging sensation that lived in her weakest part, her memories, most of all in the memory of herself in baggy dresses outside a ring of girls who were as bound together as the lights of a Christmas tree, was, even as she stood there trying to smile, fading away. Hurt's what stays inside when nothing comes by to replace it, Avis thought.

"Avis, I hated it when you were fat! But I loved you!"

Avis held out her hands, palm up, holding out the earrings. Birdey took them and allowed herself to be hugged. Sniffing, she plugged them into her ears. Her hands were trembling.

Avis said Birdey seemed nervous. Birdey said she was not. Avis said it was just like Birdey to deny her true feelings. Birdey shrieked. Avis glowered. Leo, outside in the car, shouted up for them to come out at once. He tooted the horn repeatedly until the two women rushed noisily from the house.

"I am not going to talk to that horrible man," said Nancy Beth Campbell, the pitcher, trying to do yoga on the floor of her bedroom. At nineteen, Nancy Beth was the youngest Spur and the one who was most accustomed to having her own way. "After everything he did to try to stop us, you want me to be nice to him?"

Her aunt, June Campbell, seated carefully at the edge of the unmade bed, clasped her hands together and eyed her niece with calm understanding. Nancy Beth clutched her knees and began the first phase of her deep-breathing exercise.

"Now, dear," said June, "Mr. Pelletier isn't against you anymore. Ever since Gussie got that lawyer from Boston he's a changed man."

"Then let him interview Uncle Nate. It sounds like they're having a grand old time downstairs. Daddy and Uncle Nate and that—that—" She paused, searching her mind for words. "That absolutely horrible man. Listen to them laughing down there. They're probably making fun of us."

"Uncle Nate and I are very proud of you, dear."

Agitated, Nancy Beth gave up on her yoga and fidgeted with the ends of her purple jersey.

June softened her voice until it was barely above a whisper. "Do you remember, sweetheart, when you were just six years old, and Uncle Nate bought you a special present?"

"My first golf club," remembered Nancy Beth, brightening.

June patted her knee. "Remember how proud we were when you won the trophy at the country club? The youngest girl to win one, ever! Uncle Nate almost popped the buttons off his shirt, he was so proud."

Nancy Beth stuck out her lower lip. "Well it was a different story when I quit college. Uncle Nate went through the roof. And what about the way he acted when he found out I want to join the Navy?"

"Now, now, dear. Let's not think about things like that right now. This is a big day! Oh, I almost forgot." June reached into her purse for a small silver medal, and held it out to her niece. "Don't you go arguing about this with me, Nancy Beth Campbell. I know what your feelings are about God and heaven. But you'll make me happy if just for today you'll wear this. Here. I'll pin it on the inside of your shirt and no one will know." Nancy Beth leaned forward. June fixed the medal in place, and put an arm around the girl's shoulder. "We're just as proud of you today as we were the day you won the golfing trophy."

"I can't! I can't talk to that man."

"Of course you can, dear. Just say some nice things about the way it feels when you're out there on the mound. Say how happy it makes you."

Nancy Beth flopped backward. "You don't know how awful it was, Aunt Juney. We worked so hard, and all that man did was make fun of us in the newspaper. I'm not going downstairs until he's gone."

After a moment of consideration, June cupped her hand close to her mouth and bent closer to her niece. "After the game, remind me to tell you something. A little secret."

"Tell me now!"

"I can't."

"You can! You can!"

She could. "Promise you won't repeat this?" Nancy Beth nodded enthusiastically. "Well, it just so happened that on our way over here, right after we stopped at the store to get a little treat for Jeremy Dorn—he's downstairs now with Uncle Nate—we made one other stop, to see an old friend of your uncle's. Mind you, this isn't the kind of thing I would agree to in general, but I said to your uncle that we might as well, just this once."

Nancy Beth went blank. "What did you do, Aunt Juney?"

"We made a little bet."

"You mean, on the game?"

June clapped her hands together girlishly.

Nancy Beth gaped. "How much?"

"How much do you weigh?"

"Hundred and eight."

June smiled. Putting her hands on the girl's face, she kissed her warmly. "There you are, now. You just get downstairs and do us proud."

Whooping, Nancy Beth bounded out of her room and down the stairs, where Rollie Pelletier was waiting with his tape recorder.

At Currys Crossing Hospital, two nurses in uniform disappeared into a third-floor bathroom and emerged again in purple and white. Their cleated playing shoes, tied together by the laces, dangled from their shoulders.

Every patient who could move had lined the sides of the corridor. The weekend staff had hung a sheet at one end. They had written a message with iodine.

You take care of the Belles on the field. We'll take care of the Belles in intensive care.

"Get 'em, Hannah!" called the patients.

"Go for it, Peggy!"

A doctor coming out of the supplies closet flashed them a thumbs-up signal. The lab technicians bubbled out of the elevator, cheering. The cafeteria girls in their yellow dresses waved unfolded napkins. Grumpy, icy Miss Hawkins, the shift supervisor who said publicly that a woman belonged in a softball suit as much as a fish belonged on a bicycle, came out of her office to clap her hands along with everyone else.

"Give it to the Belles right between the pitoodies!" cried Miss Hawkins.

The two nurses ducked into the stairway and bounded to the ground floor, where the admissions clerk and the guard rushed to hold the door. With perfect timing, a car filled with women in purple and white pulled up to the curb, scooped up the nurses, and screeched away as patients waved from windows.

"Of course we had special training," said Nancy Beth into Rollie Pelletier's microphone. She wiggled her feet into her purple stirrups as she talked. "What do you think, playing softball is easy? We played pinball, for coordination and timing. We danced. We practiced rhythm and reflex. We broke up into groups for fielding. We lifted weights."

"At the gym?" Rollie cut in sharply. No woman, to his knowledge, had ever stepped foot in the town gym. A crimson flush started creeping up to his ears.

Nancy Beth smiled. She gave her aunt a fast, sisterly look,

letting her know that she intended to keep it secret how June had lent the Spurs Uncle Nate's private gym in his basement. "No, sir," she said gravely. "Since we had no gym of our own, we just used each other's living rooms. Instead of weights, we lifted children. You'd be surprised to find out how hard it is to pump a ten-year-old. Especially a ten-year-old that doesn't want to be pumped."

Rollie exhaled heavily. He was not sure if he should believe her or not. He chose to change the subject. "Most of the women on your team are mothers. Right?"

Nancy Beth nodded as she tucked the tops of her stirrups over her breeches.

"Now, I don't want to come off like I'm old-fashioned, Nancy Beth. But it seems to me—"

Cutting him off, June Campbell breezed in with her nose tuned to trouble. "I don't want to be rude, dear," she told Nancy Beth. "But it's time to go." She took her niece's hand and pulled her to her feet. Nancy Beth reached behind for her cap, and pulled it on, and paused for one more good-luck hug from her Aunt Juney.

Sandy Dorn clicked the lock of her front door, tested it, and slipped the key into the pocket of her uniform breeches. "Say it one more time," she demanded.

Patsy Griffin repeated what she'd been saying over and over for the last hour. "No one's going to harm Jeremy. Jeremy's with Nate and Juney."

Sandy sighed with worry. "If only I had—"

Patsy held up a hand. "If only you'd been home that night. If only Kenny Dorn wasn't such a shit. If only, if only. Come on, Sandy, if you go into this game feeling like you're feeling now, you know what'll happen? You'll blow it. You want to let your kid see you blow it?"

Sandy reached for her cleated shoes on the porch.

"Remember what Gussie told you, Sandy. Just make like every pitch that comes at you is Kenny Dorn's face. Okay?"

"Okay," agreed Sandy with a nervous smile.

The two women linked arms and set off for the river path that led through the woods and over a bridge to the Senator Ivan A. Tolland Memorial Field.

* * *

On Anthony Street, rolling the morning paper into a hollow cone, Danny McGrath hummed a song and danced a little jig around his kitchen. His two older children came flying into the house at the sound of his voice. Uncle William turned off the television set. Allison, asleep in his lap, woke up rubbing her eyes. Danny picked her up and hugged her to his chest like a waltz partner. Assembling them all in the front hallway at the foot of the stairs, Danny put the paper to his mouth like a megaphone. Hearing footsteps, they all looked up. The top step creaked. Kate and Mundy grabbed Uncle William's hands and squeezed. The baby clapped her fat hands with anticipation.

"Look! Up in the sky!" Danny's big voice bellowed all through the house. "It's a bird!"

The children's mouths fell open.

"It's a plane!"

Uncle William made airplane noises.

"It's—" Danny performed a drum roll with his tongue as Evelyn appeared in a vision of purple and white above them. Slowly she floated down the stairs.

"It's my wife!"

Throwing back her head, she rushed down. She flung her arms open and her squealing children rushed into them. Danny ran to the kitchen for his camera and made them stand still for a picture.

"Okay, everybody get out of the way. I want one of Mama by herself."

Evelyn squinted blankly into the lens.

"Don't just stand there, Ev," Danny commanded. "Take a bow!"

She lifted her cap and the camera clicked. She swooped down with her hair falling in soft, loose ripples and it clicked again. She came up again with a huge, wide-open smile. She was shining.

CHAPTER SIX

The World Series was on television, and the children were asleep. Everyone was waiting for Evelyn to come downstairs. Danny had gone out twice for beer. The bottles clinked softly, dimly, as if they had been wrapped in blankets. Gussie was on the couch with her bad leg propped on pillows. Danny kept asking her if she felt all right, and Gussie kept answering, yes. Uncle William sat at her feet. They were taking turns naming the players. Reciting their batting averages. Calculating their runs batted in for life. During the commercials, Danny talked with Rio about insulating the basement. Then they moved on to floors, cracked windows, old furnaces, bad roofs. Behind their conversations the bottles clinked and the television announcers talked louder. Uncle William wanted to know every move Gussie had ever made as a Saint, and she told him. Danny went to the kitchen for beer. The empty bottles fell against each other. They rattled but they did not break. It was unbelievably noisy down there.

The straps against the backs of the gloves were thin. It was a miracle the way the buckles really worked. Evelyn did and undid them, marveling. It was a spectacular piece of luck that Uncle William found the bank safe in the woods. Where else would they have kept the gloves? Sitting in his armchair in his hat and his coat, Franklin Brody agreed with his daughter.

"And who's the one that dragged it home on her sled?" he asked. Behind his glasses his eyes were playful and proud.

She was unwrapping brand new, moth-resistant tissue paper. She made a special trip downtown to buy it after she unpacked her children's winter sweaters and found moth eggs in the wool. She pulled them out with tweezers but it worried her that she might not have gotten them all. She brought the sweaters to the Salvation Army bin in front of the supermarket, and promised the children new ones.

"I wouldn't bother, Ev," said her father. "I don't think it's worth all the trouble."

"Can't be too careful." She threw the old tissue paper away. The new tissue paper came in colors, pink and green and blue. She unfolded a dozen sheets and spread them out on the floor around her. Then she put her hands in the safe.

Pale blue silk with slant-eyed buttons for going to church.

Sea-green for grocery shopping.

Blue and white checkered cotton for working in the yard.

Quilted mitts in red and gold stripes for cooking.

Tangerine rubber for doing the dishes.

Avocado for the laundry.

White cotton, frayed at the fingertips, for things around the house.

Better white cotton for going to the doctor.

Brown kid for bowling with Franklin on Tuesday nights until her fingers twisted inward, her tired, pained fingers that could no longer come uncurled.

One half-finished pink mitten for a baby.

"You should've stayed with knitting, Ev. You could make some new sweaters yourself," her father tells her. She would like to ask him to be quiet but she does not know how.

Sitting in the armchair, Franklin waits and listens. Any moment the Oldsmobile will swing into the driveway. The leather gloves feel as warm and safe as skin. Evelyn is fond of them all, but it's the leather she likes best. Does her father agree?

Ruffling the edges of his stillness, Franklin begins to quiver with alarm. There is a creak in the hallway. A step. A tap at the door. A single streak of light rips the shadows apart and Franklin freezes in horror. A cry comes out from the light. The television announcer cries, "Home run!" and Franklin vanishes.

They were cheering downstairs, Danny, Rio, Uncle William, and the crowd on TV. Evelyn's lips came away from the leather gloves. The new colored tissue paper streamed out the opening of Uncle William's bank safe. In the darkness, Gussie felt her way forward with her cane. She found a switch and turned the light on. Her hands went to her mouth.

"My God."

Evelyn imagines that her father has the starring role in a Western movie. His cowboy hat is the color of snow. Unlike real life, her father is not wearing his glasses. He has fallen into quicksand.

No one is watching except Evelyn. She shouts warnings from solid ground. On the bank of the pool of quicksand there are two things. A piece of rope and her father's cowboy hat. Evelyn ties the rope to the trunk of a tree and throws the other end into the quicksand. Franklin tries to swim but he is weary. The quicksand rises to his shoulders. A wind comes up and blows in the hat. Evelyn cheers him on toward the rope. He gropes and fumbles. He reaches it, but then he changes his mind. Franklin goes for the hat. The quicksand closes with a soft, gurgling sound. Bubbles rise to the surface. Some of them pop, and some of them float off into the air. Her eyes on the place where her father had been, Evelyn simply stands there, watching.

"Come on down and watch the ballgame with us," said Gussie. "It's a great one."

The gloves had been arranged in perfect piles all over the floor. White cotton. Colored cotton. Silks. Knits. Leather. Routine. Fancy. Favorites. Evelyn tried to make up her mind whether she should tissue-wrap them singly, or in pairs, or in piles. She did up the children's sweaters in plastic freezer storage bags and look what happened. She had no choice but to get rid of them all. Mundy was deeply offended. One of the sweaters she gave away to the Salvation Army was his orange reindeer one. His favorite. He did not believe her when she promised him a new one. He was only six years old but he knew how hard it was to get his mother into a department store. Everyone knew. She tried buying whatever they needed from the Sears catalogue, but the sizes never came out right. Mundy cried for his sweater and Evelyn promised to knit him a new one herself. Kate wanted one too. Then Uncle William, Danny. If Allison knew how to talk yet, so would she. Everyone wanted sweaters, but there was only one Evelyn. She had no idea how she would ever get everything done.

She decided to wrap them in piles. She had plenty of tissue paper, perhaps too much. The man at the store where she bought it had laughed at her across the counter. Early Christmas shopping, right? It was September. Evelyn had no intention of letting people think she did her Christmas shopping in September when the crazy people did, so she told him about the moth eggs. He seemed interested to a point, but then he figured it out. She should have known better. What kind of a woman lets insects into her children's sweaters? She was tempted to rush outside to the Salvation Army bin and pull them out and show him that it was not as if she were so negligent that her children's clothes were destroyed. Her children had plenty to wear. It was not easy trying to tell strangers about the good care she gave her children. People never believed her. She reached for the pile of colored cottons. She picked out a sheet of tissue paper.

"Evvie?" Gussie laid an arm across Evelyn's shoulders. Evelyn froze. The leather driving gloves slipped off her knee and fell to the floor. Gussie picked them up and held them.

"If I help you put these things away, will you come downstairs with me? I think we'll still be able to make the last of the ninth."

Slowly, Evelyn lifted her head. She nodded.

Evelyn is seventeen, and the boy she's in love with is taking her out to a basketball game. She can't make up her mind what to wear. Gussie is no help at all. In gym shorts and a T-shirt Gussie sits cross-legged on the floor with her hands resting, palms up, on her knees. The basketball game will be the Currys Crossing girls' varsity against whatever girls' varsity had won the Western title the night before. Evelyn could not keep all the teams straight. Currys Crossing had made it through six rounds of playoffs. It took all winter, and now it was the championship. Gussie deep-breathes, psyching herself up for the game. Evelyn holds up two pairs of wool slacks on hangers. She asks which one.

"Either." Gussie catches her breath and suddenly clenches her hands. She is sputtering in Italian.

Evelyn lays the slacks on her bed. "English, for God's sake."

"Linda Drago is a shit."

Evelyn sighs. Neither pair of the slacks will do. She puts them back in the closet, and takes out another pair.

"You always say your coaches are shits, Gussie. Doesn't matter who they are or what they do. You always call them shits."

Evelyn holds up a blouse against the slacks. She puts a sweater on top of the blouse and disapproves. She puts everything back into the closet.

"Drago should have made me captain."

"You *are* captain."

"Hah. One of three. I never knew such a shit as Drago. Drago knows shit about playing ball."

Danny will arrive in two and a half hours. Evelyn will run down the stairs to meet him. She will slide into the cool interior of Danny's father's car. Warmth will come out of the defroster and the radio will play. She has nothing to wear. Is there still time to run to the store for a blouse?

"Out of the way, Ev. I've got to do some push-ups. I'm too tight."

Evelyn counts Gussie's push-ups. She holds her ankles in place for Gussie's sit-ups. Two rooms away, Franklin Brody is pounding on the door of his bedroom. Shirley has locked herself inside. The lawyer has left his bill on the kitchen table. The pounding gets louder and louder. It is amazing to Evelyn what Gussie doesn't notice when she's got her mind on a ballgame. Evelyn keeps on counting. The pounding leaves the door and comes inside her head, hard and fierce and relentless.

CHAPTER SEVEN

But the most wonderful and incredible thing of all, Avis told herself, was that something was actually happening.

Not that she had cause to complain, or to look on her life as anything but a full one. What with the children and the new babies and Leo and the house and the thousand loose ends of their daily lives she would be the last woman on earth to accuse herself of not having enough to do. Her days passed quickly. Her time was always filled. Her hands hurried from one thing to the next with hardly a moment to pause and wonder what she was doing, or how, or why. There were sheets to be washed and she washed them. There were sausages to fry, pans to scrub, friends to visit, trips to Boston, church bazaars, movies on television, dinner at restaurants with a ten-dollar bottle of wine and an orchestra: there was no end to what there was to do, and she knew it, and she was glad of it; but she couldn't help admitting to herself, sitting in the car beside Leo, with her softball glove and her cleats, that the best thing about her ordinary life was leaving it behind.

Life wasn't frying sausages. Life was blizzards and weddings and births and deaths and the first flush of spring that came in the open windows and turned your heart upside down in a tizzy and left you with your mouth hanging open and a huge growling pounding relentless hunger for something—anything—to happen. Not that nothing had ever happened to her. She had five children. Like five planets they revolved around her, now placidly, now headed straight for disaster, now back on course, scarred but intact, while she, like an amateur watcher of the night skies, stayed in one place, at home, bound down by the weight of her own body and the restless wanderings of her own mind. And somewhere along the way, while the accomplishments of her children multiplied and no other Currys Crossing mother had as much reason as she to be proud, there came a point where the secret life of her mind and the visible life of her body not only parted company but went at each other so forcefully and with such antagonism that it was all she could do to keep herself from looking in mirrors, afraid that instead of one head she might find two.

The car rolled down the familiar streets. Avis took a sideways look at her husband. Hunched over the steering wheel, Leo had his eyes on the road the way he put his eyes to everything: concentrated, straight ahead, unwavering. She could be slitting her own throat right there beside him and as long as she did it quietly, Leo would never notice. And what would he do, she wondered, if she suddenly turned to him and said exactly what was on her mind? And what would he have done, not one hour ago, coming unexpectedly into the room and finding her down on the floor, doing what she was doing: would he have said, "Oh, excuse me, darling, I see that you've got your hands in yourself; I'll be back when you're finished"?

"It's a grand and mellifluous afternoon!" Leo suddenly said, slowing the car down at a stop sign. He reached over and heartily patted Avis' knee, and hoped she wasn't nervous, and before she could answer he was back on the accelerator, humming the tune of a song she couldn't quite place or remember.

Avis sighed heavily. She was nearly fifty years old, a woman with grown children, and she was just as much at odds with herself and her moods as if she were still fifteen. They came out of the blue, no easier to control than the weather: it couldn't be; it mustn't be, that in the space of not more than five or ten minutes she was catapulted from the heights of pleasure to the bottom of despair, or was that in itself just exaggeration, one more intemperate mood, another emotion that altered not only the way she leaned back sadly against the door of the car, but the way she looked at her husband, her sister sitting quietly in the back seat, the houses they were driving past, the trees, the telephone poles, the blue uncloudy sky that even as it arched and stretched, serene and passive, seemed to be bouncing right back in her face her own leaden ponderous immense sense of— sense of what? She could not even say for herself what it was, this troubled mood that knit her bones together and pushed up against the back of her eyes: she could only grit her teeth and say to herself that she was almost fifty years old, she was practically an old woman, she was ripping apart a perfectly ordinary Saturday afternoon when there was shopping to do, and sheets to wash, and a house to air, and for what?

She was an old woman dressed up for a game of softball. In itself a thing of ridicule, it was all the more awful when she considered how she had let herself forget herself: surely she could not have been in her right mind earlier that day when she went for a run along the river, when her blood was steaming and elation ran just behind her like a frantic puppy nipping at her heels; no, she had not been herself at all since the day Augusta Cabrini came barging into her life with her scarred face and her fiery eyes and the quiet commanding dignified way she came into a room, leaning on her cane with an air not of injury but of strength; and putting out her hand to meet the hand that was offered, Avis took one long look at the big broad girl and immediately fell under a spell. Within three days she had stopped eating except at mealtimes. In a week she was shutting all the window shades in her house and turning on the record player to play her children's records: she was exercising, she was doing sit-ups and push-ups and stretches and bends; she was running in place as the furniture shook and jumping rope as the plates rattled in the cabinets, and in the morning when she awakened in stiffness and pain she heaved herself out of bed to get up and do it again.

It was too, too foolish. Her children mocked her and her husband had nothing for her but badly hidden pity. Oh, they had tried to humor her all along: Angela telephoned weekly with recipes she took from ladies' magazines; Mary-Susan sent home piles of rhythm-heavy records she collected from the girls in her dorm; the boys visited regularly to supervise her workouts, full of advice on isometrics and the proper way to pump half her weight in iron. But behind her back they shook their heads and clucked their tongues, fleeing to their own lives to

tell their friends how comical it was, how pathetic and even re-
pugnant it was to have for a mother a woman who spent all her
free time learning how to whack a ball with a bat and run
around three bases without dropping dead from exhaustion.
Leo could say all he liked about how happy the whole business
made him; but the truth was that Leo was every bit as embarrassed as if his wife suddenly took up a new religion or dyed her
hair bright orange: Avis was sure of it.

As the car pulled up to the high school and swerved toward
the parking lot where the band was already in formation, Avis
slid down a bit lower in her seat, vowing to herself that no
power on earth could make her get out of the car. Leo put on
the brakes. His door sprang open. Birdey leaned forward to
check her lipstick in the rearview mirror. Leo got out of the car
to look at the band. Birdey slipped out after him, calling her
sister to follow.

"In a minute," said Avis. She locked both doors against the
wild, colorful scene outside. Women in purple and white were
greeting each other as their children ran in and out of the rows
of the band. Photographers waved cameras, and a man with a
whistle around his neck waved his arms. Rollie the Fist wandered about with his tape recorder. The Little League All-Stars
and the Girl Scouts and the Ivan A. Tolland Memorial Baton
Corps shoved each other into lines that rippled and swayed in
long trembling fingers of sunlight; and as the clamor of the
crowd and the booms of the drums and the bleats of the horns
and the toots of the man with the whistle blended all together
in one stunning splash of sound that drove Avis flat down on
the seat with her hands to her ears, there came a polite but in-
sistent rapping against the window. She looked up.

They were flushed and out of breath but they were smiling.
Her two daughters, arm in arm, peered into the car and gestured for her to roll down the window. She knew what would
come next. Their consciences uneasy, they had followed her
here to say that they loved her but they wanted her to turn the
car around and go back home. Angela was about to say: After
all, Mother, you're nearly fifty!

But here was Mary-Susan, poking her head in with a kiss and
a hug around her mother's neck. And here was Angela, holding
out in her open palm a small silver medal attached to a safety

pin. The medal bore the face and torso of the Virgin Mary. Her hands were upon her heart. Her eyes were turned upward. Angela turned it over and Avis read the inscription. *Avis from June, Good Luck!*

"Mrs. Campbell stopped by while you were upstairs getting dressed," explained Angela. "In all the confusion, we forgot to tell you."

"Put it on, Mother," urged Mary-Susan. "Mrs. Campbell said to tell you she's proud of you."

"She *should* be," beamed Angela, adding softly that so were they all; and fixing it in place inside the neckline of her shirt, Avis had to pause a moment to let her eyes uncloud; and stepping out of the car, her spirits clacking back to life like engines she gathered up her cap and her cleats, gave her daughters a squeeze each, threw back her shoulders, and marched off to join the rest of her team.

May 10, 1975

My name is Marina Cabrini, born Oliverio. At the age of fourteen I came to America with my uncle and aunt from the south of Italy. Had I known at the time that I was bidding farewell to people I was never going to see again, I suspect that I nevertheless would have come to America. I married Victor Cabrini. I have four children. My son Carlo married and came into the business. My son Vittorio wastes his money on a house he could not have afforded in the first place, but like his brother he came into the business. My daughter Christine married. The marriage failed. She went to college and took a job in a large Boston bank with international holdings. My daughter Augusta is twenty-five. As a result of a motorcycle accident she is deaf in one ear. She is unable to walk without the aid of a cane. The scars that line the side of her face will be with her the rest of her life. But she is my daughter. I would give all I have in the world to undo what has happened to her.

She was a restless and fearless child who teetered between extremes of emotion like an acrobat. It was impossible to guess what she might try next. She raced through her infancy, climbing up on the furniture at the time most babies are trying to learn the way to hold a spoon.

She was going to be famous. She stood no higher than my hip. Throwing back her head as though she had come from a tribe of ponies, she told me how she would grow up and be famous. She used to lie on her back for entire afternoons at a time, daydreaming about unbelievable acts of human greatness. She believed that she had been born lucky. She grew up imagining herself delivering cures to colonies of lepers, or rescuing villages from murderers, or preventing the end of the world. Augusta amused us.

In those days our business was new and faltering. We were determined not to fail. I speak not with regret but with necessity when I say that I was preoccupied with different matters during much of my daughter's childhood. She was not a neglected child. She was an indulged one. Perhaps it was too great a burden to have placed on one so young; but I was only fourteen when I left my home for America. I expected as much from my daughter. We charged her with our happiness.

We encouraged her games of make-believe. Her father and I had many make-believe games of our own. Make believe the creditors are not threatening to disgrace us. Make believe the day has come when we can say that we have not failed. There was nowhere to turn but to our Augusta, our lion cub, our little warrior. Unlike her sister and brothers she had been conceived in a moment of weakness. She had been born with great difficulty. She was taken from my stomach. She was unsatisfied with my breast. She was a noisy, storming baby, but she came to make us believe that it was possible for us to be happy. Our business succeeded. We moved to a larger house. We moved the business into a house that was even larger, and I was able to have my own office at the top. Carlo married and has two children. Vittorio knows his way around lawyers, and keeps our books. Christine travels all over the world on her company's business. The circle of our acquaintances grows. Yet Augusta is much on my mind. I have often wondered where Augusta really comes from.

Memory is faithless. My traitor memory, called upon for the sight of that girl who was going to be famous, gives me only a stranger. The stranger's face is badly scarred. All her ribs are broken. I have helped clean away the blood she spilled, but nothing I do seems to touch her.

I did not see Augusta until she was more than twenty-four hours old. I was weak and spiritless. They had sedated me heavily. I had just been talking with the doctor who had taken from me not only this new daughter but the bleeding, ruined thing that was my womb. Birth and loss gathered together in the folds of my dressing gown. Into my arms came life. Against my breast came my ten-pound crying baby, and out of some deep, inarticulate part of myself came a silent cry of outrage.

My new daughter was wrapped in a hospital blanket. Her small mouth pushed forward like the mouth of a fish. The bandages across my stomach were heavy. It was difficult for me to breathe without pain. I would not allow myself to think about what had gone on underneath the bandages, but I could think of nothing else. I was alone in a room with my day-old baby. There was nothing left to me except emptiness. I laid the baby down on the bed. I touched her closed, small eyes, and her nose, and her chin. Fear was there with us. Mother and child and fear. I leaned over the bed. I unwrapped the blanket, and in the next few frantic seconds I came face to face with the wild, powerful creature who was my daughter Augusta.

I undid her wrappings. I wanted to see for myself the body that had turned against its home. This baby had kicked its way into life. It had hollowed me. It had bled me nearly dry.

Her skin was exposed to the air. She fought back at once. Her arms and legs shot out violently, beating about in little circles. Her lusty voice nearly strangled her as her face went from pale to blue. Something took hold of my heart, and I rushed to protect her. I wrapped her back in the blanket, tightly, seamlessly. I pulled her into my arms. She relaxed. The tiny corners of her mouth trembled unsurely, and gave way to an infant's sigh of pleasure. She was mine. I vowed to her that I would keep her safe. Perhaps this was love. I don't know. Nothing is simple where blood goes. Love blinds, entangles, destroys. I only know that for all of her life I have been trying to keep my promise. I have tried to keep her from harm. God forgive me if I have wronged her.

"Marina!" bellowed Victor.

She checked her hair in a mirror. She gathered a few loose things into her purse, and at the last minute, she decided to take along her notebook. She tucked it inside with her pen, and hurried to her husband, who was already halfway down the steps of the porch without her.

CHAPTER EIGHT

Gussie's body was battered in the accident but she still had an arm. It was October. Kate and Mundy were in school and the baby was across the street with Mrs. Monopoli. Cabrini Associates was out for lunch. The air was as crisp as apples and it was too good out there to waste it. Gussie lent Evelyn one of her old softball gloves and they started playing catch in Evelyn's backyard. Uncle William coached from the porch. Gussie stood on her cane, catching and throwing with the same arm, back and forth, back and forth, back and forth. Each day the distance between them grew greater, and they soon found themselves at opposite ends of the yard. Gussie started throwing grounders and pops. Evelyn complained, but she tried to catch them. Gussie's fast balls smacked into her mitt like dive-bombs but she went on trying to catch them. In the mornings, to give them more space, Evelyn raked the yard clean. The dead tree branches at the edges were getting into Gussie's hair, so Evelyn borrowed a hand saw from Danny and cleared them away. She got rid of all the dead leaves. She put the children's old toys in the trash and promised them new ones. Down on her knees she pulled up the weeds and swept away the loose stones. Once a week, although it was autumn and nothing was growing, she mowed the grass.

Gussie stayed a little longer every day. Uncle William stopped going out to find things. Mundy and Kate rushed home from school to change their clothes and join them. They fetched the balls their mother missed, screaming with cheer when she caught one. They watched her carefully. They did not entirely believe in this surprising turn of luck. Kate stole into the house when Evelyn wasn't looking and hid all the pillows. Mundy yanked at her hands every time she sat down to take a rest. When they finally realized that their mother had stopped taking so many naps in the daytime, they made themselves happy rubbing her neck and bringing her bowls of warm water to unstiffen her fingers.

Uncle William hung a chin-up bar in the kitchen doorway and taught her to use it. At Gussie's suggestion, she started baking bread to exercise her hands. Rio brought recipes. Danny borrowed a plow from the town when the snow came, and the yard stayed clear. Cabrini Real Estate Associates kept ringing the phone to get hold of Gussie, but Gussie ignored them. Evelyn ordered herself some sweatsuits like Gussie's from Sears, Roebuck and wore them all the time. Danny rubbed her down with liniment before bedtime. Their room smelled like evergreens. It was easy to fall asleep knowing that she wanted to wake up again. Her body was stronger. She imagined that she could almost hear her muscles singing. She was feeling good. Franklin Brody was proud. Shirley Brody said that in no time at all, Evelyn was going to be just as good as Gussie. She was sure of it. Franklin said she might even get a chance to paint the porch.

Ice crusted in the backyard grass and drove them into the street. Evelyn was throwing longer, faster balls, and Gussie had to strain hard to reach them. The road took a dip between the Brody and Arbis houses, and a missed ball rolled quickly down to the Campbells', ending up in the gutter there or in the traffic on Tolland Avenue, which crossed Anthony like the top of a T. Evelyn was always the one to chase the runaways when the children weren't around.

It started out slowly, a curve ball shot from Evelyn's hip, but it took off like a boomerang, sailing high over Gussie's head and straight for the traffic. Evelyn took off for the chase. She trapped the ball in a mound of dead leaves in the Campbells' gutter. She picked it up and wiped it clean on the ends of her shirt. There was a muffled, tinkling sound behind her, and she didn't have to look to recognize the sound of the wind chimes

June Campbell had brought from Rome and hung on her front porch. But Evelyn looked. The thin, bright strips of the chimes were not moving. There was no wind. The tinkling continued. It seemed to be coming from June's kitchen at the back of the house. Evelyn dropped the ball and went into June's yard. She heard a woman crying. She went closer. Inside the house a woman was crying hard, in painful, racking sobs, and Evelyn bolted for the door. It was locked. She pushed the bell. She heard it sounding in the house, but June did not come to the door. The noise stopped. The woman stopped crying. Evelyn ran around to the back. Halfway there, she met Gussie. Half of the back door was a window. They looked inside.

June Campbell's linoleum floor was covered with smashed plates of glass. The chairs of June's beautiful maple kitchen set had been upturned. Their legs were broken. The doors of the cabinets over the sink were wide open. The shelves were bare. On the table, untouched, were neat settings for tea for two. Between them there was a plate of vanilla wafers. Gussie reached for the doorknob. It was not locked. She turned it slowly, and Evelyn followed her inside.

The woman who appeared in the doorway at the other side of the room was slightly built and not very tall. She had long, strong hands and muscular legs. Her ribs showed beneath a thin cotton sweater. She was breathing hard. Her hair was wildly unarranged. In the strands clung thin slivers of June Campbell's favorite set of china. The woman's lips were pulled back tautly. Her teeth were clenched. Her name was Sandy Dorn. She lived with her son in the wood cabin on River Road. Gussie stepped toward her.

"Where's Mrs. Campbell?" Gussie's voice was low and gentle. She held out her free hand. Sandy Dorn shot past her with a twisted look of fear, and lunged for the things on the table. Evelyn backed up into a corner. Gussie, shifting her weight onto an upturned chair, swung her cane in the air and brought it down exactly between Sandy's hands and the tea things. Blocked, Sandy collapsed to the floor. She broke into cries without tears. Her small body heaved, and she held her sides in pain. Gussie went down beside her, and took hold of Sandy's hands, and held on.

"Don't pay any attention to the mess," said June, coming in

from the front of the house. She did not appear to be harmed in any way. "They were old plates to begin with. I've been telling Nate for weeks that we need a new set."

June was pale. Her eyes were red-rimmed from crying. She sighed deeply, helplessly, sadly. Gussie touched Sandy's hair, picking out pieces of glass. "Do you want to tell us what happened to you?"

Sandy shuddered and closed her eyes.

"She'll just go on upstairs and lie down for a while," said June brightly, taking charge. She helped Sandy to her feet. "You have a rest. Then we'll go back and see Jeremy again. You don't want him to see you all upset, do you, dear?" Motioning for Evelyn and Gussie to wait, June brought Sandy upstairs. When she came back they gathered in her parlor on her stiff-backed chairs.

"I really don't mind about the china," said June.

"We know," agreed Gussie. "Tell us what happened."

June took a deep breath, calming herself. "Early this morning the telephone rang just after Nate went to work. It was Sandy. I could hardly make out what she was saying. She was out of her mind with fright. She was calling from the hospital. Her little boy was rushed there in the middle of the night. His name is Jeremy. A darling, sweet boy. I knew him from the play center downtown. I've been helping out the Sisters of Saint Clement who run it. Jeremy started coming about a month ago. He was shy as a little bird. He didn't like joining any of the others, so I gave him a little extra attention. He loved drawing. That's all he wanted to do. For some reason, he took to me. I drew pictures and he colored them, and then he drew pictures and I colored them, and we got used to each other. I didn't talk to his mother much at first. She would drop him off at the center and pick him up again with hardly a word. It seemed to me that there was something very bad going on with her. She was nervous. Very nervous.

"One day, I guess it was building up inside her real bad, she talked about it to me. She told me she was divorcing her husband. He had already moved out. She was looking for a job. So I brought her home for supper and Nate was crazy about that boy. One supper, and Nate was carrying on like Sandy was our adopted daughter. He talked to his friends at the electric plant and Sandy got a job there. It wasn't the greatest job in the world but it was good money. Her hours weren't regular though. I went and stayed with Jeremy whenever I could so she could work. She hired a sitter for when I couldn't.

"She was married to Kenny Dorn. I could tell you things, believe me. Oh, he was nice enough in the beginning. He comes from nice people in Lowell. He's a big, handsome guy. Looks like he wouldn't hurt a thing. They'd been married for about six years. Something went bad. Who knows how?"

June's voice faltered. Her face looked pinched and tired. She was struggling to hold back fresh tears. Helplessly, she made a fist with her hand and waved it in the air. With a low growl, Gussie cursed under her breath in Italian.

"My God," whispered Evelyn. "Did he do something to the boy?"

June nodded weakly. "Last night, Sandy had to stay late at work. There was a power failure downtown, and she couldn't get away. It was Nate's and my card night, or we would've gone over. She called the sitter and asked her to stay, but when Sandy got home there wasn't any sitter. Kenny Dorn, last she'd heard, was up in Vermont or somewhere. Nobody knew he was back in town. The sitter was new. It wasn't her fault. She'd never even heard of Kenny Dorn. He told her he was Sandy's brother. Jeremy was already gone to sleep, so she let him in and went home. Sandy doesn't even have a brother.

"I don't know what happened exactly. Sandy was walking home from work and he drove by her in his car. She doesn't think he noticed her. He looked like he was in a big hurry to get away, and Sandy knew right away that something horrible had happened. She rushed into the house. No sitter. All the lights were out. She found Jeremy on the floor in his bedroom. He was unconscious. His little suitcase that Nate bought for when he comes to our house was half-packed on his bed. Kenny was trying to take him. He didn't like it that the judge refused him visitation rights in the divorce. Kenny tried to take him away," she added slowly, as if she were thinking of this for the first time. "And Jeremy wouldn't go."

"Is Jeremy all right?" said Evelyn softly.

"They've got him in a big steel crib," June answered. "They haven't finished giving him tests. But his head, it's his head.

They let me go into his room. He didn't wake up. He just lay there, small and hurt. I put my hand through the bars. I wanted to touch him. I just wanted to touch the darling and let him know his Aunty Juney was there. Dear God, I touched the side of his head, and it was soft. It was softer than a tiny baby's. It was just the same as touching a sponge."

June covered her face with her hands. A violent shivering came over her. There was silence for a moment, and Gussie said, "Why didn't the judge give the husband visitation rights?"

Hands over her face, June shook her head sharply from side to side.

Gussie pressed. "He hit them before? The boy and Sandy?"

Miserably, June tilted her head forward to say yes. "I didn't know. I—just—didn't—know."

"Did anybody call the police?" Gussie's voice was hard.

"Yes. Last night. They've got a warrant out for his arrest."

"Does anyone know where he is?"

"No. I don't know. All I've been thinking about is Jeremy. Nate's up the hospital with him right now. I brought Sandy home. She didn't want to leave him. She's not in control of herself at all. I thought she might feel a little better if I brought her home and made her a cup of tea, and—"

Something large and hard crashed to the floor directly overhead.

"Sandy?" called June, pushing herself up from her chair.

Evelyn was up fast. Gussie was faster, and hurried to the stairs on her cane. June tried to get past her.

"Wait. Please, Mrs. Campbell, don't go up there. You said yourself that Sandy's not in control of herself."

June scoffed. "Sandy wouldn't hurt me!"

"Please." Calmly cocking her head and turning her good ear upward, Gussie hung her cane on June's banister and leaned on the rail.

June looked at her with faith. "What do you want me to do?"

"Call Sandy. Quietly. Just say her name."

June did. There was no reply.

"Do it again."

"Sandy? Sandy dear, can you hear me?"

"Tell her the tea is ready," Gussie whispered.

"Come along, dear. Your tea is ready." June forced herself to smile as Sandy appeared at the top of the stairs.

Slowly, woodenly, Sandy came down the stairs. Her face was blotched and swollen. Her hands were fluttering at her sides in queer, jerking motions. She stared straight ahead, her eyes glazed and unblinking.

"Don't touch her," Gussie whispered in June's ear. June ignored her. She climbed up to meet Sandy. She was smiling more broadly as she held out her arms, and Sandy looked for a moment as though she would meekly go into them. There was a slight flickering in Sandy's eyes; a softening; but all at once she shrieked loudly, horribly, and fell backward onto the stairs. Gussie pulled herself up by the banister and dove, covering Sandy's body with her own. She gripped Sandy by the wrists and kept gripping more tightly. June buried her face in Evelyn's shoulders. The shrieking stopped. Like a child coming out of a nightmare, Sandy pulled her face away from Gussie's and looked at her with a sad, empty smile. She laughed bitterly.

"He's going to come back," she said in her normal voice.

Gussie pulled herself up. "You're going to be safe. Your boy will be safe."

Sandy's laugh was high and shrill. "Who's going to protect us? You?" Sandy's eyes were on the cane, the scars that lined Gussie's face, the bad leg that Gussie pretended wasn't there.

Gussie bit her bottom lip and swallowed hard. "Not just me," she answered, throwing back her head as if she'd been stung. "My team."

Evelyn and June looked at each other. What team?

"What team?" said Sandy.

Gussie slid down the stairs on her bottom and lifted her cane. She rose. She took a moment to smooth her hair, her clothes. She cocked her head, tipped up her chin, and impassively answered, "My softball team."

Sandy perked with interest. "What's it called?"

Gussie looked at Evelyn. Evelyn shrugged. Gussie turned to Sandy with a grin. "The Larkspurs."

"Larkspurs?" echoed June and Evelyn at once.

"Spurs for short," added Gussie quickly. "It's a flower my brother grows in his garden. It's my favorite one. Evelyn here plays second base." Everyone looked at Evelyn, who smiled weakly. "As a matter of fact," Gussie continued cheerfully, "I'm looking for recruits. I'm the coach. Got anyone in mind?"

Sandy gave herself a shake. She got up. "I've got to get back to the hospital. Jeremy will be wondering where I've been so long. Are you—are you serious?"

Gussie drew herself up a little higher on her cane. "Yes. When you and your boy get home again, and you are fearful in any way, you can call me. I promise you that someone on my team, or two, or three, or however many it takes, will come to your house and make sure that nothing more happens to you. To you or your boy."

June rushed up the stairs to Sandy. "I know what you're thinking, dear. Don't worry about the china. Let's go to Jeremy now. We can clean it up later."

Outside, Gussie stared into the distance, whistling through her teeth. "Well, Evvie, it looks like we'd better get ourselves a softball team," she said quietly.

December 16, 1974

Report of the First Meeting of the SAC (Spurs Advisory Committee)

Present: Augusta Cabrini, Rio Cabrini, William Brody, Hannah Wally, Peggy Glazer, Dan McGrath, Evelyn Brody

Recording Secretary: Evelyn Brody

Be the following herewith ascertained and forwarded, all having to do with the establishment of the first women's softball team in the history of Currys Crossing, Massachusetts:

1) The type of game to be played, arrived at after lengthy and turbulent discussion, is slow-pitch.

2) All women over the age of 18, regardless of personal characteristics, previous experience, and degree of physical fitness, shall be eligible.

3) Augusta Cabrini, formerly of the Phoenix Saints, has been elected coach and general manager.

4) William Brody, without whose devotion and wisdom the new team would surely fail to be enriched, has been

elected team trainer and special assistant to A. Cabrini.

5) Rio Cabrini, well-respected businessman, has been elected finance manager. He has promised to solicit funds, for what equipment and uniforms are deemed necessary, from his father and mother.

6) Hannah Wally and Peggy Glazer, both of whom are familiar with the game of softball as a result of their nursing school education, have volunteered to assist in the public recruitment of team members. Discussion ensued as to the best method of approach.

A. Cabrini suggested taking out an ad in the *Clarion*. Other members of the committee defeated that motion on the grounds that nobody would respond. D. McGrath held forth the opinion that in the initial appeal, as well as in subsequent rules and regulations, mention be made that those women who otherwise qualify for a place on the team but are, at least for the present, mothers of children under the age of eight or nine should be, for reasons he failed to put forward in any manner of coherency, rationality, or the slightest appearance of common sense, excluded from playing. The recording secretary took issue. D. McGrath suggested that the recruiting subcommittee look for players from the high school. A. Cabrini explained that the team was to be made up of *mature* women. "Oh well then," said D. McGrath. "That leaves out Evvie." Whereupon the recording secretary accidentally allowed a pitcher of iced apple juice to empty in the direction of D. McGrath's face. Upon the application of towels, D. McGrath explained to the committee that the newly-formed team would have his support, encouragement, and wholehearted assistance, but he could not find it within himself to stand by while his wife and the mother of his babies, otherwise occupied in the pursuit of a ball around a diamond, let those poor babies suffer the miseries of neglect, not to mention that she would probably never be home to cook dinners. D. McGrath proposed that the committee vote on a secret ballot to decide democratically if it wanted to have on its conscience the demise of Edmund and Kate and Allison McGrath. Before the motion was given attention, the recording secretary recommended that her husband be sent to his room and otherwise im-

peached from the committee. Both motions failed to pass.
R. Cabrini offered to take upon himself the care of
D. McGrath's and the recording secretary's children at
those times when their mother was engaged on business of
the Spurs. D. McGrath said he could damn well take care
of his own children. R. Cabrini said he would come over
and help. D. McGrath accepted under pressure. The
recording secretary vowed to herself to never, for the rest
of her life, touch, speak to, or be in the same room alone
with, D. McGrath. The discussion of recruitment continued.

R. Cabrini proposed that the committee compile names
and addresses and send out invitations to join the team.
Proposal rejected.

A. Cabrini said she still liked her idea of a newspaper
ad. P. Glazer explained that the task before the committee
was to put it to the people in such a way that they could
not possibly refuse, and reminded A. Cabrini that most of
the women of Currys Crossing would be as likely to want
to play softball as they would want to join the Marines.
A. Cabrini rejoined that she failed to understand how anyone could possibly not want to play softball. H. Wally, in
agreement with her housemate and fellow-nurse, said the
whole thing wasn't any different from getting patients to
take their medicine. It was all a matter of tact, sensitivity,
and the application of psychological pressure. A. Cabrini
said, What did they want her to do? Parade up and down
the streets of Currys Crossing on her cane, begging the
women to join up on pain of death?

H. Wally said it wasn't such a bad idea. P. Glazer proposed that the thing to do would be to go out among the
women in town and tell the truth.

The motion was denied. A. Cabrini held forth on the
subject of Sandy's privacy. A promise was extracted from
each committee member that their discretion could be
counted upon. The committee then agreed unanimously
to keep Sandy Dorn from finding out all this was for her
protection.

P. Glazer proposed going out among the women and
telling some variant of the truth. Motion passed. Debate
followed regarding the manner of getting at the women

where they were. The recording secretary volunteered to study the issue and return to the committee with a report. W. Brody called the attention of the committee to his observation that if you wanted to get to the women of Currys Crossing, all you had to do was go down to the church and play bingo on a Tuesday night.

Proposal accepted. The subcommittee in charge of recruitment decided to meet the following evening at the bingo game.

Meeting adjourned at five minutes past midnight.

Wind swished through the snow-covered branches of the trees. Twilight moved in with a hint of a moon beyond it. The snow sparkled, and it was easy to believe there was peace in this place. The name on the stone was Brody. Her father had not known where it came from, but it was the only name she had. Evelyn Brody, named for a boat and a dead man's unremembered relations, rubbed her hands together in the cold in front of her parents' grave. It was nearly Christmas. It had been snowing steadily all week. The drifting mounds peaked and fell softly in every direction.

She brought sprigs of holly and pine branches and poinsettia, carefully arranged in a wide, open basket she had borrowed from Rio. She remembered to bring some wire to hold the basket in place, for the winds were as fierce as nightmares. With her bare fingers, she scraped ice off the letters of the name Brody, and tied the basket securely to the stone. Her parents were silent, but Evelyn had something to say. She wanted to say that they'd been wrong in naming her for that boat, the *Evenly.* They'd been wrong in teaching her to expect that their lives would someday be launched on a clear, unruffled surface, utterly safe from harm. Shirley Brody was wrong to go on buying new pairs of gloves while embroidering their days with flourishes of hopefulness that always began and ended with the sound of the same word. Someday. Someday her hands would heal. Someday, her head held high, she would walk out of the mill forever. Someday, his untapped potential recognized at last, Franklin Brody would land a nice job in an insurance company or a government office. Even Marina Cabrini with her airs would come to understand that a Brody with an Oldsmobile parked in the driveway was every bit as respectable as a Cabrini. Someday, Marina Cabrini would cross the lines of their backyards and come over to have a cup of coffee. And when it arrived, this bag full of tricks known as someday would so absolutely rearrange their lives that afterward, none of them would be able to remember what had gone on before. But Shirley Brody died one night in a car crash and Franklin Brody died right after her. They left Evelyn to look after Uncle William and he was alive. They left her their house and it had not fallen down, and she told them so, fighting the wind for their attention.

She put her mittens on. Her teeth were clattering with cold. She listened for their voices. Franklin and Shirley were thinking it over.

There was a crunching of feet against snow. Danny stepped out from the shadows. He had followed her there in his truck. Danny brought a Christmas present of his own, a Christmas wreath tied up in red ribbon. He remembered, too, to bring wire. He and Evelyn had not spoken to each other for two days, but when he stooped to tie his wreath in place, Evelyn bent to help him. He touched her cold hands. He took off her mittens and brought her fingers to his lips and breathed on them. He pulled her close and kissed each one. Snow was falling. Darkness closed around them. In the silence, the two of them held each other, mourning. Then Danny took Evelyn by the arm and led her to his truck. On the seat, she found a brightly wrapped package with her name on the tag. It wasn't Christmas yet, but Danny wanted her to open it. Inside there was the sweet smell of brand new leather. Evelyn pulled back the tissue paper in the box. The softball glove was a dark, deep yellow with rawhide stitching and a thickly padded pocket. She slipped her hand in. She thumped the pocket with her fist. The fit was perfect.

"My wife the Spur," Danny muttered, clumsy with emotion. His eyes were wet. He blinked rapidly, calling it snow. Reaching with her mouth for his, Evelyn agreed. They stood together very still, warming each other, as snow gathered over the stone that said Brody, and slid down the sides of their faces, mildly, smoothly, serenely.

CHAPTER NINE

It was twenty minutes past the scheduled starting time, and in the ranks the parade was getting cranky. Feet shuffled. Shoulders rubbed. Necks craned. Voices rose. Throats dried. Hands sweated but still the marching band was quiet, and still the wait ticked on. Police officer Raymond Kuzick, leading the parade in his cruiser, watched impatiently for a signal from the drum majorette, who was watching for a signal from the driver of a red Thunderbird convertible which was parked between the band and the Spurs. The car had been taken out of storage and lent for the occasion by its owner, Tim Arbis of Anthony Street, on condition that he drive it himself and bring along his daughters, Ivy, Holly, Camellia, and Patience, to ride in the back seat with his special but still missing passenger, Augusta Cabrini. Having been to the candy cart twice each, the four girls, their wide-skirted, confection-colored dresses rising up from the seat like bubbles in an ice cream soda, stopped believing that anything interesting was going to happen and went to work twittering and bickering over many boxes of melting chocolate drops.

Officer Kuzick revved and killed his engine to irritate the members of the Board of Selectmen, who stood in a row, coughing and spitting, directly behind his car. The Little Leaguers stole batons from the Ivan A. Tolland Memorial Baton Corps, and challenged each other to duels. Rollie the Fist Pelletier made himself comfortable in a borrowed lawn chair, settling back as if he had sneaked free into a circus tent and waited for the show to begin. Some of the Spurs sat down on the ground, mildly alarmed. Birdey Nolan took off her borrowed earrings, examined her lipstick in the side-view mirror of Arbis's Thunderbird, and put her earrings back on. Sandy Dorn blew a kiss to her son Jeremy, who was nearby with Nate and June. Patsy Griffin reminded the team that there was no reason to worry, yet. Evelyn said she was sure Gussie would be along any minute. Then she said it again; but no signal appeared.

Ray Kuzick slammed out of his cruiser and hurried past the band to ask Arbis what the holdup was. Arbis said with a shrug that it was the same holdup as it was five minutes before: the coach was late. Yes, someone had phoned her house. Yes, she was on her way. Yes, there wasn't one more damn thing he could do about it except that, if she didn't show up soon, he was going to send his daughters over to Kuzick so they could smear their chocolate all over the cruiser.

Kuzick straightened, touching his hat. "Afternoon, Victor. Afternoon, Marina. You got that girl of yours with you? Seems like she's holding things up."

Victor blustered in protest, but a flurry behind him cut him off. A battered Chevy van came to a stop yards away from the Thunderbird. Rio Cabrini, behind the wheel, waved to his parents, and jumping down, he hurried to the other side to help his sister with her cane. Gussie nodded at her parents. Then she nodded at her team. Without a word, she climbed into the Thunderbird where the Arbis girls piled on top of her.

Tim sounded his horn and stretched his fist in the air. The drum majorette responded with a lift of her big baton. Ray Kuzick switched on his engine and slid the cruiser into gear. The Selectmen rearranged their neckties and the Spurs moved into line. The marching band struck up, and the parade began to move forward.

With all his heart Rollie the Fist disliked parades. Taking a circular, back-roads route, he drove himself to the field as his tape recorder purred voicelessly on the seat beside him. He had planned to start dictating his story on the first women's softball game in the history of Currys Crossing; but he was finding it ridiculously difficult to concentrate. He had not wanted to do it in the first place. This wasn't sports. This was women's business. This was—and he could not say exactly what it was, only that it had upset his digestion and fuddled his thinking and thrown him into a state of agitation he had not been in since Currys Crossing lost the New England schoolboy baseball championship in extra innings in 1962. They'd come so close! And there had never been a second season like that one. These days if you wanted to see some action you had to go over to Lowell, or Marlboro, or into the towns in the Catholic conference where the priests got their boys to offer up their points to Jesus.

Dutifully he had all the years since 1962 sat on the side with his notebook and made a respectable show of himself at tedious track meets and routine football games and Little League games and the occasional road race, and dutifully he had written arch or colorful or semiaffectionate columns, pretending to himself all along that, like the tides or the moon, good seasons come and go. He was tired of mediocrity. True, all you had to do was turn on the television for relief; but all the same there wasn't anything that came close to the feel of a roaring hometown season when the ones doing the scoring were the right ones and the phone rang regularly with calls from the papers in Boston and the thing that was ringing through the air was called pride. He reminded himself that he was not a nostalgic man. For good or for bad, he had lived all his life in Currys Crossing. He had seen it swell with promise and shrink with bad luck. He had watched flat-bellied, fast, confident boys turn into the saggy, dull-eyed fathers of other boys who came sluggishly to tryouts and went through the motions of the game more to keep from having to mow their lawns than to get down into the grit and go for a little glory.

The textile mills one by one closed down, and then the paper mill, and then the plastics mill; and the houses began to slouch, and the cars kept getting a little older, and more and more it seemed to him that the town was full of people going through the motions of dimly-remembered activities, each day getting a little bit more tired, each day getting further away from remembering the time not so long ago when the town boys almost brought home a trophy. And what had it come to—that reach, that feeling, that hope? It had come to this: they were turning the field over to the women. If he reminded them that it was fatal to give up, they would call him a bitter man. If he mentioned to the fathers in the boozy comfort of the bars that they ought to teach their sons something about pride they would slap him on the back, buy him a drink, and forget all about it until the next time. If he let them know how the baseball field that lay before him was as familiar to him as the back of his own hand, or how there had been a time, a long time ago, when his whole life had been shaped and bound up in that very place, that field, that fence, that plate, that diamond; and if he should sit down right here and talk about a time when playing ball meant having hands like miracles and eyes like radar and the feeling you could fly if only you'd been taught right—then they would shake their heads from side to side and say he was nostalgic.

Green and pampered, Tolland Field lay two blocks off Main Street between a carousel-style skating rink and the squeaky sanitation of a newly cleaned but unfilled public swimming pool. Budding old trees and tall wild bushes at its borders gave it an enclosed, safe feeling of privacy that had nothing to do with the eleven-foot-high chain link fences at either end. The well-used earth between the new bases had been swept and smoothed. The scoreboard attached to the fence behind home plate had been whitewashed, and its new, sleek black lettering glistened softly in the sunlight.

He parked his car under the No Parking sign at the head of the field, on a steep incline that his wheels took with protest. The mound of dirt was covered on top with burly, untended shrubs. He sighed, remembering a time when the hill had been mythic territory, a mountain for a boy to climb and conquer and peer through the bushes at the field where huge and godlike figures worked their paces to the beat of a masculine voice coming like thunder through a megaphone. The front end of his car tilted like an animal nosing its way up from underground. He slammed on the emergency brake and took a cardboard sign that said "Press" out of the glove compartment. He laid it across the dashboard. He didn't know why he bothered with the sign. He was the only one in town who ever parked there.

He got out into the mild air. Empty except for a man standing by the home-plate fence, the field had a look of order and
timelessness. True, the bases were closer to each other than they
would have been for a baseball game. The pitcher's mound was
closer to the plate. He would not have been surprised if they
had lined the benches with cushions to make the girls feel right
at home—but there were the same old wooden benches. There
was the same old everything, except that everything was closer
together. He sighed again. The parade was coming closer. He
rubbed the sides of his head, feeling the start of a migraine. He
half-wished he could go home, take some aspirin, and settle
down in his room to watch the Red Sox on television. He
cursed the whole day under his breath.

Cars were pulling in, and people in small chatty groups were
settling themselves on the grassy slope at the side of the field.
They had lawn chairs and blankets, picnic baskets and ice
chests, cameras and sunglasses. Rollie the Fist was trying to decide whether he should return to the privacy of his car and listen to the Sox on the radio until this joke of a game got under
way or head for the trees at the far end of the field and watch
from a safe distance, when the man he had noticed by the fence
approached him with a friendly, quizzical expression. Rollie
could not place him, but there was an easiness about him that
suggested he had as good a reason as Rollie for being there. He
was younger than Rollie by some twenty years. His dark cotton
jacket, unzipped over a neatly pressed plaid shirt, smelled
faintly of beer, but he was clean-shaven and his thick hair, the
color of ripe wheat, appeared to be recently trimmed. He had
the stocky, deep-chested look of a wide receiver and the tight
thighs of a runner. His stomach had gone slightly to pot but his
face was lean, and his light blue eyes, deeply set under thick
brows that were blonder than his hair, were guarded but
friendly. He asked for the time. Rollie wasn't wearing his watch
but answered that it must be getting on three.

"What've they got, a parade? Sounds like the Fourth of
July."

Rollie rolled his eyes and shrugged. "You can see it for yourself if you stick around a couple of minutes. This is the place
they're coming to."

"It's the softball game, right? I heard it was going to start at three but I didn't hear anything about a parade. Hell, sounds like they got the whole town out there."

"Whole town's gone nuts," grumbled Rollie. "You from around?"

A sudden flash of discomfort passed quickly as the younger man looked away from Rollie and back again. "Not exactly. I, uh, well you see there's this girl I met and I don't know her very well or anything, but I found out she was playing on this softball team called the Spurs. She doesn't even know I'm here. I just wanted to, well, I . . ." A slight flush crept into his face. He stuck his hands into his pockets and looked away again. "I thought I might drive down and take a look at the game."

"Suit yourself," said Rollie with a smirk. "As for myself, I can't see the point. These women wouldn't know a bat from a soup spoon."

"I agree. I absolutely agree," interrupted the other man. "That's why I don't even want her to know I'm here. I suppose the next thing they'll be wanting is a crack at the big time. You like the Sox?"

Rollie grinned widely and put out his hand. "Name's Pelletier. I sure do."

"Dorn. Ken Dorn," he replied as he took Rollie's hand and shook it firmly.

"Dorn, Dorn. Sounds like something I've heard before. You got people in town?"

"Naw. Least none I ever heard of. I come from, uh, Michigan. Been living up in New Hampshire. I met this girl when I was on the road for my company."

"Salesman, huh?"

"Right," Dorn added quickly. Looking over Rollie's shoulder he saw that the parade was coming toward the field. At the head of it, headlights glimmering in the sunlight, slowly rolled Ray Kuzick's cruiser. "Christ, here they come. Listen, Pelletier, you got any idea where I could sort of hang around and stay out of sight? She sees me and it'll blow the surprise."

Rollie, stroking his chin thoughtfully, eyed him with vague suspicion. "Wait a second."

"Wh-what?"

"This girl you're talking about. She married?"

"Married? What do you mean, married?"

"I mean it's no skin off my teeth, but sounds to me like you're maybe messing with a married girl and maybe her husband's close by."

Kenny Dorn threw back his head and laughed. "I live in New Hampshire! What do you take me for? Hell, if this girl is married then I'm a duck's rear end. Look, all I want to do is . . ." His voice softened. He gave Rollie a searching look of appeal and smiled. "Guess all I want to do is look at her for a while. You know how it is. Anyway, she takes this softball shit real serious. It'd throw off her game if she knew I was here. What do you say?"

"Sure. Here." Rollie reached into his pocket and took out the keys to his car and tossed them to Dorn. "It's the dark blue Dart. Behind the bushes, you can't miss it. Radio works fine, you can hear the Sox if you like. I may pop over time to time myself. Go on, nobody'll see you if you're there."

Kenny Dorn thumped Rollie's elbow gratefully and hurried away as Kuzick swung the cruiser in a wide loop and parked it on the other side of the field. The band marched onto the outfield, took up a T-shaped formation, and belted out a hearty round of its school song. Rollie the Fist covered his ears with his hands until it was over. The field was coming to life all around him as the parade broke and the marchers scattered. Up went more lawn chairs, out stretched more blankets. People who lived on the same street were carrying on as if they hadn't seen each other in years. Ice chests were flung open and bottle tops popped. Here and there, children were waving purple and white banners, and small girls in dresses were taking turns rolling each other down the grassy slope. It was plain to see that half the town or more had turned out. It was noisy, it was electric, it was suddenly full of wild cheering as the women in uniforms trotted through the crowd and took their places around the home-team bench. Rollie noted grumpily that the equipment they were dumping around their bench seemed real. Real bats, real softballs, real rubber spiked shoes, real water bottles, real batting helmets. He could not say what he had expected them to play with, but having stuck this long with the idea that whatever it was they were doing it was not real sports, he grunted to himself and looked away.

His jaw fell. His stomach lurched and tightened. He kept his eyes on the parking lot as if he could not bring himself to believe what he was looking at.

It was a van. A large, blue and white and green van with the emblem of a handbell in a circle was charging into the lot like a great roaring battleship with all its sails full and all its cannons aimed and ready. The Belles had arrived. They were armed to the teeth. They poured out of their steaming vehicle and marched to the visitors' bench, swinging their huge arms in rhythm behind their leader, Linda Drago. A deep hush came over the crowd.

CHAPTER TEN

December 28, 1974

Report of the Second Meeting of the SAC
Present: A. Cabrini, W. Brody, P. Glazer, E. Brody
Absent: H. Wally (on duty at the hospital)
Late: R. Cabrini (repairing his roof where the snow came in),
   D. McGrath (helping him)

   1) The following summary of events of the evening of
December 17, 1974, has been duly and orally presented by
P. Glazer and here recorded:
   Acting as members of the recruitment committee,
P. Glazer and H. Wally, wearing their nurses' uniforms,
appeared at the regular church bingo game to inform the
women there of the expressed purpose, and desired effect,
of coming to the aid of Miss Augusta Cabrini, recently and
seriously injured in an accident. The event of the injuries,
and their resulting trauma for one who had been until
that point a successful athlete whose career now appeared
to be rudely jeopardized if not finished forever, having
been familiar to those women present, who, if they were
not personally acquainted with A.C. herself, knew some of
her relatives or at least had heard of her, as, having been
the first and only female ever to leave Currys Crossing and
play professional sports, A.C. left behind her a reputation
which proved very useful in inciting the various townswo-

men to come to the aid of her cause. Thus, the recruitment committee, stressing the need for urgency, invited all present to their home the following evening for the following purpose: to assist in the endeavor to help A.C.

Let it be noted that the recruitment committee acted with extremely moving and effective eloquence, painting a picture of A.C. as a friend not only in need but in danger of succumbing to the mortal threat of severe psychological damage. Of singular bonus is the timely season of Christmas, during which people in general are more likely to be disposed toward goodness, and, in particular, with the chance to do good right at home, the women thus addressed responded with kindness and concern, despite the necessity of dropping their many tasks of shopping and decorating and gift-wrapping and cooking, etc.

In conclusion, this activity on the part of the recruiting committee has proven to be, in the estimation of all concerned, indubitably successful.

2) The following summary of events of the evening of December 18, 1974, has been duly and orally presented, etc., etc.:

Twenty-six women showed up. Cider and sandwiches, paid for against the account of the SAC, were served.

With the women settled amid a general atmosphere of goodwill, H. Wally introduced the recording secretary, who, although she had never in her life gotten up in front of a group to make a single sentence, never mind a prepared speech, somehow managed to get it said. And let it be noted that, despite the praise of the committee, the recording secretary feels that it would have been far more beneficial to all if somebody else had done it.

The prepared speech went as summarily follows:

That, in the belief that all there gathered wished to assist in the rehabilitation of A.C., it was the finding of the committee that the most expedient means at hand were those means with which the one to be helped was most familiar. In the agreement resulting from this statement, the recording secretary put forth the suggestion that there be henceforth organized as a perfect means to the aforestated end, a softball team, made up of women, which would se-

lect A.C. for their coach and thereafter, without letting on
that the team existed for her benefit, exist as a team, embarking on all those things which a team does.

To sum up briefly, the direct result was that by the end
of the evening eighteen of those gathered signed up. With
the exception of Nancy Beth Campbell, the youngest one
present, not one of the recruits laid claim to any previous
experience in playing softball. This in no way proved
daunting to the recruitment committee, as they were
quick to state it was the preferable thing all around: this
way they would have to invite A.C. to teach them, and,
with a discussion following on how the activity of instruction seemed a suitable, if not perfect, method by which
one could improve one's own self by teaching others, it was
agreed all around that as soon as the holidays were over
there would begin, in earnest, meetings of the new team.

As a point of interest, be it noted that a large topic of
conversation among the women was the sad and frighten-
ing event of the violence which occurred in the home of
Sandy Dorn, who was not present but is known by many
of those assembled. June Campbell, a monument to discretion, who was present but never once let on that she
suspected the true reason for the team but understood
more than anyone else the effect of the brutality upon her
friend, suggested that when Jeremy Dorn became healed
and healthier, it might be a good idea to invite Sandy to
join the team. This proposal was enthusiastically accepted.
June Campbell further pointed out that, in spite of the
fact that the team was beginning under a cloud of tragedy,
what with A.C.'s injuries and Jeremy Dorn lying in the
hospital with multiple concussions to the head and internal injuries which his physicians have not yet fully ascertained, it was her firm hope that some kind of happiness
might come soon, and it was on this note that the assembly
at the home of P. Glazer and H. Wally ended.

3) The following financial report was delivered by
R. Cabrini:

The SAC incurred a debt of thirty dollars and forty-
nine cents in meeting the expense of the refreshments pro-
vided at the recruiting meeting.

R. Cabrini reminded the other members of the SAC that he would, very soon, ask his parents for money.

4) W. Brody proposed that the members take up discussion regarding a place of meeting, especially for practices, for the team, and, reminding everyone that it is, after all, the dead of winter, suggested that we come up with someplace warm. Discussion ensued. It has been agreed to contact those women who signed up and inform them that their first meeting is scheduled for January 3 at six o'clock in the evening. Once again, P. Glazer volunteered the use of her and H. Wally's home.

5) D. McGrath excused himself at the sound of his and the recording secretary's middle child crying upstairs, and, as it followed that their other two children awakened also, the meeting was hastily adjourned.

The meeting was held at Hannah and Peggy's house. Gussie ran it herself. She didn't, she told them, blame anyone for feeling shy. It wasn't every day that somebody started a softball team in Currys Crossing. She was feeling a little shy herself. She'd been away for over six years. She was the only one in the room who couldn't walk without a cane. She wasn't used to it. There it lay like a well-behaved dog at her feet, and sometimes she thought it wanted her to feed it. It reminded her of the time Evelyn Brody invented Fred the dog. Fred was a beagle. They were seventeen years old and Fred followed them everywhere. Algebra, gym class, the lunchroom, Fred didn't care where he went as long as nobody closed a door on him.

Everyone looked at Evelyn. She blushed furiously.

And when they weren't closing doors on him, they were stepping on his tail. His paws. Even his ears. Poor Fred. Just because he was invisible, people kept driving him crazy.

"I never invented any dog," said Evelyn, but no one paid any attention. Their eyes were on Gussie.

"The first thing we do is go around the room. Everyone says her name and something about herself. It has to be something that's not showing. For example, Evelyn would not say that she has brown hair. We can see that for ourselves. Okay?"

There was a rustle, a giggle. No one moved.

"I'll go first. My name is Augusta Cabrini. I, ah, I used to have a tan." She turned with a grin to Hannah, who was seated at her right. It would be easy for Hannah and Peggy, Evelyn thought. They had gone to nursing school. They were probably used to strange situations.

"My name's Hannah Wally. I grew up in New Jersey."

"My name's Peggy Glazer. I've been on my feet all day, and they're killing me."

There was a short spurt of laughter, and a moment of awkwardness, as the attention went to the woman beside Peggy. She was dark-haired and nervous. Her small face was rimmed by a bouffant-style hairdo that looked as though it had been put together by an upholsterer of chairs. Her eyelids were streaked with green powder, and her cheeks were heavy with pink powder, and her lipstick was the color of a good-weather sunset. She cleared her throat, twisting and untwisting her hands in her lap.

"My name is Albertina Nolan," she said shakily. "But everyone I know calls me Birdey. I have five sons."

The heavyset, uncomfortable-looking woman on her right was her sister, Avis Poli. Avis was friends with Mrs. Monopoli and Joe the Rosarian. Evelyn had often seen her coming and going from their house.

"My name is Avis, same as the rental cars." She paused, rolling her eyes. "Birdey and I are sisters."

"Avis is older," Birdey cut in. Avis kicked her foot with a look that meant she would have liked doing something worse.

"I'm Grace Pandy," said a woman with graying hair and a sweet voice. Her clear, unwrinkled face turned a soft pink as she spoke. "Sometimes I make quilts."

"My name's Pamela Flynn. I'm a dental assistant with Doctor Burke. I guess I know most everyone here. I'm engaged to Bobby Ferris. He's at heavy-equipment school in Springfield. I live with my mother, who works for her, I mean Gussie's, family. We have a triple-decker that the Cabrinis got for us last year. Laura, this is Laura, she's next, she's divorced, she lives on the top floor. I would like to play third base if you let me and, oh! I said way too much. Did I? I just couldn't make up my mind which thing to pick!"

Pammy Flynn, who had probably had her hands in the mouth of every woman there, for Doctor Burke was the only dentist in town and she was the only assistant, gave her pale, thin hair a toss, wiggled her shoulders, and sat back down with satisfaction. The woman she had called Laura was sitting like tranquillity on the floor. Her long, gently curving legs were straight out in front of her. She looked at Pammy with indulgence. She was wearing a tan wool skirt over a black leotard. She was about forty years old. Her loose, thick hair was the color of chestnuts.

"Laura Bradley. I used to work as a secretary in Lowell."

Pammy Flynn bounced up and down on her heels. "But now she's got a dancing studio, don't you, Laura?" Laura shrugged. Patsy Griffin, who was next, knew everyone.

"I taught my kid, Brian, my next-to-the-youngest, how to play the bugle. The doctor told me not to, on account of his asthma. But I thought, what the hell, it'll kill him or cure him. He wanted a bugle bad." She showed her uneven, big teeth as she smiled. "Brian don't have asthma no more. He plays in the marching band at his school." Patsy patted the knee of the woman beside her. "Your turn, Mim."

"My name is Mimi Reed," she said very softly. "I like to make my own clothes." Mimi was red-haired and freckled and easy to look at. She had had a baby, her first, at the same time Evelyn had Allison. Evelyn could not remember if it had been a boy or a girl. She did not know its name. She'd been out of touch. Everyone was staring at her.

"Oh. I'm Evvie. Evelyn. Ev. I don't care what you call me," she said quickly, probably too quickly. "I did *not* invent any dog. Danny invented that dog. Danny McGrath. I married him right after high school." Ducking her head, she sat back with relief.

"I'm Nancy Beth Campbell." Blond, blooming Nancy Beth, niece of Nate and Juney, had been hanging around Anthony Street, mainly getting into trouble, for as long as Evelyn could remember. The look of her now took Evelyn by surprise. Evelyn had expected her to still be thirteen. Sitting on the floor, feet tucked neatly beneath her, Nancy Beth rocked herself excitedly from side to side. She lowered her voice and took the women into her confidence. "I'm not supposed to tell anyone this, but my father thinks I'm going back to college when semester break is over. Well, I'm not. I'm going to join the

Navy." She looked up quickly, and paused, as though she half-expected someone to slap her across the face for what she'd said. No one did. She smiled. "But first what I want to do is play some ball. I've played before. I pitch."

Gussie nodded with pleasure. There was one woman left. She was seated beside Gussie. She was thin, almost gaunt, in a pointed, hungry sort of way. Her grayish blue eyes had the dull resignation Evelyn often noticed in the waiting rooms of doctors, or unemployment lines, or lines outside a funeral parlor.

"My name is Karla Brown," she said. "I work as a cashier at the A&P." Her voice had traces of an unusual, throaty accent that Evelyn could not place. The woman was stiff and small. She was forty-eight or fifty. Next to Nancy Beth's high spirits, Karla Brown came on like a chill. Evelyn was prepared to pity her. Then she noticed her hands. Every line, every indentation, was absolutely in place. Her fingers were long and slim and beautiful. It was easy to imagine them flying across the keys of a piano, or dancing across the back of a chair, or coming around an unhappy girl like a soft, warm, living thing; like an anchor; like a home.

Gussie was talking, but her voice was dim. It sounded far away. Others were talking too, many voices, muffled. They were too low and too fast for Evelyn. She pretended they were not there at all.

The hands were smooth and very, very white. The fingernails, trimmed and rounded close to the skin, rose in perfectly formed half moons. The lines around the joints and knuckles had a carefully molded, unblemished look. They looked like they were brand new.

There was laughter, chatter, the sound of chairs pushed back and bodies rising.

The hands were lying on a stranger's knees like a pair of expensive white candles taken out of storage for a special meal. Ever so slightly the hands trembled, and Evelyn suddenly, desperately wanted to touch them. She wanted to take them into her own hands and rub them, and hold them. Kiss them. Save them.

"We're going to sue the mill!" cried Franklin Brody.

Evelyn did nothing. They might as well sue God.

It wasn't easy to breathe. Afraid, she felt her fists coming up to her eyes. She let out a strangled small cry as she tried getting up to her feet. She could not. She sank back down again, and cried into her own cupped hands.

When she looked up again the room was nearly empty. Hannah was removing the extra chairs. Peggy was fussing with Gussie's leg. She had rolled the leg of Gussie's pants to the knee and was turning the leg this way and that, examining the mess of scar and ruined tissue. Evelyn looked away. She wanted to find her coat.

"Are you all right, Evvie?" said Hannah. Her voice sounded low, friendly.

"We can walk you over to your house," offered Peggy.

Gussie struggled out of her chair and reached for her cane. "I'll do that. My brother's over there with Danny. He's going to drive me home."

"Turned out all right, don't you think?" asked Peggy brightly.

"Sure did," agreed Hannah.

Gussie crossed the room and slipped her free arm into Evelyn's. Their eyes met, and Evelyn quickly looked away. Her mouth was dry. Her head hurt.

They are all seventeen: Gussie, Ev, Danny. They are rarely apart. None of them can say for sure how it happened, but they found each other like a clubhouse. When Gussie has a practice after school, Danny and Evelyn stay to wait. When Danny is almost suspended for refusing to chain Fred the invisible dog to a fence outside the building, Gussie and Evelyn almost suspend themselves in protest. When Evelyn's mother dies, and then her father dies four days later, Danny marries her, and Gussie leaves for Arizona to play shortstop for a team called the Saints.

Damp and shivering from a locker-room shower, Gussie finds Danny and Evelyn waiting outside the door, drinking warm gin through straws. Gussie wants to be an athlete. Danny wants to be an architectural engineer. Gussie wants to be famous. Ever since she was four years old she has wanted to be famous. Danny wants to redesign every house in Currys Crossing. It is the worst-looking town in the world. Gussie wants to try out for a new softball team starting up in Phoenix, Arizona. Evelyn looks at her with amazement. It has never entered her mind before that this is the last time they are going to be together. Her mind is a little fuzzy from the gin. She is sure that in a moment or two things will go back to where they were. There is no such thing, she tells herself, as the Saints. She does not see how there possibly could be. Gussie is impatient, and makes them hurry home. It is the afternoon of the evening of the championship game between the varsity girls and whoever won another game the night before. Gussie wants to work out some more. Danny will come to Evelyn's house at seven. He will, she plans, sit in the kitchen drinking coffee with her father. She is upstairs dressing. Gussie has already left for the game. She takes her time, choosing her clothes with care. She likes the sound of male voices as they float to her ears out of the floor-boards. Danny will tell Franklin about architectural engineering. Franklin will say that it sounds like a fine thing for a boy to aspire to. It's a far cry from the mills, no doubt about that! says Franklin heartily. Danny's parents are schoolteachers, but once, for two weeks when he had turned sixteen, Danny was a floor boy at a shoe factory in Lawrence. He tells Franklin everything he knows about unions. Danny's car is parked outside the house. There is a bottle of gin under the seat. The heater is as warm as a fireplace. They will sit in bleachers and watch Gussie lead her team to another win.

Evelyn slips her arms into the sleeves of her winter coat. She has kept them waiting long enough. She comes out of her room, meeting her mother in the hallway. Nobody has been pounding on her mother's door. The house is quiet except for Danny and Franklin talking in the kitchen. Shirley Brody faces her daughter. She smiles. She takes Evelyn into her arms and hugs her. Arm in arm they go downstairs together. Evelyn is flooded with happiness. She is afraid to move or speak, because moving or speaking might drive it away. It's a fragile thing, this happiness. She will do whatever she can to protect it.

"Aren't you going to go inside?" Distantly, joylessly, Gussie's voice rumbled in her ears. Evelyn looked at her blankly. She was standing outside her own house. She did not remember how she had gotten there. She let Gussie help her in. She let Danny help her into her nightgown as if she were one of the children. She dreamed:

Gussie is clapping her hands together. It's time to go. If

they're late, Gussie says, Juney will have a fit. It embarrasses Evelyn to have to ask, but she has discovered that there is not much she remembers. She's been out of touch. There is much to explain. Gussie throws her head back and laughs at the top of her lungs. She can't believe that Evelyn can't remember it's her wedding day. Music plays. A room fills. Something happens, and the room empties. Then there is only silence.

January 25, 1975

Report of the Third Meeting of the SAC
Present: A. Cabrini, R. Cabrini, H. Wally, P. Glazer, D. McGrath, E. Brody
Absent: W. Brody (in bed with a head cold)

1) A. Cabrini reported that of the eighteen women who originally signed up, nine attended the first meeting held January 3. This figure excludes the four members of the SAC who were also present, which brings the total number of interested parties to thirteen. Of these thirteen, thirteen showed up for the first practice session, held in the backyard of D. McGrath and E. Brody on January 9, as well as for the second one, which was held in the same place on January 12. The third practice session, on January 19, ended up coming indoors as a result of excruciating cold and the presence of unremovable ice on the ground. Despite the temperature of ten degrees above zero, there were in attendance, fourteen. Accounting for the fourteenth is Sandy Dorn, whose son is still, unfortunately, in the hospital, but is, to everyone's satisfaction, doing well.

2) A. Cabrini, acting in her capacity as coach, offered to the committee the following summarily pertinent description of the three practice sessions:

The women have displayed in large, generous amounts, enthusiasm, interest, willingness to learn, and a very nice measure of good humor.

It is A.C.'s belief that the thing which is, so to speak, spurring on the Spurs, is a practically indescribable sense of novelty, as it doesn't take any research or historical investigation to know that ever since there has been a Currys Crossing it has been a Currys Crossing without a women's softball team. In fact, without a women's team of any sort unless it is taken into account that the high school extension classes for adults offer synchronized swimming and bicycle riding, which hardly anybody ever attends.

A.C. concluded by stating that, thus far, everyone concerned is having a good time, and it is her conviction that there exists every possibility of whipping into shape a real live softball team.

D. McGrath, on hearing the report of the coach, requested a further report on the actual methods being put to use in the practice sessions. Reminding the committee that the members of the team, with the exception of a handful, were not, in terms of reality, in any way suited physically to the rigors of a sport, D. McGrath pointed out that it was in the committee's interest to follow supervisorally the day-to-day activities which were intended to not only condition the bodies of the players but also to slant their abilities in the direction of athletic achievement.

R. Cabrini seconded the request.

A.C. denied it.

D.Mc., thwarted, restated himself, stressing the committee's curiosity concerning the coach's plans, strategy, and guidelines.

R.C. agreed.

A.C., in a resolute manner, explained that what went on between a coach and her players was the business of no one but themselves; and, further, that it would henceforth be the policy of the committee to restrict themselves to matters of advising, general strategizing, fundraising, and general support, leaving to the coach the matters concerned with the training and playing of the game of softball.

D.Mc. disputingly urged the committee to put A.C.'s proposal to a vote. A show of hands was called for, and H. Wally was selected to put the matter to W. Brody, who was allowed to vote from his bed.

Voting in favor of A.C. were: A.C., H. Wally, P. Glazer, W. Brody and the recording secretary.

Voting against were: R. Cabrini and D. McGrath.

The committee thus decided to disinvolve itself from all those matters pertaining to the actual operations of the team.

3) R. Cabrini reported on the state of finances. He has extracted from his father a promise to approach his wife and business partner regarding the sponsoring of the team. R.C. stated that there was every reason to believe that his mother would agree. A.C., of the opinion that the last thing in the world their mother would want to do was put out company money on a softball team, suggested that the financial manager look around elsewhere for sources of revenue. The financial manager, following a short debate, concluded that, as the business of the coach was to be left to the coach, the business of funding would be left to him. The matter was unanimously tabled.

4) H. Wally proposed that, despite such factors as the freezing weather, the unavailability of suitable equipment, the inexperience of the players and the extreme prematurity of the suggestion itself, it might be a good idea to start thinking about expanding practices to include sessions with other women's teams, and added that there existed two reasons for doing so: A) That exposure to other players would not fail to serve as a useful tool of instruction, and B) That, sooner or later, there was going to come a time when the team would enter into actual games against other teams, and it might prove beneficial to find out what other teams were out there, what they did, and how they did it.

A.C., basically concurring, reminded the committee that it was the middle of winter, and inasmuch as it would be nice for the Spurs to familiarize themselves with other teams, other teams were seasonally defunct.

H.W. pointed out that, of course they were; but not at the jail. To the mildly stupefied incredulity of the committee, H.W. explained that she had recently received word that a friend of hers had taken a position at Currys County House of Correction and was taking on the combined duties of social worker and gym supervisor in the women's division, and, furthermore, although this position was a temporary one, as her friend was filling in for the permanent worker who was out on maternity leave, her friend was embarking on a program to upgrade and expand the recreational activities of the inmates, and was soliciting the permission of officials to allow outside groups to enter the jail for the purpose of friendly competition. Such efforts on the part of her friend had been rewarded with the playing of several basketball games, and, as her friend's outside interest happened to be softball, her friend was looking around for ways to encourage and promote this interest.

Dubiously, the committee pondered this proposal, and agreed to table it until the next meeting. As the meeting adjourned, A.C. asked H. Wally who her friend was.

"Linda Drago," replied H.W.

Adjournment was at eleven-twenty P.M.

CHAPTER ELEVEN

The air was thick with the familiar smells of wood and leather and beer and the clean, raw scent of newly-mowed grass. Picking his way through the blankets and lawn chairs, Rollie Pelletier ignored the cheer that went up from the crowd as the Spurs began their warm-up exercises. His hands were thrust in his pockets. His lips were moving with silent agitation. He was trying to reason with himself, trying to overcome the shock waves in his heart that were put there by the sight of Linda Drago.

Something was up. He could smell it. It was one thing for Gussie Cabrini to organize the hometown ladies into a softball team, but it was another thing altogether to take on the likes of Linda Drago. Not that Gussie Cabrini was anyone's fool. She had a backbone as tough as trees. Pity, though, that she hadn't been born a boy. Could have made something of herself. God knew she had the touch. Rollie had watched her in her youth, her body fine-tuned and her blood out for glory. She had out-played, out-won the best the town had to offer. Pity. It was like hearing a cat tweet birdsong. She was big, too. Probably spent her whole life being the tallest girl in town. Too bad about her accident. Not that she was ever much of a looker. Didn't have half of what her mother had. A shame, a real shame.

One thing was certain, though. It couldn't be just a coincidence that the leader of the Belles was Linda Drago. Rollie remembered Linda Drago. In just one year she'd turned a whole school on its ear with her crazy ideas about girls playing football, girls long-distance-running, girls at the shot-put and the

javelin and everything else she could think of. Good thing it
had only been a year. Linda Drago might have ruined an entire
generation of Currys Crossing girls if she'd had more time.

Rollie found himself in the parking lot. Alongside the telephone company's van was Rio Cabrini's smaller Chevy. Rio sat
in the driver's seat, smoking a cigarette with nervous intensity.
Rollie took a step toward him and cleared his throat.

"Hey there, Cabrini," he said cozily.

May 10, 1975

There was a house in a development block at the edge of town that I
have thought of often. It was built in the Eisenhower years and
abandoned to a life of mediocrity on a street where all the other
houses looked the same.

The house was red with white shutters. There was a short, sparse
front lawn with a flagstone path leading to three cement steps outside the front door. My daughter Augusta, who was twelve, waited
on those steps while I was at work inside.

There had been some sort of school holiday that day. She had
followed me about, waiting impatiently for me to finish my work. Although it was springtime, the air was chilly. Against my will Augusta
wore a thin pair of old jeans and one of her brother Rio's old sweatshirts. She had removed the sleeves of the shirt at the shoulders.
Under her arms, thick, dark twists of her new body-hair mingled with
the tangled threads of the shirt and the never-ending stream of her
sweat. She generally made no effort at all to groom herself. She
rarely looked clean.

It takes the better part of a day to assess a house that is about to
be put on the market. Augusta had brought along some books and a
golf ball. She left the books in the car. She spent the entire morning
taking apart the golf ball. She scraped her knuckles ragged, pulling
the ball apart all the way to its spongy lining, which she tore away.
She started singing a song she had made up herself. The song had
three words. I hate houses.

At the heart of a golf ball there is a small, round, tough piece of
rubber. I believe it is indestructible. When Augusta reached the rubber, she began bouncing it up and down on the cement steps of the
house. As she bounced, she sang. She sang high, she sang low,
she sang with emphasis on one word at a time. Each time she
paused to catch her breath, she bounced the ball a little harder, a
little higher, singing all the while, as far as her voice would reach, I
hate *houses*, I *hate* houses, *I* hate houses.

Inside, I could hear her from every room. At last I went to an upstairs window, and called out for her to stop.

She did not. I asked her again. I asked her a third time, and she pulled back her arm and crashed the ball through the window that was directly below the one where I was standing. I will never forget the look on her face at the moment the glass shattered. Her eyes were dancing. Her face was triumphant.

The shattered glass fell inside the house as well as out. Splinters flew everywhere, but Augusta was not harmed. I turned away from the window and went back to my work.

Augusta paid for the damage with her allowance money. The incident was never repeated. The distance that opened between us that day has been steadily growing larger. I had hoped that the passage of time would help to close it, but it has not. I had hoped that it would at least grow somewhat more bearable. I was wrong.

Narrowing his eyes, Rio blew a cloud of smoke out the window of his van. "Heard you've been interviewing some of the Spurs, Rollie. Nice to know you're on your toes."

Rollie stiffened, forcing himself to smile. "Looks like you got yourself the best seat in the house. What's the matter, afraid to see a little blood?"

"I'm waiting for someone."

"Who, the Marines? That's what it'll take to get your sister out of this. I saw those Belles, Cabrini. They're no ladies."

Rio studied his rearview mirror for a long moment. He ground out his cigarette in the ashtray and nervously fiddled with the steering wheel.

"What's with Linda Drago?"

Rio rolled his eyes indifferently.

"Come on, Cabrini. It's no accident that Drago's here. I know who she is. I got a memory like an elephant."

To Rollie's surprise, Rio suddenly brightened. "Mother!"

Rollie turned around. Marina Cabrini was coming toward them from the trees at the back of the skating rink. She was dressed in black. She was the only woman Rollie could think of who could show up for a ballgame dressed in black and not offend everyone who saw her. There was a cool, liquid, admirable look to her uncreased trousers and long, elegantly tailored jacket with an upturned collar that opened against a hint of very white throat. Her dark hair had been pulled into a tight, seamless knot at the back of her neck, drawing attention to the fine, high curve of her cheekbones. She walked with a firm and easy stride, one hand swinging loosely at her side while the

other rested on a black leather purse that hung by a strap from
her shoulder. There was a drawn, weary expression in her eyes
that vanished the instant she smiled. She smelled like fine linen
and expensive flowers. Rollie smiled back, unconsciously sucking in the slight bulge of his waistline. At twenty, he thought,
Marina had been an unusually pretty girl. Now she was simply
beautiful, the way autumn is beautiful, and Rollie realized
with a sinking sensation that if Marina Cabrini should suddenly ask him to turn cartwheels across the parking lot, or get
down on all fours and bark like a dog, he would do it at once,
and never regret it.

"Hello, Rollie," she said warmly, holding out her hand. He
liked the strength in her handshake.

"Rollie's been interviewing some of the players, Mother,"
said Rio.

"How nice," she murmured.

Rio propped his elbows on the window frame and poked his
head out. "Maybe you ought to interview Mother, Rollie."

Marina shot her son a look of aggravation. Rollie shuffled.
Rio grinned widely.

"But the game is going to start any moment," said Marina.

"No way." Rio opened the door and climbed out of his van.
He patted his mother gently on the arm and pointed toward
the field. "They're just warming up. Nothing'll happen for a
while. What do you say, Rollie?"

Rollie, shrugging, waved his hand.

"It'll be great for your story," Rio added. "After all,
Mother's been in on this thing from the beginning. In fact,
Mother is the best in the family when it comes to supporting
the team. She's a regular pep club. Maybe you two could go
somewhere quiet and talk, say, right now."

"Tape recorder's in my car," said Rollie.

"Can't be too far off, right?" pressed Rio.

Rollie tipped his head to indicate where he had parked it,
missing the look Marina gave Rio. Marina took his arm. They
walked by the field in silence. She had a light, smooth touch,
and he was surprised, looking at her sideways, to realize that
she was almost exactly his height. It was an odd, slightly un-
comfortable feeling to be standing beside a woman without
having to look down on her. When they reached his car he
stopped short, looking around in confusion.

"Is something wrong?" Marina withdrew her arm.

He saw his keys on the front seat beside the tape recorder. Then it came to him. The guy with the girlfriend should have been sitting in there. He'd forgotten all about the guy with the girlfriend. There was no sign of him. "Must've changed his mind," Rollie muttered to himself. He opened the door on the passenger side, and held Marina's elbow as she stepped up and slid in. There was a bounce in Rollie's step as he hurried around the car and climbed in beside her.

But was it happiness? Avis wondered.

She was down on the ground, legs straight out and slightly parted, bending her back in the stretches that were now as familiar to her as the steps it took to cross her own kitchen. Up, down; up, down. She touched her forehead to her left knee, once, twice, three times, and as she tipped her head back, rotating it gently, there came over her another wave of giddy, sweet expectation as rich as something wonderful cooking on the stove. She pressed her feet together at the heels and started reaching for her toes. Four months ago it couldn't have been done. Only four months!

At her back the spectators were noisy and cheerful. Before her lay the empty field, its bases waiting like prizes. At either side her teammates, dressed just as she was, were putting their bodies through the same paces, straining lightly, wiggling, shaking their arms and legs in loose, easy rhythms. No one spoke. Avis grasped her ankles, bending and straightening her knees. It felt good. It felt right. It felt like happiness, but how was she to say so?

The speech she was trying to compose kept coming out all wrong. The last thing she wanted to look like was a foolish, sentimental old woman, and she knew Gussie well enough to make sure she kept her feelings in line. Gussie treated any personal outburst with embarrassment. Shy, tight-lipped Gussie responded best to feelings when feelings stayed under cover. Not that the last four months had left her unchanged. It was hard for Avis to say how, but under her eyes Gussie had slowly, quietly unfolded, opening herself the way a flower tilts its head toward the sun. You had to be careful with Gussie, simmering, big-bodied Gussie, who had stood to the side, full of mysteries, changing everyone who came her way. It was true; they had all changed. Avis herself wasn't fat anymore. Evelyn Brody was absolutely glowing, a far cry from the sullen, hesitant, brooding Evelyn who'd first come to a practice. Sandy Dorn had turned out to be aggressive and hardworking, as if she'd taken hold of her rage and turned it into the best throwing arm in the county. Shy, clinging Karla Brown found herself a voice and used it as often as anyone. Even Birdey was different. Not that Birdey could ever be anything but Birdey, but Avis had to admit that these days she wasn't whining as much as she used to. She was, in fact—but here was Birdey herself, tugging away at her sister's arm, not whining exactly, but just as nervous as ever.

"Avis! Do you see them?"

Avis followed her eyes to the Belles' bench, where the women were lacing on cleats, pulling off sweat jackets, adjusting uniforms. Some were larger or more solid than others. All of them seemed twice the size of the Spurs.

Birdey gulped. "They're going to kill us."

Avis went on stretching.

"I don't think I can take it. Not with all those people watching. My own boys are out there! What am I going to do?" Crouching down beside Avis, Birdey fluttered her hands and looked ready to cry.

Avis sat up. "It'll be all right. It'll be over before you know it."

"Ha! That's what you think."

"Look, Birdey, this is no time to get scared. Why don't you go talk to Gussie?"

"I already talked to Gussie. I told her I felt like I was going straight to the grave when I saw those Belles and do you know what she said to me? She said, 'What would you rather do, Birdey? Play this game, or give birth to five more boys?'"

"Well? What did you answer?"

Birdey threw her hands in the air. "Oh, Avis, *honestly!*" She turned her back and huffed away.

Avis went to work on her hands. She carefully kneaded her fingers, knuckles, wrists. She returned to her speech. There were three main points she wanted to cover. Thank you for getting all this started. Thank you for doing such a fine job. Thank you for existing in the first place. She felt clumsy and inarticulate. Was this supposed to be happiness?

Angela, if asked, would think so. Mary-Susan and the boys would think so. Leo who bought her a size twelve nightgown would yell at the top of his lungs: What, Avis happy? Is the pope Catholic?

Angela was home for a month with the babies. Leo had brought Avis's breakfast on a tray. Birdey had hated it when Avis was fat. Everything was new. No matter how she looked at it, it came to this: everything, everything was new. Gussie Cabrini had stepped into Avis's life and changed it. In return, Avis knew that she loved her the same as if Gussie was one of her own. The problem was how to say so. She rose to her feet, brushing the dust off the back of her uniform, and looked around for her catcher's mask.

There were five minutes left until the start of the game.

"My daughter has always been an athletically-minded girl," said Marina into the tape recorder in Rollie's car. She spoke slowly, choosing her words with thoughtful deliberation. "It comes as no surprise to her father and me that she's been able to put her talents to work right here in Currys Crossing. Of course, we have always been able to encourage her. When a parent is fortunate enough to raise a child of unusual abilities, it goes without saying that the child deserves the broadest possible range of opportunities. It's just the same as if she had been born a gifted musician."

"It's like that, is it?" Rollie raised his eyebrows.

Marina drew her lips together tightly. "My daughter has worked very hard for her team. She deserves credit."

"What about that last team of hers?"

"What of it?"

"She left." Rollie kept his eyes off Marina, staring straight ahead.

"That is right. She used to play for a team called the Saints, and she left."

"You care to comment on that?"

"I sell houses, Rollie. I don't pretend to know the first thing about what makes a person of athletic ability do a thing or not. Augusta had a successful career at one time. Perhaps it did not turn out exactly as she wanted."

"I'm sorry about her accident," Rollie said gently. "It must have been hard on you."

Marina reached up and smoothed back the already perfect sweep of her hair. "It's always fortunate, don't you think, when things straighten themselves out? In a way, what is happening here today has a great deal to do with Augusta's accident. When she was released from the hospital she wasn't sure that she would ever become involved in sports again. And now she has become a coach."

"Curative, hey?"

"In a manner of speaking. My daughter has always been a most resourceful person."

"A fighter," cut in Rollie. "But of course, as the mother of the coach, and if you don't mind my bringing it up, as the one responsible for keeping the ladies in cash—"

"I believe it's a common practice for businesses to sponsor athletes," said Marina stonily. "My husband and I were pleased to be able to help."

Rollie smiled. Her repose was a deep, well-guarded thing. He found himself wondering what it might take to ruffle her. No wonder the daughter was so tough. They were two of a kind. He wondered if Marina herself was aware of it. "You must be proud."

"As I told you, my daughter is resourceful."

"Must be." Rollie turned in his seat to face her. "Just between us, though, don't you think there's more to this than meets the eye?"

"I don't know what you mean."

Rollie snapped off the tape recorder. He grinned slyly. "You sell houses. I write sports. I don't know a thing in hell about real estate but I know a few things about playing ball. One of them is that you don't go fooling around with a hotshot team when all you've got is rookies who don't know one end of the bat from the other. Another thing is that once you've played serious ball, you don't get your kicks by playing for fun. Girl or no girl, either you play to play, or you play to win. I've got a pretty good idea how it sits with your daughter."

"You surprise me, Rollie. Not long ago you were treating my daughter and her team as if they had some kind of disease. Have you had a change of heart?"

Rollie scowled. "Just want to make some sense, Ree."

Marina pulled back her head sharply. For an instant, Rollie believed that she was recoiling from the sound of her childhood name. He'd used it unconsciously, warmed by her presence, and he regretted it as soon as it was out of his mouth. He wanted to apologize. He leaned toward her, and realized that it was not a name that had taken her by surprise. The back door of the car was opening and a man was coming inside. The man with the girlfriend. Dorn. He was wearing dark, unreflecting sunglasses and a baseball cap pulled down to cover the sides of his head. His jacket was zipped to the throat. His left hand was fisted and bulging in the jacket's side pocket. He slumped down low in the seat directly behind Marina.

Danger warnings went off in Rollie's head. His chest started aching. His stomach burned. The lump of fear in his mouth was hard and stale. His eyes told him that it wasn't just a hand in Dorn's pocket, but reason reminded him that the only time a man carried a gun in Currys Crossing was hunting season. It wasn't November. It wasn't a rifle. Less than a hundred yards away, old man Thistle was setting up his vending cart. Through the open car window, Rollie could smell the buttered popcorn and the mustard melting on steamed hot dogs. Beyond the vendor, half the town had come to watch the game.

"Close your window," said Kenny Dorn.

Rollie closed it and Marina's eyes shot open with pain. Her body twisted sideways. Dorn had reached over the seat and had her arm by the wrist, steadily wringing it harder. Marina sounded a deep, strained, awful groan.

"Hand over the keys." His voice was normal enough. He could have been asking Rollie to place the odds on a ballgame.

Marina was perspiring around the temples. Stray bits of her hair came loose. Rollie tossed the keys over his shoulder into the back seat. He did not think that he would be able to bear it if Marina's hair came all undone. He felt himself being taken over by a dull, creeping paralysis. The man in the back was talking softly, saying something about a boy. It was hard for Rollie to understand. The paralysis had reached his ears. He could not look at Marina. He could not move at all. He had a vision of himself going for old man Thistle's steaming bucket of hot dog water and spilling it over Kenny's head. He'd trap him neatly. He'd be the one standing by as Kuzick came forward with the handcuffs. No problem. And Marina would . . . The vision ended with Marina.

Marina's free hand rose up from her lap and gestured weakly in the air. She seemed to be trying to point at something. Rollie stared and stared, trying to make sense in his mind. Her hand fell. Her face contorted but she did not cry out. The ringing in his ears died down. He blinked rapidly, and shook his head from side to side.

"Let go of my arm, Mr. Dorn," said Marina.

Dorn laughed. "I wondered if you'd recognize me, Mrs. Cabrini. I sure do recognize you. That was some house you sold me. Me and the wife and the kid still in the oven. Tell you what. You were so very kind and so very helpful when you sold me that house, I'm going to let you help me again. We're going to get my boy. We're going to sit here quietly until the game gets going, and then we're going to get him." Dorn's expression was pleasant. His tone was low, almost charming. His hold on Marina grew tighter and tighter.

Rollie took a deep breath. The deadening ache in his bones was relaxing.

"His name's Joe. Joe Dorn. That's not what his mother calls him, though. His mother calls him Jeremy. Can you stand it? Jeremy. Might as well call him faggot. I've just come back to get what's mine. I miss my kid. She's tried to keep him away, but I'll take care of that." Dorn leaned forward, resting his head on the back of the front seat.

"How're you doing, Pelletier?" he asked.

Rollie brought his elbow up against Dorn's face with all the force he could raise. It wasn't much. Dorn collapsed for an instant in surprise. Rollie went for the handle of his door but Dorn got him fast with a jab of the heel of his hand into Rollie's neck. Rollie slumped down. The pain was stunning. He felt as though his head was about to fall off his body. Things grew fuzzy.

"Very convenient for you to park in these bushes, Mr. Pelletier," said Dorn, keeping his hold on Marina. "I think that things are going to work out just fine. If I were you, though, I wouldn't try anything like that again. I think we might as well just sit here, very, very quietly. Isn't that right, Mrs. Cabrini?"

Marina nodded whitely. "I will do whatever you want me to do."

Dorn seemed to relax a little. Rollie was aware of a soft sensation in his left leg. Beyond the pain in his head there was a softness, a lightly brushing feel of human warmth. He looked down, squinting. Marina was rubbing his leg with hers.

"I'd hate it if I have to use this gun, Mr. Pelletier," said Dorn. His eyes were on the bushes, as if he were trying to see through them. Miserably, Rollie watched Marina's trousered leg creeping across his own. His heart was pounding out of control. His headache was raging. He followed the movement of Marina's leg, toes upward, with a sense of doom.

"Joe's going to be glad to see me," said Dorn. "First thing I'm going to do is get him out of that suit his mother dressed him in. His mother dresses him like he's retarded. I'll take care of him just fine. You got kids, Mrs. Cabrini?"

Marina's leg stopped moving. Her face tensed beyond her pain. Dorn yanked harder at her arm.

"I said, you got kids, Mrs. Cabrini?"

"Y-yes."

"Then maybe you can get an idea how I feel, being apart from mine."

"Yes." Her leg moved again, inching toward the dashboard. Rollie gasped. He looked at her quickly, as if trying to figure out how he might be able to help.

"Hands up, Mr. Pelletier," said Dorn. "I don't want you doing anything stupid."

Rollie put his hands on either side of his face.

"Good." Dorn took off his cap. Then he took off his sunglasses. As he turned around to put the glasses on the seat beside him, Marina's foot reached the lever of the emergency brake beneath the dashboard, and released it. The car teetered for an instant on the top of the little hill. Then it started rolling.

Caught off-guard, Dorn lost his grip on Marina and clutched at the top of the seat for support. Rollie managed a chop to his chin and Dorn fell back.

"Jump!" cried Marina, reaching for the handle of her door.

Rollie shoved himself against the door on the driver's side and tumbled out sideways. He hit the ground hard. As the car shot away in reverse, its front door swung with a huge groan on its rusty hinges and thudded against the side of his head. There was a quick, fiery flash of pain that coursed the length of his body, red-hot and suffocating. His eyes turned in on themselves and he passed out.

When he came to again, he was lying on his back on flat ground. He put his hands to his mouth. No blood. All his teeth seemed to be in place. He propped himself up on an elbow and discovered that he was in the center of a small crowd. Weakly, he staggered to his feet. The clatter of voices all around him was deafening. Rubbing his head he stared dazedly at the iron railing at the entrace of the Ivan A. Tolland Memorial Field. The rear end of his car had folded like an accordion against it. Beyond the wreck, two figures appeared to be moving away. Ray Kuzick had Dorn by the wrists. He was leading him toward his cruiser. Rollie turned away. His eyes searched through the crowd and came at last to Marina, standing to one side with her husband and son and daughter. He stumbled forward to join them. A siren began to whine in the distance. Gussie Cabrini closed her big hand around her mother's hand as Rollie approached. Tilting her head, she met her mother's eyes and held them for a long, long moment. When Marina at last turned to speak to Rollie, he saw in her face a look he had never seen there before. To himself, he called it contentment. Marina let go of her daughter and took his hand with warmth.

CHAPTER TWELVE

It was a raw, lip-chapping Sunday morning late in February, the day of the Spurs' first game against the women of Currys County House of Correction. Danny, Uncle William and the children had left early with the Campbells and Jeremy Dorn for an exhibition of new bulldozers in upstate Vermont. Evelyn was home alone, trying to pull herself together in time for the game. She hadn't slept well the night before. The muscles in her lower back ached badly. She was coming down with a cold. At practice on Saturday, she had performed miserably. Her last time at bat, having come up empty for the fifth time, she flung aside the bat and grazed Birdey Nolan across the shins. Birdey, showing her bruise to everyone, quit the team. Evelyn apologized. Gussie rushed in with a lecture on self-control and Birdey joined up again, but the mood of the team was gloomy.

The house was cold although steam was clattering and hissing in the radiators. Evelyn pulled on a pair of sweatpants, four T-shirts, and three pairs of Danny's outdoor socks. Then she fixed a hot-water bottle for the pain in her back, attaching it around her waist with the cord to Danny's bathrobe. She took some aspirin and got down on the floor in the kitchen to exercise. She was halfway through her knee-bends when the doorbell rang.

Marina Cabrini, tall and frosty in a pale gray cashmere coat, unwrapped a pink head scarf as she followed Evelyn inside. She took a chair in the kitchen, refused the cup of tea Evelyn offered, and did not care to take off her coat. She laid the pink scarf in her lap, touching the tips of her fingers together as she turned her eyes on Evelyn with a long, searching look.

"I've come to talk to you about Augusta," she said at last. "I understand that there's a game scheduled for today."

"It's not really a game," said Evelyn quickly, defensively. "More like a practice."

Marina clucked under her breath. Evelyn squirmed unhappily.

"It's not a very good idea."

"The game? Oh, you don't have to worry about it at all. It's perfectly safe. I mean, we've never been inside a jail before, but they aren't murderers or anything. Drugs and prostitution, that's all. In fact, Gussie says that if they locked up every man who did the same things they lock up women for, there'd be hardly a man left free in America. It's very safe, really."

Marina lifted an end of her scarf and waved it vaguely in the air. "Please. That is not what I mean."

"No?"

"Evelyn, you are Augusta's oldest friend. I believe that your position entitles you to know the truth of the matter."

Evelyn fidgeted with the cord that tied the hot-water bottle to her body. Marina did not seem to be bothered by the cold at all.

"Tell me something, Evelyn. Don't you think that you are all a little too old to be playing girls' games?"

It was odd, how the cold did not affect her. Evelyn found herself wondering if beauty alone keeps a woman warm. Perhaps being beautiful meant being in the possession of some kind of internal electric blanket, some private insulation that kept out chilly weather. Evelyn tried to image Marina Cabrini in three pairs of her husband's socks. Her father's voice floated into her ears. He thinks that Marina is the most beautiful woman he has ever laid eyes on.

"Uppity, that's all she is," says Shirley Brody. "Look at the way she's pestering our Ev. She comes around here one more time, you know what I'll do? I'll *prosecute*, that's what!"

"Evelyn?"

Marina's eyes were on her like a pair of spotlights.

"What do you want me to do?" asked Evelyn weakly.

Shirley Brody wants to give Marina a piece of her mind. Shirley bangs away at the inside of Evelyn's head, demanding to be heard.

"Now, now," says Franklin, trying to soothe her. "Remember that she's our neighbor. She means well."

Shirley hides her hands in her pockets. She's eyeing Marina's silk scarf. She knows what would happen to the scarf if she touched it. Her tough hard broken skin would have it in shreds in a second. Evelyn reminds her of this. Shirley falls silent.

Marina gave a sigh of satisfaction and sat forward in her chair. She pressed both of her hands to Evelyn's arm. Her touch lasted for five long heartbeats. Her skin was incredibly warm. Evelyn decided that she had been right about beautiful women. She wanted to ask Marina to keep holding on.

"You and Augusta have known each other all your lives. You have a right to know about the work she is being called upon to do."

Evelyn shrugged. "We were out of touch for a while."

"But that's what I've been coming to! Augusta was not out of touch with you only. It was with everyone. Her family. Her other friends. Even, I believe, with herself. She's been through some very painful experiences. You know that perhaps better than anyone."

"Are you talking about her accident? Or before her accident?"

Marina tilted her head slightly and smiled a thin smile. "I am talking about a girl who has been unhappy for a long, long time. She ran away to the West, expecting that she might find happiness playing for that team. She found out that she'd been wrong. She is a proud girl. She is not willing to admit to her own mistakes. Her father and I stood by, doing what we could. I wrote her letters daily."

"In Italian?"

Marina, looking up sharply, gave her head a slight, puzzled nod and immediately regained her composure. "My daughter has given herself wholeheartedly to this business of playing softball with the local women. I admit that it's an interesting, perhaps worthy enterprise. But I am afraid that she is letting it interfere with her work. At this point, I am not free to give you details, except that she has been entrusted with a project involving a great deal of money. I have every reason to expect that she will do well. It is important, you see, that Augusta succeed. She has had more than enough of her share of failure."

Footsteps sounded near the front of the house. Shirley, thought Evelyn without surprise. Shirley was coming to drive Marina away. Her head was beginning to hurt. Franklin would be right behind Shirley, Evelyn imagined, making apologies. Evelyn shivered violently.

"May I believe that you agree with me?"

Footsteps. Real ones. A man's voice called out, "I'm here, Evvie!" Rio Cabrini, his red toolbox swinging at his side, entered the kitchen. He blinked at his mother in surprise. Stooping, he kissed her quickly, absently. "Hope you don't mind that I let myself in. I hadn't planned on getting here until after the game today, but I found I had some free time." He turned to Evelyn and said, "I came to fix the hole in your roof. It's freezing in here."

Evelyn looked at him blankly. Marina rose.

"I have enjoyed our visit, Evelyn. Don't bother getting up, I know my way out." She lifted her scarf and flung it across her shoulders. Rio saw her to the door, and returned to Evelyn with a grin.

"There's no hole in the roof, Rio."

"No?" Leaning against the sink he lit a cigarette. "If I were you, I wouldn't let Mother know."

"You knew she was here?"

He nodded with a little laugh.

"Was there another fight? I mean, with Gussie?"

"Another one? I don't think there ever is another one. I think the same fight just keeps going on."

"She wants Gussie to quit the Spurs."

"What a surprise."

Evelyn untied her hot-water bottle and flung it past Rio into the sink.

"In a way," he said lazily, "your name sort of came up in a conversation I had with my father."

"Mine?"

"I showed Papa the minutes you've been keeping of our meetings. They're not bad, you know? Papa says he always knew you were a woman of a thousand talents. He said to tell you that he can't wait to read the next installment. Don't pay any attention to anything Mother said to you, Ev. Just ignore her. She won't mind. Half the human race is trying to ignore my mother. By the way, Papa's going to back the team."

"With money?"

"With money."

Evelyn jumped from her chair and ran to him, throwing her arms around his neck.

"Don't tell Mother," he whispered, returning her hug.

"There's nothing in the world like the game of softball," Gussie told the Spurs, who had gathered in Evelyn's front room. It was nearly time to leave for the game at the prison. The women were doing their best to ignore the excellent smells coming from Evelyn's kitchen. She was slow-roasting a chicken for her family.

"I bet you all find it hard to believe sometimes. Especially on those mornings when you wake up so sore you can hardly move."

There was a murmur of agreement. Avis Poli, living for the last month on a diet of lettuce, baked fish, and unbuttered vegetables, was starting to look pinched. Her nose kept aiming toward the kitchen.

"Smells good," whispered Avis. "Parsley and onions, just the way I like it."

Birdey Nolan reached into her purse for a small plastic bag filled with celery sticks. She handed Avis a long one.

"Little bites and long chews," Birdey advised.

Gussie cleared her throat. The effort at speech was pinkening her with embarrassment. Evelyn had a good idea what Gussie was trying to say. Good luck, team. Give it all you've got. Go, team, go!

"Remember that movie about Helen Keller?" said Gussie. "Remember when Annie Sullivan is trying to teach her about the word for water? She has the water running over one of Helen Keller's hands while she spells out the word in the other one. Remember how Helen finally gets it?"

"I cried for a week," said Birdey, putting the bag of celery back in her purse.

"I felt the same way the first time I ever saw a softball game," said Gussie.

Birdey's eyes filled.

"Why softball?" Gussie let her eyes linger over every face in the room. "Who knows? All I can say for sure is that it feels good when you play it, and it feels good when you watch it, and it feels good when you think about it. With softball, see, it's all in the *team*. It's all in the *idea* of a team. Most people think it's just a different version of baseball. It's not. Playing baseball is like playing with bullets. In softball, you've got a ball you can really get your hands around. You've got more of a chance at the plate and you've got something that's real beauty when you do it right. I was only about four or five years old when I found out about it. My father took me to Lowell for a tournament the mills were sponsoring. The guys who were playing were factory workers, the kind of guys I'd seen all the time, but out there under the lights they looked different. It was almost like they were dancing in a ballet. We saw four games that night. Papa had to drag me away. After that, I was gone. I guess I never spent much time thinking about anything but softball. Softball was *it.*"

Flushed and self-conscious, Gussie looked down toward the floor. "I guess what I'm trying to say is that, this being our first game against anybody but ourselves, I just hope you have a good time. You know the rules, you know pretty much what you're supposed to be doing. I just wish it wasn't so damn cold."

It was the first time Evelyn had ever heard her say so many sentences at once. For a long moment, no one spoke. The only sound was the steady crunching of Avis's celery.

Gussie looked around again. She opened her mouth in a big broad glow of a grin.

"Let's go!" she said.

Avis was the first one out the door. As the women headed for cars, Gussie stopped Evelyn.

"My mother came to see you," she said flatly. "Look, you don't have to try concealing anything. I already asked Rio about it. I had a feeling she might be trying something. I suppose it makes sense she'd try it on you. What did she say?"

"It's not important."

"Ev! Please!"

"She's not exactly crazy about the team. About softball. About the *idea.*" Evelyn mimicked Gussie perfectly, but she didn't seem to notice. "Gussie, forget about it. She doesn't mean any harm."

"Pah! The only thing my mother *ever* means is harm."

A familiar jolting look came into her face. Evelyn knew it well. It was her I-am-about-to-curse-someone-in-Italian look. Evelyn gave her a nudge toward the car.

"Save it, Gussie," she told her. "Save it for the other team."

They arrived at the jail about an hour before the starting time. At the entrance they were stripped of all personal belongings, including all jewelry and hairpins.

Their gloves, bats and balls were confiscated.

In a small, windowless room with gray walls, somewhere deep inside the building, a female guard body-searched them. She led them through a maze of damp cement passages, each one narrower than the one before it. They finally came into an empty room no bigger than Evelyn's kitchen. They were told that this was the women's gym.

Linda Drago met them there. She wore a loose pair of insulated sweatpants and an oversized shirt that said QUESTION AUTHORITY. She looked like she had just shot a quart of vitamins into her bloodstream. Evelyn wondered how the guards felt about her shirt. Drago threw out her arms to Gussie, cane and all, and looked at the Spurs over Gussie's shoulder.

"Welcome to our country club," she said with a laugh. "I was hoping they'd let us use the men's gym today, but no go. Looks like we'll have to play outdoors."

"No problem," said Gussie a little too eagerly. Most of the Spurs were already shivering.

They followed Drago outside to a small playing field completely surrounded with spiked steel fencing. Over their heads, the sky was sickly, emptily white. At their feet the ground was bare and hard. They looked from each other to the fences and back again, smiling uncertainly.

"Sorry about the bases," said Drago. "We haven't got any."

"No problem," mimicked Evelyn, and made them all laugh.

A door behind them swung open, and the prison women came out with a female guard who was a head taller and thirty pounds heavier than Gussie. As they came toward the field, Evelyn tried to guess who was in for prostitution and who was in for drugs. She gave it up quickly. The women wore thick jeans and sweatshirts, and did not look any different from any woman on the Spurs.

The two teams shook hands as their coaches drew bases in the dirt with the tip of Gussie's cane. Gussie leaned on the female guard and Drago drew the baselines. The women's spirits were high. They went into the game with a great deal of noise and laughter but didn't keep it up for very long. It got colder and colder. Hannah Wally hit three home runs. Sandy Dorn played shortstop like an octopus and came up with four solid singles. Laura Bradley got two singles. Peggy Glazer got one. So did Karla Brown. Nancy Beth Campbell, the pitcher, hit a single that was called foul by the female guard, who was umping. The Spurs poured onto the field to protest the call but the guard held firm. Gussie let her have it. Birdey Nolan amazed everyone with a gorgeous line drive to left field but her shoe fell off as she was rounding first base and she did not feel inclined to run without it.

At the end of the game, when the score was twenty-nine to three, Drago invited the Spurs to come back and do it again.

"Not a bad team you've got here," she told Gussie, thumping her on the back. "For a bunch of housewives." Drago flashed the Spurs one of her healthiest smiles, winked, and found herself flat on her back on the ground.

"You tripped her!" cried the guard, rushing forward. "With your cane!"

Gussie spread her arms apart, looking at her cane as if it were an abused pet. Spurs crowded around their coach.

"Must have been a rock," said Gussie. "Poor Drago must've tripped on a rock."

The guard looked all over, and could find no rock. Gussie did not find it surprising.

"Anyone who'd call that single a foul ball needs to have her eyes examined," said Gussie placidly.

The guard said, "Hey! Who you talking to like that?"

Gussie said, "What's the matter? You deaf too?"

Drago picked herself up off the ground and brushed herself clean, looking around for bruises.

"I'd like to hear you use that tone of voice if you were playing against the Belles," said the guard.

Pammy Flynn said, "Belles?"

"Best goddamn team on the Eastern seaboard," said the guard.

Gussie threw back her head and laughed at the top of her lungs. She laughed so hard she nearly fell over, and leaned on Pammy for support.

The guard stepped up close to Gussie. "You know what the Belles'd do to a half-assed team like yours?"

"Wh-what?" said Pammy nervously, with her eyes on the guard's hip. The gun in her holster was real.

"The Belles'd whup you so good you'd get fed to a toothless baby, that's what."

The Spurs leaned back as if they were trying to get out of the way. Evelyn stayed close to Gussie. She felt frozen to her bones. Her nose was runny and she was sniffing. She tried to think about her chicken dinner. The guard wore a pair of thick black leather gloves lined with brown fur. Her hands were enormous.

"Let's go home," said Evelyn.

Ignoring her, Gussie whispered in Drago's ear, and it was Drago's turn to laugh out loud. Gussie whispered something else. Drago put out her hand.

"You're on, Cabrini," said Drago. The two coaches shook on it.

Huddled closely together, the Spurs left the field and claimed their things from the guards at the prison entrance. In the doorway Gussie told them what she had done.

"We're going to play the telephone company. In May. I guess we've got some work to do."

Except for Evelyn's sneezing, they were quiet on the way home.

February 27, 1975

Report of the Fourth Meeting of the SAC
Present: A. Cabrini, W. Brody, R. Cabrini, H. Wally, P. Glazer, D. McGrath, E. Brody
Visiting: June Campbell

    1) R. Cabrini reported to the committee the generous offer by his father, Victor Cabrini of Cabrini Associates, to sponsor the team. As the man's good nature and generous

spirit are known to everyone concerned, it is our stated trust that his support will not end with financial matters, but will extend to all aspects of the team's various activities.

2) D. McGrath presented a list of items drawn up by him and W. Brody pertaining to necessary equipment for the team. A. Cabrini promised to look it over.

3) J. Campbell, in a characteristic act of kindness, spoke to the committee on her reason for attending the meeting: to extend to the team the offer of the use of her basement for workouts. J.C. explained that her husband owns some exercise equipment which is rarely in use during the day when he's at work and the weekends when he's golfing. As D. McGrath pointed out, the Campbells' basement is equipped as well as any gymnasium, and with the town gym being off-limits to women, the Spurs had much to gain by accepting J.C.'s offer. The motion passed unanimously. J.C. stipulated that the only condition was that no one could let her husband Nate find out about it, as he is somewhat touchy on the subject of women performing such acts he would rather see done only by men. A. Cabrini assured J.C. that most of the women of the world are quite skilled at keeping secrets from men, and the Spurs were no different. D. McGrath swore on the eyes of his children that even though he works side by side with Nate Campbell, he would die before he let Nate know that the Spurs were using his basement.

4) H. Wally presented the schedule she created for visits by the Spurs to Sandy Dorn's house. (J.C. told the committee that Jeremy Dorn is at home and doing well.) According to this plan, there will be a Spur sleeping on Sandy's couch every night except weekends, when Jeremy stays with the Campbells. Excepted from the list of women spending the night at Sandy's were: E. Brody, Mimi Reed, Albertina Nolan and Patsy Griffin, all of whom have children of their own under the agreed-upon age of sixteen.

H.W. said that in addition to the sleep-overs, Sandy's house will be covered in the daytime by Patsy Griffin, driver of the school bus, who has already begun checking the place twice daily; Grace Pandy, who has offered to bring her quilting things and work there, and Laura Bradley, who would like to use Sandy's house now and then to practice her dance routines. E. Brody regularly goes over there with her children, and Karla Brown will visit as often as she can.

It was the opinion of the committee that the situation was pretty much under control.

5) A.C. reported the Spurs' grim defeat at the prison, and quickly expressed her conviction that the team would do better next time. She has arranged for another game to be played next Sunday.

6) A.C. then proposed the following: that the Spurs play a game against the Belles of the New England Telephone Company from Hartford, Connecticut.

A discussion ensued.

In favor of the enterprise were W. Brody and all the female members of the committee. Although she had no vote, June Campbell suggested that the Spurs would never be able to find out what they could do until they tried, and this sounded as good a way as any.

Against it were: D. McGrath and R. Cabrini, who compared the idea to such things as a very small country going to war against a very large one; a bunny rabbit coming up against a shotgun; and the biblical narrative of David and Goliath.

J.C. reminded the dissenters that it was David who won.

A.C. made a motion to contact Linda Drago, coach of the Belles, with an acceptance.

Motion passed, 5–2.

CHAPTER THIRTEEN

The people of Anthony Street had spread their blankets and lawn chairs at the bottom of the slope directly opposite third base. June Campbell helped Jeremy Dorn draw a picture of his mother holding a baseball bat. Teresa Monopoli knitted and Allison McGrath slept, a rounded bundle of baby fat at her feet. The men stood around the ice chest. Now and then Tim Arbis and Danny McGrath wandered off in search of their children, but gave them up as lost in the crowd.

The echoes of the police sirens still rang in their ears.

"Thank God they've got him," whispered June for the third time since she'd seen for herself that the man in the back of the cruiser was Kenny Dorn. Relief made her light-headed and happy. She had no idea what the police would do to him when they got him to the station but she hoped that whatever it was, it would turn out to be permanent. She hadn't had a decent night's sleep since the day Sandy Dorn called her from the hospital.

"Thank God," she said again, giving the boy a hug.

Nate Campbell popped open another can of beer. He was trying to win an argument. "Luck, that's all it was," he growled. "You ask me, it was a damn fool thing to do in the first place. She could've hurt herself. Or Pelletier."

Tim Arbis laughed. "Pelletier's got a hide thick as my front door. He'd never even notice."

"She lets up the brake and vroom!" Joe Monopoli slapped his thighs with glee.

"Drop it, will you," said Danny. "The kid'll hear. He doesn't have to know about his old man."

Nate stared off across the field. "Look at this, will you? Isn't this just like women? They keep you waiting every time. If this was a normal ballgame we'd be at the bottom of the fifth by now. What're they doing down there? Powdering their noses?"

"Probably they're trying to work up some guts," said Tim. "Scary-looking bunch, those Belles. Their coach looks like she ate a bowl of bullets for lunch."

"Her name's Drago," said Danny. "She used to be a gym teacher at the high school."

"That was before Tennessee Tim's time," drawled Nate, deliberately exaggerating his t's.

Tim ignored him. "You mean her and Gussie're friends?"

"I wouldn't call them friends, exactly," said Danny. "Not since the girls' basketball team lost a shot at the championship. Drago was the coach and Gussie was the best thing that ever happened to that team. You remember, Nate?"

"Hell, McGrath, you think I got nothing better to do with my time than watch a bunch of girls play ball?"

"What happened?" Tim leaned forward, ignoring Nate.

"It was the play-offs." Danny's eyes clouded for a moment. He looked as if he were losing himself in a memory.

Nate pounded him on the back. "If it was girls' basketball, Lover-Boy McGrath was probably up there in the bleachers, cheering them on. Very big on that sort of thing, weren't you, McGrath?"

Danny flushed. "It was after the play-offs. We were one game away from the state title. We were up against Springfield. We were leading by four in the fourth period. Gussie was wild that night, she was all over the ball like it had her name on it. I'd never seen her play so great. She wanted that title. She wanted it real bad. She—"

"They were ahead by *two*, not four," interrupted Nate. Everyone looked at him and he shrugged indifferently. "Might as well get the facts straight."

"It was tense," continued Danny. "And next thing we knew, Drago called a time-out. Took Gussie out of the game. The crowd went crazy. You could've heard 'em boo Drago all the way to Boston."

"I lost twenty bucks on that game," said Nate.

Joe the Rosarian smacked his lips sadly. "Me, it was forty."

Tim scratched his head. "What do you mean, took her out? Sounds like maybe she threw the game."

"Sure did look that way," said Danny. "Without Gussie, we got screwed. Lost by twelve points."

"Fourteen," sighed Nate.

"Drago tried to feed Gussie a line about how Gussie needed a lesson in humility or something," said Danny. "I don't remember much else that happened after the game. It's all kind of blurry. The night of that game, see, it was the night that Ev's mother—"

"Hey!" boomed Nate suddenly. "Give that man a drink!"

Victor Cabrini came up to the Anthony Street group, kissed the women, grasped Monopoli by the shoulders in a hearty hug, and accepted a can of beer. Under his purple baseball cap his face was beaming.

"Wife okay?" asked Tim.

Victor nodded. "Fine. All fine. You see that car hit that railing? You see how my wife came through like a hero? Hey, Rosarian! What do you think of my wife?"

Joe Monopoli touched his beer to Victor's in salute. "*Vroom!* I never seen anything like it!"

"Cabrini," said Nate, scowling. "How about you go down there and get this show on the road? Tell your girl to get her team going. At this rate they won't even start till Christmas."

"Keep your pants on," said Victor. "When they're ready, they're ready. My girl's got everything under control. If I said it once, I said it a million times. 'Augusta,' I tell her, 'no playing till you're good and ready. You run off half-cocked, you get the stuffing beat out 'a you.' She's a good girl, she listens. Anyhow, it's all held up on account 'a that bastard, that Dorn."

"Keep your voice down," whispered Nate. "His kid's right over there with Juney. Let's keep the kid out of this, okay?"

Victor shrugged. "Okay, okay. Any minute now, they'll start. Look at my girl, talking to her team. She's got 'em roaring to go."

Nate looked. "Now what? Where's she going?"

"She's presenting her roster," said Danny.

Nate bent his empty can in half and reached for another beer. "What the hell for?"

"It's a formality," said Danny impatiently. "There she goes, straight to Drago."

"This is one conversation I would truly love to overhear," said Tim, clucking softly as the two women came together behind first base and reached out to shake each other's hands.

Opening his notebook, Rollie Pelletier wrote the date across the top of a blank page and the words *Spurs vs. Belles.* His hands were trembling. He ached all over. He wanted a stiff drink and his armchair in front of his television set. He wanted to return to what was ordinary. No women's teams, no lunatics hiding out in the back of his car. Dorn, God, Dorn. The pain had been tremendous. He wondered what kind of a job he'd done at concealing it.

He cringed at the uneven slant of his handwriting. *May 10, 1975. Spurs vs. Belles.* For an instant, he could not identify the curious surge of feeling inside him, unless, after all, his heart was worse off than he realized. He rubbed at his chest. No pain; only flutters. Then he remembered. It was his birthday. He drew heavy lines to underscore the date.

The crowd rustled with tension. Out on the field, Gussie Cabrini shook hands with the opposition. The two umpires, Jake Trombley and Curtis Fletch, Rollie's very old friends, were bending their heads together near the plate. Trombley was the best ump Currys Crossing ever had. Not that he got much chance to show his stuff. The Little League these days cared more about their stereo systems than their batting averages. The men's leagues had ended years ago. Fletch, who'd been working games all over the state since Rollie started as a copy boy with the *Clarion,* swooped down to brush the plate clean. Their regulation black and white striped uniforms sent shivers of anticipation down Rollie's spine, and he found himself gripping his pencil with vigor. *Spurs vs. Belles,* he wrote again, this time in a straight line. The gears of his mind clicked away with a nearly-forgotten delight as he added a small note on the weather:

It was a perfect day for a ballgame.

"Me?" called Avis. "You want me?"

Summoned, she trotted across the infield and came up to the two coaches. "What's up?"

Gussie looked at her calmly. "Linda seems to be having a problem with our roster. She's asked for some verification. I told her I'd get the most honest woman on the team."

"You've only got one pitcher," cut in Drago sharply. "I thought by now you'd have turned yourselves into a real team. How am I supposed to believe you only have one pitcher?"

"I already told Linda how smart she is, knowing how to count and everything," said Gussie.

"You are beginning to get on my nerves, Cabrini. I've got the best team in the East. I bring them all the way up here and I expect to play some serious ball. We can't even start because you've got this cops and robbers routine going on in the bushes. Now you tell me you're planning to play with one girl."

"Nancy Beth's pretty good," said Avis, folding her arms across her chest and glaring at Drago.

Drago glared back.

"I'm ready whenever you are, Linda," said Gussie.

Drago turned on a heel and headed back to her bench. Gussie waited until she was nearly there.

"Hey, Drago? One more thing."

"What?"

Gussie flashed a brilliant, lop-sided smile. "Nice blimp. It was very touching to us all, that blimp."

"I thought you might like it," called Drago.

"I sure did. It was you all over." She lifted her cane and put it down again with a soft thump, and took Avis by the arm.

"I think Linda's a little nervous," whispered Gussie.

Avis cleared her throat. They had about a hundred yards left before they reached the home-team bench. Her threefold speech was ready and waiting at the tip of her tongue.

"Gussie?" They stopped walking. "Gussie, there's something I want to tell you."

Gussie gave her a sideways look.

"Let's play some ball!" shouted Drago.

"What I want to say is that—"

"Spurs! Spurs!" came the voices of the spectators. "Spurs! Spurs!" Hands clapped. Someone tooted a horn.

Avis flushed with impatience. "There're three things I want to say." She took a deep breath, as if she were standing in front of a microphone trying to deliver an after-dinner talk. The hand on her arm squeezed gently. Lifting her eyes, Avis met Gussie's eyes and held them for a long moment. She felt tears starting, and looked away. With the tenderness of an Angela, Gussie touched Avis's eyes. Then she moved a finger to Avis's lips, hushing her, softly, sweetly.

"Let's *go,* ladies," cried Drago.

"Let's go," barked Jake the umpire.

"Go! Go! Go!" chanted the crowd.

Avis stepped away, sniffing.

"Let's go," said Gussie with a grin.

Avis snapped her mask in place, heading for the plate as the Spurs' fielders spread out to take their positions. Gussie walked Nancy Beth to the pitcher's mound and called out last-minute cheers to them all. Avis slipped her hand into her mitt, crouching to prepare for Nancy Beth's warm-up pitches.

The Belles' first batter approached the plate.

Jake Trombley, getting down behind Avis, asked if she were ready. Avis nodded. She flexed her catching arm and lifted it.

"Play ball!" cried the ump.

Avis gulped. A rumble came into her belly. It was on.

CHAPTER FOURTEEN

By the end of March the Spurs were meeting every day for practice. They were getting to be old hands at it, they had a routine. Weekdays, except Wednesdays, there was batting and fielding at Tolland Field. Gussie painted orange Day-Glo spots on the balls so they could see what they were doing after sunset. At the end of these sessions they dragged themselves to the riverbank for a run. They were like witches, running loose in the night while their children slept and their neighbors clucked with disbelief behind partly shuttered windows. Their bodies grew younger.

On Wednesdays after supper they slipped into Jake Trombley's restaurant by the Catholic church. Jake was Karla Brown's first cousin. If asked, Jake said he had hired the whole team as cleaning ladies. They stayed until midnight, playing pinball at the four machines at the end of the lunch counter. Waiting for their turns to play they kept the jukebox going, moving their bodies to the rhythms of old rock and roll. Victor Cabrini came by every week with rolls of quarters, passing them out like a Santa Claus at a company banquet. He often stayed to watch, grinning from a stool at the counter as the pinball lights flashed and the bells jingled and the rock and roll played on, sending their hips swaying and their arms cutting wild circles in the air. Their timing and coordination got better.

On Saturday afternoons June Campbell let them into her

basement to work out on her husband's weights. Nate Campbell played golf on Saturdays, and June kept watch upstairs in case he came home early. He never did. They learned that pumping dumbbells was not much different from lifting heavy, bedridden children. They bench-pressed. They lay on their backs beneath steel that pressed against them with the urgency of lovers, and they pumped their hearts out. Afterward they gave each other massages. Evelyn was good at massages. She worked a tight muscle like a lump of bread dough. Birdey Nolan told her that she had hands like an angel, and wouldn't let anyone else, even her sister Avis, lay a finger on her. Gussie kept charts to follow the number of pounds each woman lifted. Uncle William sat on the floor as they worked the weights and called out encouragement, straining his face in sympathy. They got stronger.

On Sundays at two o'clock they piled into cars and drove to the jail for a game. They kept getting beaten, but each time they were beaten by a little less. During their third game Evelyn got her first hit: a crackling line drive that brought her all the way to third base. Her children, embarrassed by their hitless mother, went wild at the supper table. Kate taught the baby to say one of her first real words. Allison loved the sound so much that she talked herself to sleep with it.

"Triple, Mama, triple!" said Allison.

Her family was looking at her with new eyes.

Rio finished his kitchen, a white and silver affair, dirtless and gleaming, with sliding glass doors that opened onto his garden. They had a party to celebrate. The team bought him a forty piece set of Tupperware with a lifetime guarantee.

Gussie spent all her time on the team now. She quit working for her family, moved out of her parents' house, and went to live at Rio's. When she wanted to relax, Rio put a paintbrush in her hands and steered her to another unfinished room. She saw her father on Wednesday nights at the restaurant. She did not see her mother at all. Evelyn wondered if they had been fighting again.

"Don't ask," Gussie said.

Evelyn told no one, not Danny, not Rio, certainly not Gussie, about the card that came from Marina Cabrini on the twenty-

eighth of March, the day of Rio's party. It came in the mail as
Evelyn sat in her kitchen, trying to gift-wrap Rio's Tupperware. She didn't have a box big enough to fit all the pieces so
she wrapped each one individually. It took up her whole morning. Allison helped. Evelyn wrapped, Allison unwrapped. Evelyn tied a bow in place and Allison tried to chew it apart. In the
end Teresa Monopoli came over and took the baby away. Evelyn was alone. The mail slid through the slot in the front door.
There was only one piece, a greeting card, a one-dollar Hall-
mark with gold edges and thick, raised lettering. On the front
there was a picture of geraniums in a basket. The geraniums
were red as blood. Over them rose a pair of hands joined fingertip to fingertip in prayer. They were perfect hands, pale,
beautiful, holy. They pulsed with health and life. They ra-
diated a kind of glow that made Evelyn flush and weaken. The
card said, *Thinking of you on the Anniversary of Your Bereavement.*
Inside, there was a handwritten message.

> My dearest Evelyn,
> With fondness and sadness I pause to honor the memory of
> your dear parents. I have arranged a memorial service
> which the priests will perform quietly later today. A small
> token, I know, but one your treasured parents might have
> appreciated. If I can be of any help to you, especially at
> this sad time of year, please do not hesitate to call on me.
> My days are not so busy that I could not find a moment
> for you, or as many moments as you like.
>
>   Affectionately yours,
>   Marina Cabrini

So she sends you a greeting card, big deal, Danny would
have said. It's just a gesture.
She sat looking at the card for a long, long time, tracing and
retracing her finger over the outline of the praying hands. Then
she threw it away. She threw it away in tiny pieces, in shreds of
gold, shreds of message, shreds of white hands and red geraniums, all gone into the trash with the scraps of the children's
breakfast, and she found herself rewrapping the pieces of Tupperware she had already wrapped. She found herself sur-

rounded by Tupperware in layers and layers of colored paper,
mixing bowls and pitchers and tumblers and cheese holders
and the lettuce crisper and eighteen plastic containers in eighteen different sizes, each with a leak-proof lid of its own. She
rewrapped them all. She kept on wrapping. When she ran out
of tape she used glue. When she ran out of wrapping paper she
used aluminum foil.

"Mama cried all day," said Kate when Danny came home
from work.

"Cried and cried," said Mundy.

Danny looked at the calendar and sighed.

How clever of Ev! said her friends that night at Rio's party.

Rio couldn't stop laughing. His kitchen filled with heaps of
wrappings. It was just like Christmas, they all said. The tallest
women on the team helped Rio put his Tupperware high up
into his cabinets. All the cabinets were white with silver han-
dles. All the women wore dresses. It was Saturday night.

The husbands and boyfriends wandered through Rio's
house, talking about ceiling beams and plaster while the
women gathered in the kitchen to talk about batting stances
and the theory of the double play. They weren't used to seeing
each other like that, dressed up, smelling of perfume instead of
sweat, and they were shy with each other. Self-consciously they
sipped fruity wine until someone rolled up a discarded piece of
Evelyn's wrapping paper, and someone else found a broom.
Under the bright lights of Rio's kitchen they struck up a mock
game of ball. The men came in and stole the equipment, daring the women to chase them outside.

Running in their high heels, their skirts whipping around
their knees, they yelped like girls. The wind stung Evelyn's eyes
with needles of pain and her ankles wobbled in her uncomfort-
able shoes. She fell behind the others. She kicked her shoes off.
The wind bent the trees, throttling the branches, and it did not
seem as if a single trunk would be able to stay in place. In the
distance rang the shouts and laughter of the women chasing
the men with the ball and broom. Evelyn looked about in confusion. The trees that lined Rio's street bowed and swayed. All
the branches whistled. The voice of Shirley Brody rode the
back of the wind, shrill and magnificent, but Evelyn could not

understand what she was saying. She began to walk past the
broad shivering trunks of the elm trees. An elm tree was the last
thing Shirley Brody ever saw. Its bare branches looming in the
headlights must have come at her like weapons, pointing, awe-
some, blinding her eyes with fright. Or perhaps they came to
her like long soft bare arms, like the arms of a lover, singing a
song that sounds in the wind in March, and Evelyn began to
run. She wondered if Shirley had screamed. She wondered if
Shirley had smiled. She rounded a corner, and another. Streetlights flashed past. Here and there in the lighted windows of
houses a face bobbed against a pane of glass, not friendly, not
unfriendly, just a face, as if seen from a rushing train. She hur-
dled cracks in the sidewalks with a recklessness that left her
breathless. She twirled through space, imagining herself speed-
ing down the baseline for first, tearing for second, lunging for
third, and in her ears roared the sound of a crowd, *Home run!*

She imagined her fingers coming to rest against the smooth
safety of home plate. Out of breath, her mouth foaming and
her legs stiff, she lay where she had landed. She told herself that
she would get up in a minute. She would find her shoes and she
would straighten out her hair and her dress. She might even
put on some lipstick. She would go back to Rio's, to Rio's
party, where there was warmth, where there was light, in a
minute.

Not sleeping, not waking. There is nothing but voices, two
voices.

They're at it again, this man and this woman. They've been
at it so long that they know it by heart, two old soldiers meeting over and over like wind-up toys, battering their little toy
heads with their little toy guns. Their passion glows in their
eyes and rock-hardens the words they hurl at each other over
the head of the girl who desperately tries to make them stop.
Franklin shouts. Shirley shouts. Uncle William rushes past,
reeking of urine, an unhappy old man who wets his pants every
time they fight.

Doors slam. Evelyn covers her ears with her hands, her
young, strong, beautiful hands. She is standing at the top of the
stairs, like the girl in the fairy tale locked up in a tower. Shirley
wants to tell her something, Shirley whose hands beneath her
gloves are darkening, twisting. Evelyn keeps her hands on her

ears. A moment ago, Danny's brown jacket slumped over the railing at the bottom of the stairs. He had come to take her to a basketball game. She is seventeen. He has left without her.

Shirley wants to go out in the car.

Franklin says, *No*. His *no* floats smokily through the house and vanishes.

Evelyn looks at him in his armchair. He tells her, *I knew it. I knew she'd pull something like this.*

This time Evelyn has an answer. She answers, What do you know, you can't even remember your own name. You don't even know what country you come from.

Ah, that hurts, says Franklin. That hurts.

You're dead, Evelyn reminds him. You're past that.

He denies this. She hears him denying it all the time. She tries to keep her ears covered because she wants to keep his voice away. Her voice. Their voices.

This is a dream:

Two women, next-door neighbors, put down their baskets of laundry and meet by the low fence that separates their houses. One of the women is Shirley Brody and the other is Marina Cabrini. Evelyn is the one who eavesdrops. Not for nothing is she the daughter of a quality-control inspector. Nothing gets by her. Her eyes and ears are cat-sharp, moon-clear. She makes herself small and she eavesdrops.

What the women are saying is dangerous and shocking and thrilling. Evelyn tingles all over with wonder.

They want to swap daughters.

Impersonally, Shirley tucks her hands under her armpits. It's an involuntary gesture, she wants to keep them hidden. She says: The problem with Augusta is that she eats too much. With Franklin just being promoted, we don't want for much, understand, but we just bought a new car. Augusta's big. Eats lots of meat, I'll bet. Could be a drain.

Marina considers. Her beautiful face sinks into repose the way sunlight goes into a river. She speaks: Augusta will come to you with her own food allowance.

Shirley's eyebrows shoot up like they do at the market when she's sizing up tomatoes. She's impressed.

Marina says: The problem with Evelyn is that she's an only child. I've got three others. She might not fit in.

Shirley, bargaining hard, grows shrewd. Look here, Ev's got

her great-uncle Willie. He's like a brother to her. Anyhow, Ev's a born fitter-in.

Evelyn turns meek with love. She crosses her fingers. She makes a vow to herself that she will teach Gussie to love her mother's hands. She promises to visit her father and Uncle William every day. It's a perfect scheme. She can't see why they hadn't thought of it before.

Shirley says: Augusta will have her sports. As her mother, I will give her the best equipment, and even if I have to go half-way around the world for it I will make sure she gets the proper training.

As my daughter, Evelyn will have a life of beauty, says Marina. She will have money and property. One day she will become a partner in the business I have with my husband.

Marina holds out her hand over the fence to clinch the deal.

Shirley balks. She hadn't counted on a handshake. Stiffly her hands press against the sides of her body. She takes a step backward. Marina Cabrini looks on with confusion. She has no way of knowing this, but Shirley Brody has not touched anyone for years. Will she now?

Evelyn pokes her head out of her hiding place. Silently she cheers her mother on.

Marina Cabrini smiles, waiting. Her hand lingers in the air like the white curved neck of a swan. Shirley begins to turn away.

Shake, Mother, shake! pleads Evelyn. She's cheering. She's begging.

Shirley goes back to her laundry basket, calling her daughter to come and help.

Marina stares sadly into the yard. Evelyn creeps out from hiding. Marina tells her with her eyes that she has tried her best. Shirley calls. Shirley calls and calls and calls.

A woman's voice, low and familiar, called her name with urgency. Sliding into consciousness she allowed her eyes to open. Marina Cabrini floated by, swooped down, and fussed with her blankets.

"Evelyn? Do you know where you are?"

Her dream clicked into place like an instant camera, spitting out a picture that slowly undissolved. Sharp lines appeared, color, clarity. A little miracle. So dreams really did come true. She wondered if people already knew this. She wondered if she had been singled out for this extraordinary revelation because of something clever she had done, even if it was something as simple as opening her eyes.

"In Gussie's room. I'm in Gussie's room."

Guiltily, shamefully, she remembered her mother bending over her laundry basket. Do the dead in their mystical awareness monitor the dreams of the living? If so, do they forgive?

Clucking with displeasure, Gussie's mother sat down at the edge of the bed. "It's lucky for you that I found you when I did. Do you remember what happened to you? I thought not. It seems you had too much to drink at my son's party. It's all the fault of this softball business. It's madness."

Her head felt amazingly light. All this focus was making her dizzy.

"You collapsed outside my house, Evelyn," said Marina wearily. "Your husband and the others are downstairs. They've been frantic. I can't think what you were doing out there without a coat. Without shoes!"

"My mother named me for a little fishing boat that was called the *Evenly*," she told them. She was up on pillows on Gussie's old bed. The room was small but the women had all squeezed in. Their party dresses were limp and wrinkled. Nancy Beth Campbell couldn't stop yawning. Marina, hastening away, had left a chill in the air but it felt like a party all the same. It felt like she had just been dragged in from a night in a horrible storm, and she told them so, and the laughter that rose from their faces rose like bubbles of love: they had been out in the cold for hours trying to find her.

"What this girl needs is a compass," said Avis Poli.

"Compass, hell. She needs a two-ton anchor," cracked Patsy Griffin.

"Enough with the jokes," said Gussie commandingly. "Let Evvie talk."

Evelyn talked. The night wore on and the wind howled against the walls with its noisy remnants of memory and the women huddled close together. She kept on talking, bargaining with the dead to stay dead as she emptied her pockets of secrets.

The women watched and listened. Birdey Nolan held her hands, and called them beautiful. Gussie's eyes filled with feeling, and she hid them. Now and then a face lit up with recognition. Now and then someone bowed her head or hoarsely cleared her throat, and Evelyn kept talking, spinning a web of talk for her friends, and sometime in the night she found that it was not just her own voice anymore. It was all their voices. They were talking all together the way they did at their practices, playing, this time, with bad dreams and fear and ghosts and pain, and it wasn't only suffering any longer, and it wasn't only Evelyn's. The Spurs gathered together all her secrets, pulling them into bundles like pieces of laundry. There was nothing more to hide. They remembered that there had lived among them a woman called Shirley Brody who hid her hands, dying slowly while her daughter looked on. They remembered that a man had sat upright in a chair, his jaw drooping: a sad, lonely, frightened man whose daughter had done what she could to try to save him. Dimly, the shadows pulled away, and the women blinked at each other in the dawn. Tenderness and grief and magic came together in their voices, covering them like the sunlight. Giddily sleepless they broke apart as their thoughts hurried home ahead of them. There were children to dress and breakfasts to fix.

Before leaving, Evelyn wandered through the Cabrini house, hoping to find Marina. She wanted to say that she was sorry for disturbing her the night before. She wanted to thank her for sending the greeting card, but Marina was nowhere to be found.

Gussie stood on the front porch to see the women off. Her shoulders slumped wearily forward. Her knuckles were white where she held her cane. She shivered a little, and her big, solid body swayed slightly from side to side. She looked fragile and worn. Her eyes were cloudy with sleeplessness. The scarred half of her face, caught in the thin, frosty morning light, had the look of an old piece of wood filled with nicks and chips and slivers. Evelyn wanted to touch her, smooth her. She came up beside her and said her name. Gussie turned. The good side of her face softened as she opened her mouth in a smile. Their eyes met, and held, and Evelyn's body began to stir in a slow, certain knowledge that she was about to understand something she had not understood before. It was coming to her gradually, the way heat begins to come up from a radiator, and just as she felt it inching into conscious thought, into an almost-clear word or two, Gussie abruptly looked away.

"Better get some sleep, Evvie. We've got a game at the jail this afternoon, remember?" She reached for the door and went inside, dragging her bad leg behind her.

CHAPTER FIFTEEN

Grinding herself a toehold on the mound against the black rectangular pitching rubber, Nancy Beth Campbell shook both of her arms loosely and glanced over her shoulder. The Spurs' outfielders had fanned deeply back, settling into half-crouches like four purple pegs across a game board. Evelyn played close to the bag at second. Laura Bradley, at first, was still stretching her long legs. At shortstop, Sandy Dorn seethed with energy. At third, Pammy Flynn, working her jaws over a thick wad of chewing gum, flicked her thumb up with cheer. Nancy Beth turned toward the bench for a sign.

Gussie moistened the left corner of her mouth with a deft, cat-like darting of her tongue. High arc.

The Belles' big batter loomed like a rock. Nancy Beth held the ball in front of her body, crooked her elbows, and counted to three. Then she brought back her right leg, swung into her windup, and released her first pitch with a neat twist that sent the ball soaring in a slow, untroubled, four-foot arc that fell in a casual drop dead-eye across the center of the plate. The eyes of the batter filled with surprise.

Strike one.

Nancy Beth took off her glove and wiped her hands on the sides of her breeches. She was sweating profusely.

In the parking lot next to the field, her back turned to the opening moves of the game, Marina Cabrini took hold of Rollie's arm. Three photographers buzzed around her with clumsy passion, and a chubby, bad-smelling reporter waved his pencil an inch away from her nose, demanding to know what it felt like to be held hostage by a kidnapper with a gun. She flinched as if she'd been slapped by the flashbulbs.

"There was no gun," she sighed.

Rollie lifted his gaze to the sky and let it fall down hard on his friends from the *Clarion*. Winking, he elbowed his way through the little crowd, pulling Marina along with him. They broke free to a clearing.

"You're spoiling their fun, Marina. A story like this happens maybe once in a lifetime. Gets them all excited."

"I want them to leave me alone."

"I'll tell them." Rollie traced a little cross over his heart. "But if I call off the press, I want you to do something for me."

Marina eyed him warily.

"Tell me the truth. Do you honestly believe that your daughter's got a chance against Drago? And don't talk to me like somebody's mother. Talk to me like we're doing business."

Marina looked out to the ball field for a long moment before turning to Rollie. She met his eyes squarely. "Are you asking me if I think they're playing to win or playing to play?"

Rollie grinned. "That's about the size of it."

She took her hand off his arm and said firmly, "I believe that they are playing this game to win."

Rollie clicked his tongue against his teeth and pulled his notebook from his back pocket and strode back toward the group from the *Clarion*. Casting a suspicious look at the photographers, Marina tucked a few loose strands of her hair in place, and hurried off in the opposite direction.

The Belles' first batter popped out to center field and threw down her bat in disgust. Avis peered out from her mask at the new one.

"You girls're off to a marvelous start," she said pleasantly. "Bet if you try hard enough, you can get out, too."

"Oh, eat it," said the batter, digging in her heels. She was a thin, agile woman with the rosy skin of a young girl. Gripping the bat with ease, she let two outside pitches slip by, both balls, and jumped for the next one. It fouled outside third.

Gussie moistened the right corner of her mouth. Low arc. Birdey Nolan in left field stepped back two paces. Nancy Beth delivered. Birdey ran backwards as the ball came soaring into her line of vision. She cupped her glove to catch it, and stopped abruptly with her free hand over her eyes. The ball bounced at her feet. The batter made it to second.

"The sun! The sun got in my eyes!" cried Birdey.

Gussie pulled her cap down low until its visor covered her eyes: If you do that again, I will remove you from the game.

Birdey swallowed hard.

"Plays at first and third!" cried William Brody from the bench.

Avis barely had time to buckle down again when the next batter cracked a line drive to center field. Acting fast, Patsy Griffin scooted in for it and held the runner at second. Nancy Beth wiped her hands again. Avis unconsciously moved back a bit in self-protection, adjusting her mask at the sight of an extremely wide woman who swung the bat as if it were no heavier than a spoon. The entire outfield moved back. The sudden noise of wood hitting cowhide for a sure home run made Avis's head ring. She wondered if her eardrums had been pierced, and rose weakly to her feet, watching helplessly as Belles rounded bases and slipped home free. Three to nothing. Linda Drago waved a fist in the air. Belles thumped each other on the back.

Four to nothing. Five. Six.

Nancy Beth took off her cap and rubbed the sides of her head as if she were in pain. The infielders started up a lively chatter to rouse her spirits but she silenced them quickly. Squaring her shoulders she delivered a choppy low ball, barely inside, that came back to her in a pop fly. Two out. The infield applauded. Gussie scratched the injured side of her face in warning: That was nice but don't let it go to your head. Nancy Beth walked the next two batters.

"Plays at first, second, and third," called William Brody, hopping up and down.

Avis took off her mask, signaled for a time-out, and walked briskly to the mound.

"What the hell are you doing?"

The infield closed in like a hand. Red-faced and pouting, Nancy Beth kicked at the dust. "I'm okay."

"I'm down there losing my hearing. I'm standing there like an idiot while they score like crazy and you say you're *okay?*"

Laura Bradley from first base stepped between them. "Avis, this isn't like you. She says she's okay, she's okay." Laura slipped an arm around Nancy Beth's shoulders. "You're doing fine, honey. We got them twice, we'll get them again."

Avis sputtered hotly: "Try a little control, Nancy Beth, will you?"

Birdey trotted in from left field. "Go back to the plate, Avis, and leave this poor girl alone." She sent her sister a withering glance. Avis went taut with anger.

"This isn't any time for a blow-out," said Pammy Flynn uncertainly.

Avis snarled. From the Belles' bench came sounds of hooting.

"Ladies, ladies," soothed Laura. "The last thing we can afford to lose is our tempers."

"My temper's *fine*. It's her pitching we've got to worry about," huffed Avis.

"Avis!" Birdey looked at her like a horrified mother. "Avis, you've got to tell Nancy Beth you don't mean that!"

Sandy Dorn clasped Avis's hand. "Really, now, let's not have a scene."

"Let's just get back to work," suggested Evelyn.

Avis showed signs of softening. Eyes to the ground, she mumbled from behind pressed lips.

Birdey brightened. "And you, Nancy Beth, you tell Avis that you won't let her feel like an idiot anymore with all these runs pouring in."

Shrugging, Nancy Beth said, "Okay. I guess she's maybe sort of right. Sometimes I get a little hasty."

Birdey nodded her approval. "Good. Now let's get back and clobber Ma Bell, okay?"

Avis put her mask back on. The women returned to their places. Nancy Beth carefully put the front of her left foot to the rubber and looked to her coach for instructions. Gussie pulled down her cap until it completely covered her face. Shuddering, Nancy Beth went into her windup on a spurt of guilt and delivered a steeply peaking pitch that skittered across the plate and nearly removed the batter's nose.

"Stee-rike!" howled Jake Trombly at the plate.

The flustered batter went next for a low, outside rumbler coming on like a bowling ball.

"Stee-rike two!"

Nancy Beth licked her lips and bore down. The outfield moved in. Avis was afraid to breathe. She didn't want to throw off her concentration. Tiny balls of sweat formed across the top of her mask and dripped slowly into her eyes. Nancy Beth threw once more. Pammy took a dive to stop the fast ground ball and whipped to first in time.

"*Out!*"

Avis exhaled.

Restlessly, Tim Arbis began to pick at the threads of his earlier conversation with Danny McGrath. "Gussie Cabrini, she played a lot of ball in high school?"

Danny, trying to unwrap a box of chocolate cookies for his youngest daughter, wagged his head. In her earnestness, Allison was ripping open the other end of the box with her teeth, holding on to her father's ankles for leverage.

"Gussie's a big girl," mused Tim. "Strong, too."

Allison spat out a mouthful of cardboard that dribbled down the sides of her chin like pieces of wet cigar. Nate Campbell watched her with horror.

"Clean up your baby, will you, McGrath? You're raising her like a little pig."

Allison's end of the box popped open. Grubbing with her fat hands she quickly filled her mouth, and acting on the perverse instincts of the very young, she wobbled on her new, unsteady legs to Nate and dropped herself, trailing crumbs, into his lap. Nate groaned but he let her stay there.

"She must've been pretty pissed off, getting taken out of a game like you said," Tim pressed. " 'Specially when they lost it."

"What's it to you, Tennessee?" said Nate.

Tim shrugged. "I got four girls. One or two of them might end up the athletic type. Just want to know what I'm getting into."

Nate snorted loudly and gave Tim a bug-eyed stare over the top of Allison's fuzzy, peach-colored head. "Who're you kidding, the athletic type? Your wife the fashion queen know anything about this?"

"Don't pay any attention to him," cut in Danny firmly. "Your girl Camellia's got a good set of legs, like my Kate. Hockey legs, I think."

Tim scrunched up his eyes, deep in thought. "Don't like the idea of a high school where coaches throw games."

"It's too bad about Drago," said Danny. "The coach they got now's a bimbo. Her idea of fitness is a walk around the gym with a book on your head."

"Nothing wrong with that," said Nate, accepting the piece of cookie Allison was shoving between his lips. "Teaches 'em poise."

"Poise, shit. I want my girls to be able to take care of themselves. I'd kind of like it if they play some ball. My Holly's in a growth spurt. Think I'll teach her some dribbling, maybe hang a hoop over the garage. So they fired this coach, this Drago, huh?"

Danny looked away. "Yeah, but I don't remember a whole lot of what happened. Around that time, I mean."

Tim hooted. "I get it. You were too busy messing around with your girl. I used to be seventeen too, you know."

"Lay off him, Arbis," Nate cut in.

"What'd I say? Huh?"

Danny leaned back on his elbows, squinting into the distance. "Nothing. You didn't say nothing. The fact is, I wasn't so busy messing around with my girl. I was helping her bury her mother. Four days later I was helping her bury her father. Then . . ."

Turning up his lip, Nate interrupted Danny with a low howl. "C'mon, McGrath, this is a ballgame. None of that stuff, okay?"

An appalled look came over Tim's face. "Sorry, Dan. I never knew."

"Ev took it real bad."

Nate wrapped his long arms around Allison and nuzzled her hair with his chin. Danny hunched forward, speaking in almost a whisper.

"Ev and I got married right after. We tried to keep the whole thing quiet. They were suicides, both of them. We played it down, see, so they could have their funerals in church."

"No need to say anything, Dan," said Tim. "I shouldn't've bugged you."

"It's okay. You live next door to us. Might as well know."

"Looks like they're all done squabbling, or whatever they're doing out there," said Nate too loudly. "Let's get this game going! Hey, ladies!" Allison clapped her chocolate covered hands together, and wiggled happily in Nate's arms. "Come on, McGrath. Pay some attention to your wife out there."

"Ev took it real bad," Danny repeated.

Tim reached into the cooler for three more beers and passed them around. No one said anything. In the awkward hush, Allison gave a little grunt. Nate gasped. He held her out at arm's length and passed her to Danny.

"Why don't you raise this kid right, McGrath? This is disgusting. Clean her up, will you?"

The bottom of the first whizzed by quickly. Hannah Wally, the Spurs' strongest batter, took to the plate with a great show of force and was immediately tricked into swinging at a vicious backspin. She was out by a foot at first. Karla Brown hit straight into the waiting arms of the pitcher and found herself tagged in the hip halfway down the baseline. Sandy Dorn nicked a weak little pop over her shoulder, cursing the catcher, who went down on her knees to scoop it up the instant before the ball reached the earth. It was fast and efficient and merciless. The Spurs pulled their gloves back on and told each other not to worry.

Rollie the Fist opened his notebook, thought for a while, and began to write. His lips moved along with his pen.

Defensively speaking, the hometown girls' biggest weakness is their inexperienced inability to function together as a team. Any good ball club knows the first rule of play: The whole is greater than all its parts. And any good ball club would never allow a left fielder to do what the Spurs' left fielder did, namely, cry because the sun got in her eyes when she missed an easy pop fly. Not that it could have done much good, as

"Hey, Rollie!" Chocko Nolan, suntanned on the outside and beer-drenched on the inside, crouched down on the grass beside Rollie. "How's it goin'?"

Rollie covered the page he was writing on with his hand. "Not bad, Chocko."

"Only got a minute. Wondered if you might want to lay a little something on the game. I got ten bucks says the Spurs'll get creamed."

"You serious?"

Chocko puffed out his cheeks and spread his arms wide open. "Swear to God, Rollie. I know what you're thinking, though. You think maybe I got an unfair advantage, seein' as how my old lady's on the team, right?"

"It's your marriage, Chock. Me, all I have to do is write about them."

"I'm interested in a healthy little bet between a couple of friends. You got eyes. You can see for yourself what's goin' on."

"It's only the second inning."

"I don't care if it's the sixth. The telephone company's blowing our girls apart. I'm a practical man, see? You can play it safe and play some numbers. What do you say they'll get beat by? Fifteen? Twenty? We got to do it by fives or tens so the arithmetic works out right."

"Fifty," said Rollie decisively.

"Hey, Rollie, they're good. But not *that* good."

"Fifty on the Spurs to win."

Chocko whistled between his teeth, grinned, and stuck out his hand to shake on it.

Left on his own again, Rollie bent over the lines he'd written. He reconsidered each word, reconsidered his tone, reconsidered the woman running for the ball with the sun in her eyes, and finally drew heavy lines to wipe out his paragraph. He turned to a fresh sheet of paper.

Defensively speaking, the weakest point of the Spurs is inexperience. However, with a fast, sure-eyed shortstop and a solid guard at first base, the Spurs make up in spunk what they lack in authority.

Rollie looked up. His head was swelling with sentences. Things were not looking good on the field. Seven-zip. One out. The outfield was looking a little jumpy but the infield seemed on their toes. Shortstop sure was acting sharp. Shortstop, he remembered, was the wife, or ex-wife of Dorn. Kidnapping his own kid, Christ. Must be a load off her mind. Unless they let him go. He was no fool. Must have a lawyer. Cute kid she's got, too. Good arm. Spunky all over. Good word, spunk. Infield was getting tighter all the time. Especially first base. First base just bagged a runner like a pro. Very nice play. Two down. Holding them at seven. Whoever she was at first, she had a pair of legs like in the movies. Too bad she wasn't wearing shorts. Not gym shorts. The silky ones. Clingy. No good hiding it in those baggy breeches. She must be five-ten, easy, with most of it in her legs. Atta girl, she's going for another one. Don't blow it, darlin', I got fifty bucks riding on you. Ah, sweet! Out like a light. Very, very nice.

CHAPTER SIXTEEN

This was no dream. She was wide awake. Like two glittering fishes just below the surface of a sun-drenched pond two words leaped out at her, presenting themselves for inspection inside her head. She looked upon them with awe.

For me.

She lay very still for what seemed a long while, whispering them over and over. She wanted to make certain she was getting them right. But she knew. She knew it all. She was as sure as if Gussie herself had appeared by the side of her bed to say what she had done. Part of her wanted to wake Danny with the news. Part of her sank back in the pillows, lulled and serene, hypnotized by the charm of those two words. Sleep came, burrowing her deeply in untroubled dreams, but not for long. The screech of the telephone next to her bed had her flinging off blankets like a woman on fire. Danny rolled over, smacked his lips a few times, and turned his back to the phone. Evelyn answered it. It was Rio. It was three-thirty in the morning.

"Evvie? Sorry about this, but you've got to come over here. Can you? Gussie needs a ride to Sandy's house and my van's in the shop. Something is wrong with Jeremy. Can you come right away?"

Sandy. Jeremy. Rio's van. Slowly her mind blinked open.

"What happened to Jeremy?" She remembered that Sandy was working the night shift at the electric plant.

"Pammy Flynn's there with him," said Rio. "She called here

a minute ago. Jeremy woke up screaming, and she can't calm him down."

"I'll be right over."

She dressed fast, pulling her running sweats and an extra sweater over her pajamas. She put on sneakers and wrapped a woolen scarf around her neck. She tiptoed past the rooms where her children were sleeping and hurried into the night. The sky hung low, and she could hardly tell the stars from the pop-eyed glow of the streetlights. She got into her car. As she turned the key it came to her that this was the first time in her life that she was driving a car alone at night. The headlights cut into the trees with white, wild urgency, and as she drove away, exhaust smoke trailed behind her like small pale balloons, disappearing into the chilly silence of Anthony Street. Except for the noise of the car, all was still.

Gussie was waiting for her in front of her brother's house. They drove to River Road in silence.

Pammy Flynn was scared. "He stopped crying," she said weakly, leading the women into Sandy's house. "He's just sitting in there with his eyes wide open. He hardly even blinks. It's like he's watching a scary movie on television, except the television isn't on."

Gussie took off her coat and gloves. "Where is he?"

"In his bedroom. Just sitting there. I tried everything. I got him some milk. I sang songs. I even let him wear Sandy's softball glove. It's his favorite thing, but he wouldn't touch it. He wouldn't listen to me at all." Tears slipped down the sides of Pammy's pale face. "It's awful. He's so little!"

Gussie patted Pammy's arm. "You did fine. It's going to be all right. You said when you called me that you didn't hear any noise. It didn't sound like anyone was trying to get into the house, right? Tell me, did Jeremy do anything unusual before he went to bed? Or say anything?"

"No, I don't think so. Unless you count the polar bears."

Gussie cocked her head to one side. "The polar bears?"

"We listened to the radio at suppertime, and there was this news report about this polar bear that had a baby. It was a big deal, on account of it being rare for one to be born in captivity. I don't know where, some zoo I guess. But it turned out that the baby died when another polar bear rolled on top of it and, well, smushed it to death. Jeremy didn't say anything, he just kept eating his hamburger, but he had a funny look. So I asked him if it bothered him, hearing about it, and he said no. But later on he said, 'Pammy, you know what I'd do if I was God?' And I said, 'What would you do if you was God?' And he said, 'I'd make it so babies got born with weapons.' So I asked him how come and he only jumped out of his chair and started dancing around to the music. All he talked about the rest of the night was his play center. He went to bed when I said to. I fell asleep on the couch. All of a sudden there was this sound coming from his room, this shriek. He'd fell out of bed. He was thrashing around on the floor, screaming at the top of his lungs. So I called Sandy but she was way in the plant and then I called you.

"He's not so good, Gussie. He's not good at all. I wish there was some way I could open up his head and see what's goin' on in there. Know what I think? I think that time that Jeremy ended up in the hospital wasn't the first time he got beat. Maybe it happened a lot. I've been watching him real careful. Sometimes when I come into a room too fast, or I raise my arm in front of him because I have to get something off a shelf, he gets real jittery. Like tonight, when he was dancing around, he looked so cute that I stopped doing the dishes to come over and give him a hug. I guess I must've caught him off-guard. I put out my arms and he real quick covered up his face and backed away from me. I pretended like I didn't notice. I just said, 'Jeremy Dorn, you are so good-lookin' that I have got to give you a hug this very minute.' He was okay after that, he let me."

Clumsily, Pammy wiped away her tears with the bottom edge of her T-shirt. Gussie bore down on her cane and crossed the room. Jeremy's bedroom was just off the kitchen.

It was a bright, airy place with two windows that looked out on the river. The curtains were drawn shut. The walls were covered with circus posters and baseball stars and pictures Jeremy had drawn himself. A long bookcase was crammed with books and toys. Plastic airplanes and ships and racing cars hung on strings from the ceiling. Everything was orderly and colorful and lively. The boy who lived there was sitting in the middle of the floor, wrapped in one of Grace Pandy's quilts. He stared into space with his head tipped slightly back. His mouth was slightly open. Drops of spit trickled out one side but he did not seem to notice. Gussie went in, slowly. Evelyn went in behind her. Gussie took a step closer to the boy, and gently called his name. There was no response. She called him again and this time his body began to tremble in a violent spasm. He grew rigid all over. A snarl broke loose from his throat. Gussie went closer. The boy spoke.

"You better not step over this circle." His small voice was rasping, wheezy. Gussie stooped down and laid her cane on the floor. The boy drew back. His face was as hard as an animal's. "Don't you get any closer, you."

Hesitating and unsure, Gussie met Evelyn's eyes. She moved her lips slowly, mouthing a sentence. She had no idea what she ought to do next.

"Talk to him," Evelyn whispered. "Talk like you talked to Sandy that time at Juney's house."

Gussie shrugged, baffled. Jeremy was a child. What did Gussie know about a child?

Evelyn sat down on the floor.

"You better not step over this circle," said Jeremy again.

"You mean this circle?" Evelyn traced a little O in the dark blue rug.

Jeremy lowered his eyes and mutely shook his head. Evelyn drew a larger O. Jeremy unclenched his fist and swung his arm widely around. Evelyn nodded solemnly.

"Okay. You mean *that* circle." Evelyn pushed Gussie's cane out of the way. Gussie scooted across the floor on her bottom and pulled herself up on Jeremy's bed.

"Make a circle with your arms," Evelyn told her. Like a ballerina in a dance class, Gussie raised her arms in front of her, crooked her elbows and touched her fingers together. Obediently, she held her arms in place.

"You had a bad dream," Evelyn said.

The boy shook his head.

"Oh, yes you did. You can't fool me."

Jeremy's mouth twisted at the edges. Sadly, he brought his fists to the sides of his head, and for an awful moment Evelyn expected him to start pounding himself. She sprang forward, catching hold of the boy by his wrists. He struggled but she pulled him onto her lap, wrapping her arms around his chest and holding him tightly. Gussie waited on the bed with her arms circled in front of her.

"Dreams can't get inside circles," whispered Evelyn in Jeremy's ear.

He lurched, protesting. "Can too."

Evelyn tipped back his head and made him look at Gussie. "You see that circle up there?"

Jeremy watched suspiciously. Gussie's arms were firm and rigid, a perfect, huge O that hung like a hoop at the entrance to his pillow.

"I'd like to see a bad dream get through that one, Jeremy Dorn."

Gussie's eyes were on the boy. "Want to come in?" she asked a little shakily.

Evelyn gave him a nudge. The boy gripped her hard. She pushed him off her lap. With a yelp, he bounded up to his bed, leaped through the circle of Gussie's arms, and brought her down with him on to his pillow.

"You stay right here," Jeremy commanded. Gussie did as she was told. She heaved her bad leg up to the bed and pulled the blankets over them both. Jeremy buried his face in Gussie's neck. His breathing was easy and regular. He was almost smiling.

"Let me get this straight," said Sandy Dorn, refilling the women's coffee cups. "Pammy called Gussie at Rio's. Then Gussie called Ev—"

"No, Rio called Ev," cut in Pammy. "Rio's car's broken. I think it's the fan belt."

"Rio called Ev," Sandy continued. "And Ev came over with Gussie because Jeremy had a bad dream."

"No, no, no," insisted Pammy, salting her eggs. "It was worse than a bad dream. Jeremy was more like, like hysterical."

"Nothing wrong with him now," said Patsy Griffin, who had come over to take Jeremy for a ride on her bus.

Sandy went to the refrigerator for some more milk. Lowering her voice, she turned to Gussie. "What did you do?"

Gussie broke a piece of bread in half and dipped it in her eggs and grinned. "Ask Evvie."

"What did you do, Evvie?"

"Talked."

Sandy put the milk carton down on the table. Her fingers were trembling but the worry had gone out of her eyes. "About what?"

Jeremy came bounding into the kitchen. He went at once to Gussie's lap. She squeezed him with affection.

"What do you want to talk about, pal?"

Jeremy was beaming. There was no sign at all of what had gone on the night before. He wiggled closer to Gussie and squealed, "Softball!"

"First we'll talk about first base," Gussie told him. "Then we'll talk about second base. Then we'll talk about third base. And then we'll talk about—"

"Home run!" cried Jeremy, clapping his hands with delight.

When breakfast was over, Evelyn followed Gussie into Sandy's front room.

"He's going to be all right," said Gussie. "Did you call home to tell Danny where you are?"

Evelyn nodded. Gussie reached for her coat. It was lying where she had thrown it the night before, across the back of the couch, an arm's length away. Bending forward, Gussie lost her hold on her cane, and stumbled. She slipped and began to fall. Evelyn was at her side in an instant. She propped her up again, amazed at her own strength. Her hand lingered on Gussie's hand on her cane.

"Damn thing," sputtered Gussie, embarrassed. Evelyn left her hand where it was. She was standing so close that she could almost hear the pulse of Gussie's heart. Its beat was the beat of two words, strong and simple and alive. For me. Gussie turned her head to one side. They looked at each other.

"I don't care why you left the Saints, Gussie. All I care about is that you're here. I know what you did for me. The team. Playing catch in the backyard. All of it."

Gussie drew her breath in sharply. She winced as if she'd been stung. "It wasn't that I left the Saints, Ev. They benched me. Took me out of it. I wasn't good enough."

Evelyn pressed a finger to Gussie's lips, hushing her. There was nothing more they needed to say. Linking arms, they went out into the sunlight together, waving to Jeremy as he climbed aboard Patsy's bus.

April 2, 1975

Report of the Fifth Meeting of the SAC
Present: A. Cabrini, W. Brody, R. Cabrini, P. Glazer, D.
McGrath, E. Brody
Absent: W. Wally (on duty)
Visiting: Marina Cabrini

1) A. Cabrini read to the committee an article which appeared in the *Clarion,* written by Rollie "The Fist" Pelletier, who states his intent to legally prevent the Spurs from using the public ball field on account of their sex. He expects the whole town to rally behind him. He is in for a surprise.

The committee voted to take immediate action.

2) R. Cabrini presented an itemized list of recent expenditures: five bats of varying weight; two catcher's masks; two dozen softballs; three hundred yards of adhesive tape. There are no invoices outstanding.

3) The committee voted unanimously to accept the design for uniforms created by Grace Pandy, who makes quilts. Following a lengthy discussion, with W. Brody holding out for his favorite colors, pink and blue, the committee decided on the colors the Spurs should wear. Purple and white.

P. Glazer volunteered to collect the measurements of the players.

R. Cabrini and D. McGrath presented financial estimates for uniforms, and urged the committee to hop to, as there was not much time left until the game against the Belles. The uniforms will be purchased in Boston. The game was scheduled for the tenth of May.

D. McGrath, in a move that took even his own wife by surprise, motioned for a postponement of the game. R. Cabrini seconded. W. Brody, who was mad at everyone for voting down his choice of colors, said he wanted to third it.

A.C. reminded him that there was no such thing as thirding a motion, and he would have to stick to procedure. W. Brody said that he was eighty years old. What did he care about procedure?

A.C. brought to the attention of the committee the fact that last week at the jail the Spurs lost by only two runs. Postponement was out of the question.

4) A discussion occurred, with the following results:

A) The dissident male faction of the committee argued that they were only thinking of the good of the team. In their minds the Spurs were not ready. In their minds Gussie, being new, was doing a fabulous job as coach but all the same it was all too new. Postponement was the only logical course to take. Maybe the team would be better off waiting until, say, September. The men did not feel obliged to stand by and watch a massacre.

B) A. Cabrini tried to expel all the men from the committee.

C) D. McGrath tried to expel A.C. from his house.

D) Marina Cabrini, attending the meeting at the invitation of herself to see how her money was being spent, mentioned that all of this was not very different from real estate. You put up your cash, and you take your chances.

R. Cabrini said it was an interesting thought, but inapplicable.

E) D. McGrath proposed a vote, reminding the committee that according to the bylaws, voting by the present company was binding, and could not be undone.

F) The committee voted, under protest. The result was 3 for postponement and 3 against postponement. The recording secretary proposed running up to the hospital to get Hannah to break the tie, and D. McGrath said it was not allowed in the bylaws. All eyes turned to Marina Cabrini.

G) "One puts up one's money, and one takes one's chances," said Marina. "Postponement is out of the question."

The meeting adjourned on time.

CHAPTER SEVENTEEN

Avis's daughter Angela, sitting on her heels between her father and sister, quietly chewed on her fingers when Avis stepped up to bat. It was the bottom of the second inning. Pammy Flynn, greedily lunging for the wrong pitches, had struck out. Nancy Beth Campbell had popped out to center field. Patsy Griffin, first Spur of the game to land safely on base, looked worried and jumpy on first. Avis sprang up and down on the balls of her feet as she lifted her arms and pulled back the bat. Angela put three fingers into her mouth. Leo Poli muttered under his breath, praying that heaven would come to the aid of his wife. Mary-Susan Poli nervously plucked at Angela's sleeve as if she meant to unwind every thread.

"Look 'em over, Ma," said her brother Paulie between his teeth.

"Two down," his brother George reminded them.

"C'mon, Ma!" whispered Frank. His breath was hot on Angela's neck. "Swing!"

Avis swung. With a loud crack the ball sizzled to the left and crossed the foul line. George Poli swore. Frank Poli sucked in a mouthful of air and spat it out noisily. Angela turned around and told her brothers that if they didn't be quiet she was going to chop off their noses. Avis swung again and missed.

"If only we could help!" whined Mary-Susan.

Angela started chewing on her knuckles. The pitcher pitched. Low and outside. Ball one. Avis rearranged her cap.

She wiggled her hips and pulled at the neck of her jersey. The next ball missed its arc and rolled delicately past her feet. Ball two. Mary-Susan let go of Angela's sleeve and grabbed her by the elbow and clung.

"Mother of God. I can't stand it," groaned Leo, wiping the sweat off his head as the umpire called ball three. A murmur of excitement swept through the crowd the way wind goes through clothes on a clothesline. Angela shut her eyes. Mary-Susan's fingernails dug into her skin. She let them.

Whump came the sound of the hit. Angela leaped to her feet. Her brothers screamed in her ears. Patsy tore down the baseline for third. Avis chugged along toward second. She made it. The ball sailed in from right field, luxuriously high and slow, and landed in the mitt of the catcher a clean, long yard away from the plate. Patsy slid home on her bottom. Angela's heart unfroze. The cry of a bugle rang through the cheers of the crowd and filled the air with its echoes as the Spurs came off their bench to welcome home their first run.

May 10, 1975

There is a parcel of land on River Road which I have had my eye on for some time. Choice waterfront property, even on such an inconsequential river as this one, is not an easy thing to come by. I inquired into its ownership, and discovered that the land might be put up for sale in the event of a satisfactory bid. I am talking about two square miles of uncleared trees. The ground is level and rich. Its chances for water and sewerage are excellent. Its owner, the Boston bank where my daughter Christine is employed, has long been plagued by the economic setbacks of small towns such as this one, where the mills have closed and prosperity, if there had ever truly been such a thing, lived only in people's minds, like the idea of democracy.

There had been some talk that the town would buy the land for a public beach with a boating dock. One of the members of the Board of Selectmen, as corrupt as any man I have ever encountered, belonged to a family which dealt in the buying and selling of beach sand. According to my information, negotiations between the town, the bank, and the Selectman's family had already been started. The price of the beach sand alone was a staggering amount. I was able to slip into the breach in the negotiations. Augusta was still in Arizona when I entered my bid.

What I envision for this property is an ambitious and, I believe, rather sophisticated scheme of living arrangements, with half the proposed housing units going up for sale, and the other half maintained as rentals. The mills are not going to be empty forever. There is a new breed of technology on the way, eager for space and all the trappings of established society. I hired an architect whose work I have admired in the past, and I began inviting the bids of various builders and contractors. My head filled with plans the moment I awakened each day. I imagined the foundations newly dug, and the smell of new wood, and the sounds of hammers echoing for acres. All of my powers have been put to the test on this. I have determined not to fail. My husband has given himself to the more practical side of our business, and chooses to occupy himself with day-to-day necessities. He has left the new development entirely in my hands. My son Vittorio has proven himself less than adequate even at the task of redecorating his own house and cannot be trusted with large enterprises. My son Carlo cares only for the expansion of his wardrobe and the slimming of his waistline. Christine travels a great deal. That left me only Augusta, who was playing ball in Arizona. I believed that a girl of her talent and abilities would leap at the chance I was offering her. There is not a considerable difference between property development and the game of softball. A young woman of character and confidence should easily be able to manage to switch from one career to the other, and I expected nothing less of my daughter.

When I passed papers on the land, I set out to let her know.

Cut down at first with a weak grounder, Laura Bradley finished off the second inning. The score was seven to one. The Spurs went back to the field with rearrangements. Hannah Wally, pulled in from right, played third. Pammy Flynn was benched. Grace Pandy, trying to gulp down her terror, was sent out to replace Hannah. Karla Brown came in from short field, and Peggy Glazer replaced her. Nancy Beth Campbell, reminding Avis that she'd better leave her alone this time, went back to the mound. Her first two pitches put Belles on base at first and third.

A Belle singled. Eight. A Belle doubled. Ten. A Belle popped out to Hannah. Another Belle singled. They held the runner at second. A Belle popped to Grace Pandy, but Grace ducked. Eleven to one. Nancy Beth looked grim. She pitched a ball that nearly struck the next Belle on the head, but the Belle went for it, and clobbered a drive to left that moved about ninety miles an hour. Birdey Nolan dove through the air like a goose with its wings up and to everyone's amazement she came up with the ball. She whipped it to the infield, and danced all over the outfield when the double play actually worked.

Eleven to one. Rollie Pelletier's stomach was kicking up. He felt a flutter of hope as Evelyn Brody, leading off for the Spurs, came up to bat looking like she knew what she was doing. Wrong. Her little grounder rolled right into the glove of the first-base Belle. She didn't even bother trying to run for it. Up next, Birdey Nolan let go a glorious belt to right field. She was halfway down the baseline when an octopus of a Belle reached up and snatched it out of the air. Two up, two down. There was a sour taste in his mouth. He wondered if all his internal juices were going rancid.

Grace Pandy stepped into the batter's box, her knees knocking together with terror. She went down fast on three called strikes.

In the next inning, with Hannah Wally taking over right field and Pammy back to third, Nancy Beth put some grit in her arm and held the Belles to one run. The Spurs came up with a run of their own on a bases-empty homer by Hannah.

It was twelve to two at the end of four. There were three innings left. At this rate the numbers were staggering. Rollie put his hands on his stomach and groaned.

May 10, 1975

Secretly, when Augusta was away, I used to read the sports pages of newspapers and magazines. I do not suppose that I ever really expected to find news of her. A small organization of female softball players, based in the Southwest, which defrays its overhead with exhibition games and follows no standard of behavior but its own, hardly has a chance of exposure in the newspapers. But I went on looking. I followed the activities of obsessed, bud-breasted little gymnasts working their way through their hoops and across their exercise mats. I studied the faces of adults who presented them trophies, looking for signs of girls' mothers. I memorized tennis circuits. I knew the gross annual earnings of every professional female golfer in the country. I monitored the progress of high school sprinters, college crew teams, swimmers, skiers, horseback riders, figure skaters. Lingering over newsprint photographs of other women's daughters, looking into their lively, hopeful faces, I kept Augusta alive to me.

Now and then there were letters. Impersonal letters, scribbled between training sessions in her sloppy Italian. They were no more than bulletins on the weather, the state of her throwing arm, her batting average, her diet, her bank account. After a time, they did not come very often. They were almost always addressed to her father. I do not know what first prickled my skin with the hint of danger. Perhaps a tone in one of the letters. Perhaps desperation in her complaints about the weather. There is nothing in Arizona but desert. I cannot imagine why she ever went there in the first place.

She was twenty-four years old. Her father tried often to telephone her, but she was difficult to reach. Her team was on the road a lot. The Olympics came to television, and her father and I watched every one of the women's events. Anxiously, we looked through the faces of the crowds, hoping to catch sight of her. Her father entertained our clients with lavish stories of her success on the ball field. Her sister Christine, travelling to the west coast on business, stopped in Phoenix to visit her, but found that she had missed Augusta by only a few hours. Christine had not been able to find her. She left behind a note to say she'd been there. Inside the note there was a large check written on my private account. A week later, Augusta returned the check, with no explanation.

When I secured the property on River Road, I determined to go to Arizona to see her myself. I entertained no fantasies of stepping off a plane into her open, happy arms. What I had not expected was that she would refuse to see me.

I was in Arizona for five days. It was hot, intensely hot. You could smell the heat in the air and you could feel it coming up from the sidewalks, destroying all signs of human ambition and choking dry the sparse vegetation that desperately tried to grow. Walking outdoors was the same as trying to walk through a furnace.

I tried to see her. I left messages at the locked door of a stucco hut where she lived alone. The house was always empty when I visited. I left messages on the bulletin board of the gym where she trained, and at the laundry where she had her clothes cleaned. I attempted to see the coach of her team, but I was informed that the coach had left the country. There was not a single response to any of my attempts to reach her. In the room of my hotel I tested and retested the answering service, certain that she had been trying to telephone me. After three days, I learned that the team was resting in a motel in the north, prior to an overseas journey in which they planned to play exhibition games before audiences who had never seen a woman play ball before. I learned the name of the motel, and rented a car, believing that my daughter was planning to undertake a trip out of the country without a word to me.

It was a run-down, gaudy motel with half the letters missing from its cheap neon sign. I found some of the team around the swimming pool. They were large, friendly women who made a great deal of noise, but they would not tell me anything about my daughter except that she would be sure to be unhappy that she had missed me. One of them, a girl whose face and name I cannot remember, agreed in the end to talk to me. We met in a cocktail lounge where she drank goblet after goblet of a pink, sweet confection heavily laced with vodka. She became extremely drunk. From the stream of trivia that poured from her lips I was able to learn that Augusta was in fact in Phoenix. Early the previous season, she had begun playing badly. At first it was a matter of small errors in the field—a missed catch, an offbeat reflex, a hesitancy, as if she had suddenly grown afraid of the ball and came to doubt her own powers to protect herself. She showed up late for practices. She missed games. They fined her. They benched her. As the season wore on she sank into a slump so profound that the managers of her team threatened to drop her. I suppose they did what they could to help, for Augusta had been one of their best. When the new season began, and she showed no sign of recovery, they cut her from the team, and planned a trip abroad without her.

I flew home the next day.

Early one evening, a month or so after I had returned, I was sitting at the table with a newspaper when I heard the sudden roar and sputter of a large motorcycle. I believed it had merely been passing our house, but it came to a stop in our driveway. A moment later, Augusta walked through the door.

Everything there was to see was in her face. It was as thin as if an iron-handed giant had taken hold of her, and squeezed, and stood by laughing as her spirit slowly left her. Her skin, browned by the desert sun, was the color of unpolished copper. She wore it like a mask. Her lips were taut and pale. Beneath her eyes, where laughter had once crossed her face in youthful, happy crinkles, I looked upon the dark circles of bad days and sleepless nights. Her beautiful, thick, crow-black hair had been clumsily chopped short, and stuck up in coarse, unwashed spikes. Around her neck she wore a necklace of bright pieces of animal bone. Their sharp edges pointed against her neck like tiny spears. She was dressed in dirty white pants and a black leather jacket which was unzipped to the crevice of her breasts. On her feet was an old pair of heavy leather boots. She carried an overstuffed canvas bag. She dropped it onto a chair as if she had been away from home for only a weekend. I rose from my chair. She fixed me with hard, mute eyes, daring me to come closer.

I wanted to bathe her, feed her, to comfort her. I wanted to offer her a new career and watch her eyes come to life. The words stuck in my throat. Clumsily, I attacked her instead.

"That motorcycle, is it yours?" She responded that it was. She had flown to a friend's in the Midwest, and came the rest of the way on the motorcycle. She had no license to operate it. I told her, may God forgive me, to remove it from my property at once.

A year has passed since that day. The next time I saw her I was leaning over her bed in the hospital. She was unconscious. The details have not grown less clear. Her bruised skin goes on swelling. Her groans of pain sound louder. Her black hair makes a tangled web on the pillow and her eyes keep on failing to open. Her battered body has lain across the bottom of my heart all this time, still and cramped and heavy.

I made an office at home for her. She was moved from intensive care to a private room at the sunniest end of the hospital. There was no reason to suspect that she would not eventually recover from her injuries. I had her bedrooom painted. I filled the house with vases of freshly-cut flowers from her brother's garden. When she was finally released from the hospital, she appeared to be willing to succeed in the position I had created for her. She was given every chance. Not once, although the subject was often on my mind, did either of us mention the trip I had made to Phoenix. We were polite with each other, the way co-workers in an office are polite. I honestly believed that her interest and efforts were genuine; but her heart was somewhere else.

I have for a long time enjoyed walking by the river in the morning. If I am early enough I can be there for sunrise. I have been over the property many, many times, but I never tire of walking it.

One morning, instead of parking my car outside the woods as I usually did, I drove in on the old dirt road that leads to the electric plant. I parked in a clearing not far from the cabin where Sandy Dorn lives with her little boy. My daughter had often spent the night there, but I never encountered her coming or going.

Perhaps it was a trick of the light. The morning sun was stroking the cabin windows with red and gold, and it drew me nearer. The smell of good coffee was coming from the kitchen. Inside, a young woman by the name of Pamela Flynn was dozing in a chair at the table. There was a fresh pot of coffee on the stove. I walked around to the other side of the house. The grass was wet with dew. I walked carefully, quietly. I passed the window of a bedroom which had not been slept in the night before. I approached another one. The boy's room. Its heavy drapes had been drawn, but I was able to look in through the slit between the two sides of fabric. It was gray with shadows. My eyes went to the boy's bed. He was fast asleep. He was sleeping in the arms of my daughter. Half-sitting, half-lying, she held him closely. Now and then she rocked him. Her lips were moving as if she were singing him a song. Her eyes were closed but the look in her face was a look of triumph. The solid flesh of her body all around him seemed to be the beginning and end of all things that are safe and warm and fearless. Something within me stirred. Something unchoked. Something moved in me like the heart-stopping feel of a fetus that rolls its padded self benignly against the walls of its home. I did not want my daughter to see me so closely by. I began to turn from the window. The sun had broken through the tops of the trees, and long fingers of light were criss-crossing the yard and the cabin with watery brilliance. I was turning away into the sunlight. It was most likely an act of my imagination, or one more trick of the light, but I believe that I saw my daughter wink at me. A long, deliberate wink. I have been over and over this in my mind. The boy was fast asleep. There was no one else in that room. There was only Augusta, winking, and I, watching. I can almost swear that she winked. I am nearly sure of it. Sometime, I would like to ask her.

CHAPTER EIGHTEEN

Nailed to the trunks of trees and utility poles, plastered over shop windows, tacked to the walls of public offices, dangling from the ceiling of the A&P with the weekly meat specials, purple and white posters announcing *Spurs vs. Belles* went up all over town. The fire chief, who was Grace Pandy's brother, put one on the back of the hook and ladder. The police station took three. The Catholic church took a dozen for the walls of the bingo hall. Pammy Flynn's dentist handed them out to his patients. Victor Cabrini enticed every one of the tenants of Cabrini Associates to display at least one in a prominent place on their property. It looked like the circus was coming to town. Quiet jubilation seeped through the air, and every Spur was catching it. They were giddy and nervous and clumsy and alarmed. They heard rumors that the telephone company had promised all the switchboard operators in New England an extra coffee break for a month if the Belles had another undefeated season. Linda Drago's picture appeared in a business magazine under the headline CALLING THE STRIKES AT MA BELL. Drago mailed a copy of it to Gussie with a one-word note.

"Worried?"

Gussie wrote back with a word of her own.

"Never."

It was April. Warmth came back into the air like the unexpected touch of fingers covered with fur. Weeds first, slivers of green started poking up from the mud in the gardens of Anthony Street. Evelyn bought a shovel and overturned a wide strip of earth in her backyard. Her lower back, thigh, and shoulder muscles stretched and hardened some more, and the biceps of her arms bulged so nicely she got into the habit of rolling up the sleeves of her T-shirts to show them off. When she finished with her own yard, she took care of Teresa Monopoli's tomato patch and dug some holes for her husband Joe's new rose bushes. She trimmed June Campbell's shrubs and cleared out a place for Hannah and Peggy to start a Japanese rock garden. Tim Arbis offered her a reconditioned Plymouth if she'd dig up his yard for a swimming pool, but Evelyn thought that might be taking things a bit too far.

Rio Cabrini tore down most of the walls in his upstairs bedrooms, and Gussie found that the noise and the plaster were ruining her concentration. She moved out and went back to live with her parents. There, in the room her mother had designed as her real estate office, she settled down to work with a sketch pad filled with fielding diagrams, a chalkboard covered with the vital statistics of every Spur, and Uncle William. The two of them declared themselves off-limits to everyone and would not even answer the telephone. At practices they strategized some more. On the third Sunday of the month the women in prison beat the Spurs by one run. They thought that Linda Drago was beginning to look a little worried.

The day after their close defeat, without telling anyone, even Evelyn, the reason why, Gussie called an emergency meeting of the team at noon in her office. Spurs dropped what they were doing to attend.

Pammy Flynn showed up in her pink and white dental smock with pictures of Tina the Tooth. Hannah and Peggy wore their duty-stained nurses' uniforms. Karla Brown wore the gold polyester blazer of the A&P. Sandy Dorn wore her tool belt and Edison hard hat. Laura Bradley was in a leotard. Nancy Beth Campbell showed up in her seamless white yoga jumpsuit. Birdey Nolan's hair was in curlers. Avis brought along the four ounces of tuna with lemon juice she was allowed for lunch. Patsy Griffin was smeared with grease because her bus had blown a tire on the way over. Grace Pandy sat quietly in a corner, sewing patches onto a quilt. Mimi Reed, looking perfect in a plaid, crisp cotton dress, brought her well-behaved little boy and a shopping bag full of rubber animals. Evelyn brought Allison with her big lungs and a great deal of Anthony Street dirt. She did not think that any of them looked as if they belonged on a softball team. She thought they looked like a Hollywood game show.

Uncle William waved Gussie's cane in the air to call things to order. Allison waddled under a table to fight with Mimi's son for the toys. Avis started chewing her tuna. Gussie propped herself up on the arm of a chair, holding an oversized brown envelope. Slowly she undid the clasp.

"There're two things we've got to take care of," she announced. "First this."

She pulled from the envelope several sheets of paper, lifted the top one, and unfolded it. She cleared her throat and read out loud with a clear, strong voice:

Dear Spurs,

I don't know if you know who you're messing with when you mess with Gussie Cabrini, but I'll be thinking of you May tenth. And I never heard of any Linda Drago but I'll tell you something. I sure have heard of the telephone company. Stick it to them, girls. Get 'em real good.

Jojo Souther

"A Saint!" cried Uncle William.

A murmur swept through the room.

"Jojo plays first base," said Gussie with a pleased, almost shy smile. "She grew up on a ranch outside Tucson. People say she can run about as fast as a pony."

Everyone looked at Laura Bradley, first base of the Spurs. Laura laughed heartily.

"I'd be no match against a horse," she said.

Avis swallowed a mouthful of tuna and waved her hand for attention. "So you've been writing to your old friends, Gussie?"

Gussie shrugged. "Just once. I thought they might like to know what's going on."

"More!" interrupted Uncle William. "Read some more!"

Gussie turned to the next note. "This is from Eliza Dawson. Eliza plays right field. She comes from the Bronx and she's been playing ball since she was about four years old. Got herself named to the Associated Press All-Stars four years in a row. Her note's real short."

> Hey, Cabrini:
> Tell your girls to keep their heads up and their gloves low and not to believe a single thing you tell them.
>
> Miss you,
> Eliza.

"This next one's from Caroline Goldy. She pitches. I wish you could see her, she looks like the queen of the prom. Her backspin can knock your teeth out."

> Dear Spurs,
> I'm writing to you from a hotel in Tokyo, Japan. We just got here from a tour of four villages. You have no idea what it feels like to be stopped on the street by strangers who want to take your picture. Not because you're famous or anything, but just because you're tall. We all feel like we're a sideshow but we're having a great time. The whole team is going to get together May tenth and make like cheerleaders. Good luck. Tell your coach to write to us right after the game so we know how it went. Or maybe somebody should write for her. She's a pretty good ballplayer but I don't think she ever got past the third grade.
>
> All my best,
> Caroline Goldy

Quietly, Gussie looked down at the next note and began to slip it back into the envelope.

"Hey!" called Uncle William. "Aren't you going to read some more?"

"I guess that's enough." Gussie looked up, swallowing deeply. "This one says pretty much the same as the others."

Uncle William stuck out his lower lip.

"One more, Gussie," pleaded Nancy Beth.

Folded inside the large sheet of paper was a photograph. Gussie held it up for the women to see.

Four women wearing the uniforms of the Saints stood in a cluster of dwarf-size, knobby-jointed evergreens. In the distance were the dim outlines of steep mountains, soft with fog and snow. The women were all laughing. The Spurs recognized Caroline Goldy, whose long yellow hair dusted the shoulders of her T-shirt. Jojo Souther was not more than eighteen, and grinned into the camera like an advertisement for a farming commune. Eliza Dawson wore her cap high on top of a mass of blackly swirling curls. Her skin was the color of hot cocoa richly laced with cream, and her big, frank eyes danced with amusement. They were friendly, interesting faces, but they all seemed to shrink into the background with the midget trees the instant the eye landed on the face that dominated the picture.

It was a large, deeply brown face that vibrated with an energy the camera had somehow managed to capture. It gave the impression that it wanted to spill over onto everything in its path, as dangerous as thunderstorms and all at once as easy as melting snow. There was energy in the woman's strong, high cheekbones, energy in her wide-bridged nose, energy in her full lips and slightly furrowed brow, and none of the Spurs were surprised when Gussie told them her name.

"Calamity Ann Reese. Center field."

From all around the room came hushed exclamations of awe.

"Calamity Ann started out her athletic life with the shot put," said Gussie with a small catch in her voice. "She was in the Navy for a while, and then she found out her true love was softball. She's built like a tank. Stops grounders with her bare hands if she wants to. She looks mean, doesn't she? The truth is, she's got a heart made of sweetness. When I was in the hospital she wrote to me almost every day."

"You must miss them," said Avis softly.

Gussie looked away. She put down the photograph and read Calamity Ann's letter to the Spurs.

Honey,
One thing I have always had in my heart is the feeling that you've got the soul of a coach. You're bossy like a coach, and stubborn like a coach, and arrogant like a coach, and when you've got to be, you're just as deep down crazy like a coach. I hope your women know what

they're dealing with. Tell them Calamity Ann sends them every single wish she can think of for kicking the guts out of the telephone company. Tell them to play their little hearts out. When I get my eyes on you again, girl, I am going to come right at you and take you up off the ground, cane and bruises and all, and I am going to give you a hug like no hug you ever got before.

The letter fluttered a little in Gussie's hands. The women were silent until Uncle William started hopping up and down on one foot.

"The other thing, Gussie! Don't forget the other thing!"

Gussie folded the letter around the photograph and slipped it back into the envelope. She turned to Uncle William.

"They wouldn't be interested in *that*," she said teasingly. "And it's already time to get back to work."

Uncle William let out a howl. Allison stuck her head out from under the table and howled too. Mimi's son started to cry. Avis put the lid back on her tuna container, spread out her arms, and pulled the children to her lap.

"What other thing?" demanded Nancy Beth.

Gussie looked around the room in wide-eyed surprise. "Other thing? Did I say there was another thing? What's the matter? Aren't the Saints enough for you for one day?"

Uncle William rushed past her to the closet door and impatiently opened it. Grunting with the effort, he dragged out a large cardboard carton. Its flaps were closed tightly under many layers of adhesive tape. He heaved it out to the open and the women hurried to help. Gussie stood on her cane to one side, watching silently.

The top of the box came undone.

"Our uniforms!" screamed Birdey.

The knot of women around the box came apart with a flourish of purple and white. Hats were flung in the air. New white breeches with purple stripes down the sides were passed from one hand to the next. Purple stirrups appeared and were thrown up with the hats. Karla Brown took off her grocery blazer and ducked her head into a purple shirt that said *Spurs*. Wiggling her hips she paraded around the room to show it off.

"Ev?" Gussie came up beside her. "Do you like them?"

Evelyn smiled. In a minute she would join the others. She would step away, reluctantly, from the warm strong feel of Gussie by her side. For now, all she could do was stand there, wrapping her arms around herself as if she wanted to hold on forever to the happiness that was suddenly, beautifully hers. She turned. Gussie's eyes were dancing. In a minute she would fold herself into herself again but for now her eyes were dancing.

"Aren't you going to try yours on?"

"In a minute," Evelyn answered, squeezing herself. "In a minute."

CHAPTER NINETEEN

It was the top of the fifth. Avis returned to the plate and put on her mask. A Belle with curly red hair came into the batter's box.

"Maybe you should ditch the mitt and try catching with your potholders," said the Belle in a low voice.

Avis held out her hand to take Nancy Beth's warm-up pitch. She returned the ball to Sandy at shortstop.

"I figured we'd beat you girls, but I had no idea it'd be this easy. Why don't you do yourself a favor and quit before you're dead?"

The ball criss-crossed the field, to first, to center, to left, to third, to right, to second where Evelyn dropped it, to first, to the mound, and back to Avis. The batter idly lifted her bat, swinging it in the air like a cavewoman.

"I'm starting to feel real sorry for you girls," said the Belle. "I'm starting to feel like an assassin."

Avis cupped the ball in her mitt and took a walk to the mound.

"What's up?" Nancy Beth was beginning to show signs of fatigue. Her thin face was crimped and pained. There was a dull look in her eyes but she smiled bravely.

Avis cocked her head to indicate the Belle at bat. "I want you to put some elbow grease in this one. She likes to go for the backspins. I want you to destroy her."

Nancy Beth shrugged and took the ball. "I'll see what I can do."

Back at the plate, Avis grinned through her mask at the Belle. Nancy Beth went into position. The two umpires crouched in readiness. The Belle took her stance.

"Too bad you called yourselves Spurs," said the Belle over her shoulder. "Unless you're planning to whip up a dead horse."

"Oh, eat it," said Avis. Nancy Beth's first pitch thumped neatly into the pocket of her mitt.

"Stee-rike!" cried Jake.

Avis returned the ball, buckled down, lifted her mitt.

"Stee-rike two!"

The next pitch met the bat in its center and shot out with a loud thud. Avis lifted her mask to watch it soar. The red-haired Belle was streaking down the baseline as tiny clouds of dust rose up behind her.

"It's all yours, Birdey," prayed Avis.

Birdey moved back fast. The batter was inches from the bag. Avis felt her teeth gritting together. The crowd fell silent, and Birdey went up off the ground, plucking the ball out of the air with the ease of a woman reaching into a tree for a piece of fruit. Avis hugged herself, cheering. One out.

The Belle coming up had already singled and doubled. She was a solid woman with a rectangular body and short, boxy hands that gripped the bat the way stranglers grip throats in the movies. Her name was Melinda. Avis was getting to know them all by now. She knew what this one would do: choke up and throttle the first decent high pitch, shut her eyes against the impact, and slam to center. Nancy Beth looked to the bench. Gussie's tongue was in the right corner of her mouth. Low arc. Avis approved. Nancy Beth stepped into her windup, delivering the lowest legal pitch of her life. Jake called it a strike. Gussie kept her tongue to the right. In three more pitches they had her. Two down.

The next Belle was wide-bottomed and exceptionally slow on her feet, but she knew how to hit. It didn't matter how the ball came in and it didn't matter where she aimed. She'd hit anything. Pulling back, the four outfield Spurs left their two-on-two formation and went into a solid line.

The pitch was low, inside. The Belle slammed it hard and the ball took off close to the ground, sizzling past Nancy Beth, tipping off Evelyn's glove, and heading straight for the unguarded space where half the outfield would have been if they hadn't pulled back.

Patsy Griffin came flying forward. She fell to her knees, stopped the drive, and threw to second from a crouch. The big batter lumbered for the bag. Evelyn lowered her glove for the catch as she looked for the runner. Then Evelyn went for the tag a long, awful moment before the ball was even in her hands. The Belle was safe at second.

Evelyn weakly picked up the ball and shot underhand to the mound. Avis felt a curse coming to her lips but she stopped it. Evelyn looked ready to cry.

The next Belle was chewing fruit-flavored gum, about seven sticks of it at once. She was tall and awkward, and she was desperately in need of an orthodontist. Her overbite was so bad that her teeth reached nearly to her chin. Avis called her Fang. Passionately working her jaws, Fang went up on tiptoes for a high pitch and sent it back, straight up, stiffly peaking above second base.

The runner at second paused, watching. Evelyn tipped back her head. The ball started falling. The upturned glove started trembling. Evelyn took a small step forward, then a small step back again, and the ball landed with a dull whomp on the ground at Evelyn's heels. Patsy moved in to retrieve it. She threw to first but the Belle was on.

"Damn," said Avis, kicking the dust by the plate.

The outfield Spurs moved in toward Evelyn in a huddle. Patsy flung an arm around her shoulder. Laura joined them, and Sandy, and Pammy. Nancy Beth took a walk around the rim of the mound with her head low. Her arms swung limply at her sides. She looked ready to keel over any moment.

"Damn," said Avis again.

"McGrath! Where you going?" demanded Nate.

Joe Monopoli clapped his hands together like a four-year-old. His eyes were runny from beer and sunshine. "Tell 'em, Danny-Boy, tell 'em!" He threw his bald head back and laughed at a joke known only to himself.

"I got to talk to my wife," said Danny.

Nate caught him by a belt loop at the back of his pants and pulled. Danny stumbled backward. Nate reached out with both hands to hold him steady.

"Let go," said Danny through clenched teeth.

Nate held on. "You're not going anywhere."

"Sit down, Dan," said Tim Arbis quietly.

Danny shuffled his shoulders and smoothed his rumpled shirt. "I just got to talk to her for a second. I got to tell her to calm down. She gets flustered out there, see. She gets herself all wound up and she gets scared. I got to tell her to take it easy or she'll blow the whole thing. I'll be right back."

"Sit down, Dan," Tim said again.

Danny stamped his foot. Nate took him in a chest hold from behind and Tim grabbed his ankles. Monopoli clapped his hands together. Danny sat.

Avis took off her mask and stretched her legs, bending each one carefully at the knee. They were starting to cramp. She shook out her arms and reached up to rub the back of her neck where the muscles were tightening. The Belle in the batter's box was called Karen. She liked pitches with very high arcs. She liked to ram them to right field.

"What're they doing out there?" Karen talked loud enough for the whole crowd to hear. "Swapping recipes?"

Avis ignored her. Her eyes ached from the strain of so much concentration. Her head throbbed from her eyebrows to the backs of her ears. The pain in her lower stomach shot upward in fiery spasms and it was only the top of the fifth. She felt like a middle-aged woman who is up to her neck in housework. A woman whose children probably mocked her behind her back. A woman whose husband surprised her with a silk nightgown when all her life all she'd ever worn was flannel. She'd worn flannel on her honeymoon and she'd wear flannel until the day they put her in the ground. Leo had never complained before. All he could say now was how he couldn't keep his hands off her. Perhaps she didn't know Leo at all. Perhaps she didn't know any of them. She felt old and tired. Old and tired and foolish. She sank to the ground. She took off her mitt. She felt beaten.

Rollie Pelletier doodled in the pages of his notebook. He drew vague, sinister, blobby creatures that lurked in the margins like little nightmares. In the center of a page he drew a big diamond. Where the mound should have been he drew a rough outline of the human heart. He advanced the shapeless monsters until they came at the heart from all three bases. Then he drew cylinder-shaped bombs falling in thick clusters from the sky. Around the bombs he drew rain, strokes of lightning, lines to represent thunder. When the huddle in the field broke up at last, and the second-base player returned to her position, looking, he thought, utterly miserable, he tore the page from his notebook and crammed it into his pocket. Belles were on first and second. The Belle at bat stuck out her bottom and lunged for a lifeless pitch and drove it dramatically into the outfield. Rollie closed his eyes. The runner began advancing. He was not going to look again until the entire game was over, but a scream from right field made him change his mind.

"I got it!" screamed Birdey Nolan, waving the ball over her head.

Peggy Glazer blew life into the tired will of the Spurs with an earth-shattering home run in the fifth. Sandy, coming up behind her, doubled. Pammy Flynn tried hard, but popped out to the Belles' new pitcher. Nancy Beth, holding up her bat as if it weighed five times more than she did, struck out. Patsy came up, huffing and puffing, and made the crowd roar with a line drive that sent Sandy tearing for the plate. Patsy landed at second and Sandy upped the score to twelve to four. Avis roused herself for an infield hit. Patsy stayed at second while Avis stood on the bag at first, touching her ribs to see if her racing breath had broken anything. Then Mimi Reed, batting for Laura Bradley, singled nicely to load the bases. Evelyn was up.

June Campbell wiggled in her chair. "Look, it's Evvie."

"Mama's *up!*" squealed Kate.

Mundy McGrath bit his lips. He stepped away from his sister and stood sideways with his feet slightly apart. He closed his seven-year-old hands around an imaginary bat and pulled it back in the same angle as his mother. He furrowed his eyebrows and glared at the pitcher like she did.

Danny lifted Allison to his shoulders and pointed. "There's Mama, see?" Allison played the bongo drums on her father's head.

"Triple, Mama, triple," cooed Allison.

Mundy was all set. The ball left the pitcher's hand. It came in on an arc that peaked too early, too high, and Evelyn let it go by. Mundy did the same.

"That's the girl. Look 'em over," muttered Danny.

Mundy moved his hands closer together. The next pitch was well inside the plate. Evelyn and Mundy swung and missed. June Campbell groaned out loud. Danny gritted his teeth.

Kate said, "Don't worry, Daddy. She'll get the next one."

Evelyn and Mundy reached for an outside pitch and cracked it too far to the left. Strike two. Evelyn lowered her bat, Mundy lowered his. In came the pitch. They swung. They connected.

"I told you!" sang Kate.

Evelyn waited an instant too long at the plate, trying to see where the ball was going, as if she could not believe that she had hit it. She missed her stride on the run for the base and they got her easily. Shoulders slumping, she walked slowly to the bench. Mundy threw himself down on the ground and buried his face in his hands.

It was the top of the sixth and the Spurs once more took the field. Chatting themselves up, they tossed the ball from infield to outfield, outfield to the mound, pitcher to catcher, around two bases and back again. Linda Drago strode to the edge of the diamond with her hands on her hips.

"Hey, Cabrini! What's the matter? Forget how to play this game?"

Pointing wildly, Drago drew the attention of the crowd to the hole at second base where Evelyn should have been. The Spurs went on tossing the ball. There was no response from the bench, where Evelyn sat in a slump. Her arms were hanging limply at her sides. The corners of her mouth turned down with defeat. Slowly, as if the effort was almost too much to bear, she began to shake her head. Gussie laid her cane on the ground. Stooping, she sat beside her.

Evelyn dug her cleats in the dirt. She lowered her eyes. She could not say exactly where it had started going wrong. She had come out of her house in her uniform, full of hope, with Danny and the children around her like bubbles. She had taken her place at second base. She had squared her shoulders, exhilarated, with the rest of them. She had tuned her body to the rhythms of the game, and through it all, as she went through each one of her paces, she had kept her eyes on the bench. On Gussie. Squinting in the sunlight Evelyn had watched every move she made. All her senses were alert, on edge. Something was wrong with Gussie. Evelyn had watched the lines of her face and the curl of her hands and the signals she sent to the mound. She had watched carefully, patiently, constantly, as if Gussie might vanish the instant Evelyn moved her eyes.

"Ev?"

Gussie was saying her name. Details swirled in her head with the urgency of leaves in autumn, and Gussie was saying her name. Each detail presented itself to her with stunning clarity. She was illuminated with understanding. She saw it all. The long evenings of practice. The jukebox. The bread she kneaded with her own two hands. The meetings, the box full of uniforms. The look on Gussie's face as she caught and threw the ball on Anthony Street, one hand on her cane, daring fate to defy her. Gussie who had tripped Linda Drago on the prison grounds. Gussie who had puffed with pride, feathering herself with the thrill of the odds when all the odds were against her. Evelyn could see it. Another defeat, another fast removal. Her silence. The funny way she had of cocking her head to one side when she didn't want to listen. *Remember the movie about Helen Keller? Remember when she learned a word?*

"Evvie, look at me." Reaching forward, Gussie moved her hand to Evelyn's face, holding her the way an egg-cup holds an egg. Evelyn shook her head and Gussie's hand moved with it.

"You've been jumpy, Ev. I don't blame you. The pressure is intense."

Gussie with her strength, who hated talking. Out of the blue she'd come home, back to Anthony Street on a motorcycle. No explanation, no apologies. In the hospital she had turned her face to the wall. She would not wave to Evelyn's children from the window. *Looks like we'd better get ourselves a team, Ev.*

Some team.

"Don't worry so much. Okay, you made a few mistakes today. I don't think you've been concentrating. Drago's scary, but you shouldn't let her get to you."

Gussie who had the cunning and secrecy of a thief could no longer fool her.

"You're holding up the game. It's practically over anyway. Just take a deep breath and get back out there, okay?"

She could see them waiting for her in the field, blurs of purple and white. They looked weary. They looked hopeless. On the mound, Nancy Beth was rubbing the shoulder of her throwing arm. She had used up her strength. Her arm looked ready to come out of its socket. It was nearly over, all of it. Gussie who had stirred them with belief was giving up on them. Afterward, she would probably disappear. Perhaps she would go back where she came from and try to appease them with postcards of the Arizona desert. *Honey, you've got the soul of a coach,* said the woman they called Calamity Ann.

Some coach.

"Everyone's waiting, Ev."

She had made them believe her, Gussie with her bag full of tricks. She had painted the balls orange so the women could see them in the dark, a regular wizard. In Evelyn's dream, Gussie had leaped onto a motorcycle surrounded by women in uniforms. The women's arms were open. Their heads were thrown back with laughter.

At the end of the dream, at the end of every dream, there was silence. There was only silence, opening its huge jaws slowly, in the place where the dream had been.

"Evelyn!" Gussie's breath came and went sharply, rapidly. In her eyes, rearing itself up like a ghost, there was sadness. There was loss. Her lips began to quiver, strong, solid Gussie, a coach who wanted to cry. She had lain beneath the crush of a motorcycle. Under her skin she was soft. She had not been wearing a helmet: doomed, destructive Gussie, thrown off a team for not trying. She thought she wasn't good enough. *They benched me, Ev.* Up from the wreck rose her wounded leg, her tanned and beautiful leg. In their youth she had run like a colt, her mother scowling in the window. She had defied them all, then. She had run like a mare with the wind on her back and the strength of forever in her body. Then, there had seemed nothing she could not do. She had said so herself, and Evelyn had believed her.

Evelyn felt her voice growing in her throat like a fist. "You told us that we had a chance of winning this thing."

Startled, Gussie backed away.

"We've still got two innings to go. Nancy Beth is exhausted. One more pitch and she'll be finished."

A soft red flush crept into Gussie's cheeks. She pressed her lips together tightly. What kind of a coach goes into a game with only one pitcher?

Evelyn faced her. At their backs the murmur of the crowd gathered and swarmed like a press of insects, but the silence between them was immense.

Shuddering, Gussie turned away. Gussie who had told them they had a chance, and had not believed it herself. Her face was rigid, pained. She fisted her hands and thumped at the edge of the bench.

"I've been watching you, Gussie." She was the daughter of Shirley Brody, Inspector. Her own hands were young and strong but she had inherited her mother's eyes. She felt suddenly large with confidence. There was nothing she could not see.

"Go back to the field, Ev."

In Arizona Gussie had given up. Her big heart had gone out of her the way a candle goes out, poof! They called it a slump. Somewhere, Gussie bought a motorcycle and learned to drive it. She came home in a roar of defeat, Gussie who had taught her to throw a softball, who taught her to look a ghost in the eye and tell it to go back where it came from. Evelyn shook her head. Within her, images of the past faded and crumbled. Her mind was working fast. She was planning.

"Let's go!" screamed Drago.

The crowd was buzzing. The umpires put their arms in the air and pointed to their watches.

In Evelyn's dream, Gussie had gone away in a cloud of dust, leaving Evelyn helpless. But this was no dream. Gussie turned to her with a sigh.

"It's only a game, Ev. What the fuck do you want from me?"

Everything, nothing, everything. Evelyn leaned forward. She put her hands on Gussie's hands and uncurled them. Gussie with her ruined leg and her scars. Gussie who had lived with despair. Gussie who had peopled her dreams, stared down her ghosts, awakened her; Gussie who sat beside her, biting her lips to keep from crying as she asked her what she wanted. Evelyn smiled. At least they would not go down without a fight.

"I want you to pitch," she said.

* * *

Rio Cabrini and his brother Carl, approaching their parents from opposite directions, reached them at the same moment. Marina sat on a wood and canvas chair with Victor beside her on a matching one. The canvas was purple and the wood was white. Across the back of each were large white letters in elegant script that said, *The Spurs.* The chairs were a gift from the team. Marina leaned back and her son Carl hurriedly touched his mouth to her cheek. Rio stood behind with a hand on each chair.

"They winning?" asked Carl.

"Almost," said Victor distractedly.

"What's the holdup?"

"Evvie's down on the bench. I don't think she's feeling so good. Gussie's pepping her up."

Carl gazed out to the field. Nothing was happening. He put his hands into the pockets of a well-pleated pair of gray flannel slacks.

"I thought Christine was coming," said Marina.

Carl took his hands out of his pockets and slapped himself on the head. "Mama, I'm sorry, I forgot. Christine called me at my house. You'd already left. She says to tell you and Papa she can't make it, she's got to go someplace. Business, you know?"

Marina nodded and looked away. Carl tapped his father's shoulder.

"Chocko Nolan's laying money all over town against the team. Rosarian told me. You got anything to do with that?"

Victor stretched out his hands, palms up. "Who, me?"

Carl looked at Rio. "What about you? You in on Nolan's thing?"

Rio's face suddenly stretched. His jaw dropped. His eyes widened with amazement. Carl shrugged.

"What did I say, huh?"

"Holy Mother of God," said Victor in almost a whisper.

Marina gave a start forward in her chair. Her hands closed tightly around the wooden arms. "Augusta!" she said softly.

Carl looked to the field. The regular pitcher was coming off the mound. His sister appeared to be taking her place. From all sides, Spurs ran forward to gather around her.

The crowd was up on its toes, tingling.

"That's Gussie," said Carl dumbly, as if no one else could see.

Victor began to come up from his chair but Marina stopped him with a single touch.

"I think she's going to pitch," Carl told them.

Victor grabbed his wife's arm. "Look at *her!* Ha, look!"

Linda Drago, standing at the edge of the diamond, staggered as if she had just been shot in the back. She came forward a few steps toward the mound, changed her mind, and returned to her own bench where Belles closed in a huddle around her like surgeons.

"Play ball!" cried Jake the umpire, waving his hands in the air. A Belle came into the box. The cluster of Spurs around the mound was breaking up. The crowd sat down noisily, ready for anything.

"Gussie?"

"What."

"You all right?"

She shook the handle of her cane, eyed its tip in the ground. She clenched the ball until her knuckles turned white. Tilting her head to one side, she gave Evelyn a long slow look. She was pale and sweating hard already. "I'm fine."

"Avis is going to throw real easy. Don't worry. Sandy and I will cover you."

She dug her cane a bit further into the dirt, shifting her bad leg behind her like a prop. "You'd better not screw up, Ev."

"I'm not going to screw up."

"You know what I'll do if you screw up?"

"What?"

"I'll take you out of this game. You'll never play ball again."

"Never?"

"Never."

Beside her, Evelyn slipped her hand into her glove. Gussie swung herself around to look at her outfield. Then she took a look at her infield. Then she waved to Linda Drago.

"Ready whenever you are, Belles," she called. She gave her cane a tug, as if she were testing the leash of a dog. The fear in her eyes was naked, raw, glittering. She swiped at the sweat on her forehead with the back of the hand that held the ball. She squinted at the Belle with the bat. The Belle glared back.

"Gussie?"

"What."

"I don't care if we win."

"Get to your base, Ev. Neither do I," she lied, shuffling herself into a windup.

Evelyn walked backward to the second-base bag and crouched, waiting.

Nate Campbell lit a cigar. Leaning back, he rounded his lips and puffed out a long chain of smoke rings.

"You want another beer, Nate?" asked Tim pleasantly.

Nate jabbed the lighted end of the cigar into the air and waved away the smoke with irritation. Tim repeated the question. Nate put his cigar back into his mouth and sucked hard.

"No good," said Joe the Rosarian. "He make up his mind he ain't gonna talk, that's it. He ain't gonna talk."

"Come on, Nate," said Tim.

"He's fired." Nate blew another chain of rings.

"Ho! He talked!" hooted Joe.

June Campbell leaned forward in her lawn chair. "Really, dear, I think you're taking things a little too far if you fire Danny. Of course, you don't really mean it, do you?"

"He's fired." Nate flicked a gray mound of ash to the dirt and turned to his wife. "Tell him he'd better not show up for work Monday morning. He'd better not ever show up again."

"Have a beer, Campbell." Tim held out a cold, sweating can and pressed it into Nate's hand. Nate pushed it away as if it were covered with germs.

"Get away from me, Arbis. You knew all along. You knew, Rosarian knew, my own wife knew, the whole town probably knew. But most of all, McGrath knew."

Tim opened the beer and started to drink it himself. "I did not know. She's as much a surprise to me as the day I found out my first girl was growing inside her mama."

Nate scowled. He allowed a huge ring of smoke to form like a halo over Tim's head. "Well, McGrath knew. All he had to do was say, Hey, Nate, did you hear who the relief pitcher is? That's all. I gave the man a job. I brought him along all these

years and I'd expect that he'd let me know what's going on so I
don't feel like the whole town knows what I don't. My wife I
can maybe understand. She's female. Females got to have codes
of secrecy or they're not female. Anyhow, Gussie Cabrini
would've broken Juney's arms if she told me. I can understand
that. Rosarian I can understand too, he's Italian. But not
McGrath. McGrath I just cannot figure out."

"Oh, Nate," sighed June.

Tim reached into the cooler and tossed a beer to Danny.
"How's it feel to lose your job?"

Shrugging, Danny let Allison cool her face on the sides of the
can of beer. "Tell Nate he don't even know enough to know
he's alive. I'm on the goddamn committee and I didn't even
know."

Nate looked down at his cigar. It was out. He propped his
thin long legs in front of his face, leaned his head forward, and
closed his eyes with a great show of indifference. "Somebody
wake me up when this thing's over," he said. "Anybody except
McGrath."

Top of the sixth, no outs, bases empty, recorded Rollie Pelletier in
his notebook. *Relief pitcher holding her own. The crowd's behind the
hometown girls in a big way.* He stopped writing. Be nice to get a
shot of her on the mound, cane and all. Good for the front
page. Very dramatic. The advertisers'd love it. He looked over
his shoulder for the photographers. The photographers had
long gone, no surprise. Never could find them when he wanted
them, not in thirty years. He'd have to take the picture himself,
get her to pose on the mound after the game. She was looking
as strained as if she'd just come back from the dead but it
wouldn't show in the shot. He looked down. His lips moved
along with his thoughts. His brow furrowed. He crossed out
hometown *girls* and wrote *women.* Then he crossed out *women*
and wrote *team.*

The Spurs fanned snappily over the field. The score was
twelve to four. On the mound Cabrini sent in warm-ups. She
had a nice clench to her jaw. Win or lose, he'd have to give the
girl her due. The girl had guts. Spunk. He found himself wishing he could have seen her in action before her accident. That
leg looked like it was gone for good. He'd seen it before, limbs

gone, athletes turned to bums. He'd seen it in the war. War, hell, he'd seen it right here in town where it didn't take shrapnel to ruin a man's shot at a little glory. All it took was a little booze, a little paunch, a little defeat in the daytime that turned into big defeats in the darkness and next thing you knew you had a town full of losers. Not this girl. He'd had his eye on her for years. Gussie Cabrini was a fighter. Not much to look at, though. Pity.

She wound up, delivered like a pro. That leg must be killing her. From where he sat he could see her face twisting and clenching with pain. He had to give it to her, he thought, lifting his pencil to the page.

Like a pro, he wrote, licking his lips with the good, clean feel of the words. Like a pro.

Her cane shook with the force of her delivery but it held her. The pitch went weakly by the knees of the Belle for a ball. Avis returned gently, and she took the catch with her bare hand. She put her good foot up against the pitching rubber. She delivered again for another ball. The third pitch found its course, and the fourth, and the fifth, and the Belle went down on a strikeout. The following Belle helped herself to a triple. Four Belles and two runs later, they had them. The back of Gussie's shirt was soaked. Her hair was soaked.

"If you think I'm going to bat, you're crazy," Gussie said back at the bench, her face white with strain. Her scars stood out like ragged pieces of skin hastily sewn in place.

Birdey Nolan went up for a double. Hannah went up for another but they held Birdey at third. Peggy popped out. Sandy winged a belt to left to bring in two and Pammy grounded out at first. Mimi Reed, batting for Gussie, safely singled to bring Sandy home. Patsy made the sign of the cross on her forehead as she came up to bat, but Gussie denied that it had anything to do with the long low drive that brought in Mimi. Avis went up with all of her hopes in her swing, and lost them in a flimsy pop to second. Spurs patted her back as she reached for her mask. Muttering unhappily she dragged herself behind the plate for the last time, watching Gussie limp her way back to the mound. Fourteen to eight. It was the top of the seventh, and last, inning.

*   *   *

Carl Cabrini put his hands in his pockets and wandered off to look for Chocko Nolan. Victor muttered in Italian as a Belle hammered his daughter's pitch to a double. One on. The next Belle pushed her to third with half a mile to spare. Marina held up her hand.

"Vittorio," she said softly. Rio lowered himself to the ground at her feet. She kept her voice down. "There is something I want you to do for me."

Victor roared, pressing his hands to his eyes and fearfully peeking through them. A Belle streaked across the plate. The ball winged in from far out in center field too late to do anything with the runners at first and second. The score was fifteen to eight. Gussie ran her free hand through her hair, rubbing her head with her eyes closed. She shook her shoulders and adjusted her cane. Before she held up her hand for the ball she reached behind and tucked her left leg in place as if it might be of some use to her.

"Go the distance, baby, go the distance," prayed Victor out loud.

"What is it, Mama?" said Rio.

The Belle with red hair came up and went down fast on a high pop to short field. Tagging up, the second-base runner took off for third. Pammy Flynn tipped her glove for the ball, caught it neatly, and chased the Belle to the bag. Curtis Fletch, the umpire in the field, called it out. The Belle protested. Drago flew off her bench. Belles swarmed to the side of the field and Victor rocked back and forth in his chair, shouting in English and Italian that the Belle was as out as a no-good lightbulb.

"Augusta listens to you," said Marina.

Rio lit a cigarette, watching her. She stared straight ahead. Her legs were crossed at the knees. Except for her right leg she was utterly still. Only her right leg moved, as if it had a twitch. Up and down she bent her leg, nervously, intently, over and over and over. Rio stubbed out his cigarette. He reached for her hand.

"Mama. Tell me what you're thinking."

"She's out!" cried Victor, thumping the arms of his chair. The protesting runner, shaking her fist at all the Spurs, stumbled back to her bench. Drago sat down again, moving her lips with indignation.

"What a bunch of bums, the telephone company," said Victor. The wide-bottomed Belle strode to the plate, exchanging nasty looks with Avis Poli. Gussie came up with a wide, slightly curving pitch that went outside for a ball. Victor groaned.

"I am going to give you something," said Marina. "I want you to pass it on to Augusta."

Rio looked at his mother blankly.

"Strike one!" yelled Victor. "Atta girl. That's my girl. Go the distance!"

"Give me what, Mama?"

"A notebook. I have been writing in a notebook," Marina said.

"You mean, like a diary?"

Whomp went the crack of the ball against the Belle's bat. It fouled down the third baseline. Pammy Flynn scooped it up and hand-delivered it to Gussie.

"One more," begged Victor.

"Something like that, yes," said Marina.

"Can I read it, too?" Rio looked up wistfully, a little hurt.

Marina stared into the field, biting her lips.

"Hold on, honey," cried Victor.

"That will be up to Augusta," said Marina.

Rio lit another cigarette. "Do you have it with you, Mama?"

"Ball two," said Victor. Sweat was pouring down the sides of his face. "I can't stand it."

"Yes," said Marina.

"Do you want me to give it to her after the game?"

"Three!" Victor came up from his chair so fast he tipped it over. "Struck the bum out!"

Marina smiled a soft slow smile. She answered, "Yes."

"Hey, Arbis," said Nate. "Tell McGrath I changed my mind. I want him to go have a talk with his wife. She's on deck. She's got maybe one more shot at bat, and she hasn't been doing so well. Maybe he hasn't noticed how she's been swinging like she's blind."

Tim nudged Danny with his elbow. "Nate says to tell you he changed his mind."

"Tell him to tell me himself."

Tim poked Nate in the ribs. "He says tell him yourself."

"He ain't talkin'," mumbled Joe Monopoli with his mouth full of beer. Suds clung to his upper lip and dripped from the black hairs of his nostrils.

"Wipe your face, will you, Rosarian?" Nate turned up his nose as if something was stinking. "Arbis, tell McGrath that time is ticking away. I've been watching his wife practice for the last five months. I know what she can do. Tell him I'm worried. Tell him to go give her a little pep talk. A little kissy-face or something."

"Nate's worried," Tim told Danny.

"Tell him fuck off. Evvie's okay."

"He says to—"

"What am I, deaf?" snapped Nate. "I *heard.*"

Bottom of the last, wrote Rollie. *Fifteen to eight. Batting looks like this: Laura Bradley, Evelyn Brody, Albertina Nolan, and after that, if, dear God, there's an after that, it's Hannah Wally, Peggy Glazer, Sandy Dorn.*

He put down his pencil. His wild heart was driving him crazy. Laura was nervous at the plate, he could tell. Her long legs were wider apart than she usually stood. She looked over the pitch with a careful eye; good. Ball one. It could have been Rollie's imagination but the tip of her bat seemed to be shaking. He silently advised her to take it easy. No sense in letting herself get intimidated. She rocked a little on the balls of her feet, positioned herself, swung. Nice connection, nice force. Single. An easy, beautiful single and her legs had only to be pointed in the right direction to take her safe to the base and then some.

Nice.

"Time!" called Linda Drago, waving her hand to talk to her pitcher. She took a walk to the mound. Waving again, she brought half the fielding Belles in around her.

Evelyn took her stance at the plate, raised the bat, gave it a few practice swings. Behind the bag at first, Uncle William raised his fists in the air to cheer her. Behind her, Spurs were purring encouragement, and beyond the bench sounded the voices of Anthony Street, forcefully urging her on. Nate Campbell was loudest of all.

The huddle of Belles broke. Evelyn wiped her hands on her breeches, looking at the bat as if she could will it to perform with her eyes. She breathed deeply to relax herself, but even over her breathing and the thumping noise of her own heart, she could hear the silence that suddenly descended, everywhere. She could feel it. She could almost taste it, and it almost made her feel sick. She looked out to the mound and straight into the eyes of Linda Drago.

"Oh, God," said Evelyn, frozen.

Drago motioned her aside for warm-ups. The silence was thicker than fog, thicker than clouds, thicker than the hard knobby lump that formed in her chest and rose to her throat and she believed that she was going to be sick all over the plate.

"Oh, God," she said again as Drago's deadly accurate pitches whomped into the catcher's mitt. She dizzied. Once more, floating to her ears the way nurses rush into a room with trays of pills, came the sounds of her team, desperately trying to believe in her. Easy, Ev. You can do it, Ev. Go, Ev, go! And over the sounds, pure and lovely, rang out a shrilly musical cry.

"Come on, Mama! Smash it!" cried her daughter Kate. Evelyn felt her blood begin to flow.

Drago cocked her elbows in readiness. Tension rode the back of the place where the silence had been, drumming its long cold fingers inside her head. She lifted her bat. Her son lifted his. Danny and the rest of Anthony Street stopped breathing. Drago's pitch came in high. Evelyn could hear it sizzling from the instant it left her hand. She swung. Mundy swung, and they fouled hard to the left. In only seconds the ball was back with Drago. She went into her windup like a killer cocking a gun. She delivered. Mundy thought he ought to let it go by for too high, but seeing his mother lunge, he lunged. They smacked it. The cracking sound echoed in her head, and kept on echoing as she flashed down the baseline and overran the bag by what felt like a hundred yards. She was safe. Laura waved giddily, happily to her from second, the Spurs were falling all over the bench with delight, and her whole family was screaming.

Drago sent her a steel-eyed glare. Evelyn returned it. Birdey was up. Drago let her have a limp, low pitch that to everyone's amazement Jake called a strike. Birdey shook her bat as if to hit him across the head for the call.

"Sorry," said Jake. "But that's what it was. Strike one."

Seething, Birdey watched helplessly as another strike limped past her. She turned her head, looking for her team. Gussie stood apart from the others around the bench, leaning wearily on her cane. Only Gussie's eyes were moving. Moving upward. Birdey did as she was told, and moved her hands up a little higher on the bat.

"Ball one," called Jake.

Drago bent low, delivered, and this time Birdey was ready for her. She slammed into the ball, sending it high out to left field. Laura came home. Evelyn came home. Birdey flung herself to the ground with her fingers in a passionate grasp of the third-base bag and the score was fifteen to ten. Hannah Wally came up to defy Drago's steel eyes and cunning arm, and homered, eleven, twelve, and the crowd grew hoarser and hoarser.

Drago, muscling up as if she were only now beginning to get serious, caught Peggy on a grounder at first. Sandy Dorn, up next, squeezed in a single. Pammy Flynn, hardly daring to let herself look at the ball, tried desperately to hold back her terror, and went down fast on strikes. Two. Mimi Reed with her team begging in her ears singled solidly to center, and Sandy moved to second base.

Drago called time, strolled down to her catcher, whispered something, shook her head, whispered something else, and went back to the mound fisting her free hand in her gloved one. They could hear the thumps her fist made all the way to the edge of the field where Anthony Street sat. Patsy Griffin stepped up to the plate, crossed herself and loaded the bases. Stillness fell like twilight, and Avis was up, heaving her bat with all her might. Her whole body ached. Her bones dug one into the other, sharply, horribly. She turned to face the mound. Drago looked at her with what seemed to be pity. The voices of the Spurs, the voices of the crowd, the voices of Leo and the children rising high above the others ran one into the next, mixing themselves into her bones, and blended all together in a huge, splashing, crushing, crashing wave of hurt. She tipped the bat to her shoulder. Drago pitched for a strike. She lifted.

Drago pitched. Strike two. At her back she could feel the faces of the crowd crumbling with disappointment. She imagined the sounds of people at the fringes, giving up and already leaving. Car engines revved up in the distance. The three Spurs on base poised themselves on their toes, bending low. The sun was hot on her neck. The blue of the sky made her eyes ache. She was not sure she could keep them open much longer. Drago rose out of the mound like an executioner. Avis raised her bat. Drago pitched. The ball came in like a bullet. She tensed. Pain fisted in the pit of her belly and hammered its terrible fists against her. She crouched a little lower. She could feel every one of her muscles contracting and pulsing, hard and throbbing and furious. She let out a rasping, hollow cry that seemed to break from her throat with a life of its own. Leaning forward she thrust everything that was left inside her into her swing. Drago's pitch met Avis's bat and exploded.

She put her hands to the sides of her head and forced herself into a run.

The ball rocketed out, out. Outfielder Belles leaped to the chase, dropping their hats as they ran. Mimi Reed came home, Sandy came home. Avis lurched for second. Patsy came in with the tying run. Belles fished in the bushes at the farthest end of the field for the ball. Spurs left their bench and swarmed as near to the plate as they could get. Electrified, the crowd stood itself on end, roaring. Avis covered her ears and rounded third, and fisted her body as if she were trying to ram a wall. She lowered her head like a great, charging bear and rushed on. Fluid, blurred splashes of purple and white leaped and swam before her. The second-base Belle moved out for the relay. Drago left the mound, inching toward the plate with her glove raised high over her head. The ball came out of the bushes. The ball sailed into the field. Her knees were giving out. Madly, violently, she heaved herself forward and dove, sprawling across the plate on her belly as Drago stood above her begging for the ball. She felt herself sinking. She let her arms and legs flatten out against the earth. She turned her face away from the crowd that was gathering all around her. She had had enough. She wanted only to be still. She would not have minded it at all if they left her alone, and let her stay where she was forever.